Roslyn McFarland

All the Lives We've Lived

All the Lives We've Lived
ISBN 978 1 76041 785 7
Copyright © Roslyn McFarland 2019
Front cover photo: *I Don't Wear Goggles*
by Phil Desveaux (www.idontweargoggles.com)
Author photo: Jo Gardiner

First published 2019 by
GINNINDERRA PRESS
PO Box 3461 Port Adelaide 5015
www.ginninderrapress.com.au

For Angus

'All the lives we ever lived and all the lives to be are full of trees and changing leaves.' – Virginia Woolf

'No man ever steps in the same river twice, for it's not the same river and he's not the same man.' – Heraclitus

Let Me Tell You

I fear nothing. I am wise beyond my years, and my years are beyond measure. I sleep within a constellation of stars and live in the depths of dreams. I can be seen on black, moonless nights, drifting over the crow-black, slow-flow of this curiously named river, Salt Pan Creek. I pockmark its waters like a midnight breeze that can freeze a man's soul.

I am elusive but can also be seen in many guises. Some say they've seen me – a wizened crone with witch's hat and broom. Silly fools. That was Old Mother Roach. The last of her gypsy tribe, who've fished up and down this river for many a decade. Out of habit, as well as from necessity.

Some swear they've seen me as the ghost of a headless woman hovering by the river's shores. That's magical thinking for you. Though I move in shadows, I can see light beyond the darkness. I create clearings in the thick and tangled voodoo scrub of ideas. I conceal nothing. So, step right up. Take a closer look. You may well find truth. There's no two ways about it.

I have been known by many names. But please, I am no Arachne, that weaver and spinner of yarns. Nor am I Cassandra, teller of prophecies, babbling from deaf door to deafer door. Some may think I'm a rare bird, a fish out of water, for I exalt the spirit of this place, this land, this river. I am its guardian angel. I know its history, its essence, its character.

When things went wrong, I've known. And when flags were raised and barrels loaded, when lives were lost and lies were told – I know well the sad and dirty work of empire. I've also known the tales of all the mean and gentle folk, who've lived nearby these waters. I hold up the mirror and let in the light. Do as I do.

I have no name. But you can call me Aletheia.

In the Beginning

First, he hears them coming from across the river, the slap-slap chorus of oars on water. Swift and silent, he sweeps through the bush and once he's reached the top of the escarpment, he sees that the strangers have landed down below. One of them stays behind with their big canoe, while the other four men scramble up the hill and start to make their way towards his vantage point beneath the silvery-grey canopy of the turpentine forest. He waits and watches as these strange people hack their way through the dense, ferny undergrowth. They must be stopped.

And then on cue, the dogs begin to bark and a dozen of his men, yelling and waving their spears, step from their hiding places. One of them throws his spear wide of the trespassers, who seem to take this as a warning and begin to retreat. He is pleased, because these people need to realise that they're not wanted here. They must stay away, well away. For good.

Another spear is hurled, this time aimed directly at the four foreigners. It just misses its mark, and one of the men calls out to another, who aims his weapon and fires a shot that reverberates around the mighty sandstone cliffs that line the ancient river in these parts. This is Bidjigal country, and these marauders have no claim here. Their smoking, noisy weapons do not bode well. Pemulwuy sees his men are troubled. He knows that if they are to rid their homeland of these invaders, he must act quickly.

A sudden flap of wings, then a stream of murderous caws cracks the sky above the treetops. It's a sign his men know well. They smile and turn to follow their leader back through the forest to their camp by the river, just a couple of miles north as the crow flies.

Going Back

Kate pulled her car into the curb, turned off the ignition and looked across the road towards the brick-veneered box that she'd once called the family home – the house where she'd grown up. She and her brother Mark had assumed the new owners would bulldoze the place and build one of those noxious McMansions to match so many others now in the street. But no, here it was – still standing. Indestructibly ordinary.

The old picket fence needed a coat of paint. And the paltry patch of kikuyu that was the front lawn hadn't been mown for weeks. Fronds of hairy paspalum were flourishing between the paving stones, which formed the pathway that edged the scrawny garden bed, now dotted with scrappy orange and yellow nasturtiums. Her father's prized rose bushes were nowhere to be seen. The place looked almost abandoned except for what looked like a brand-new kid's tricycle lying on its side on the front porch.

It all seemed rather sad. Kate closed her eyes. Where had the years gone? And what on earth had she hoped to achieve by coming back here? Wallowing in the swamp of nostalgia, for what? Then she heard it. The old pianola in the front room. She was practising her scales, her tiny fingers moving up and down the cream coloured keys. Up and down, up and down. At the open window, the chiffon curtains puffed up and out, then fell in the breeze. She could only have been ten years old.

But no. It was an earlier time Kate wanted to recall – during the height of summer in the year she turned six. It was the day her family had first moved into what was then a fibro house. She'd shut her eyes on that day too, but then, her eyes were stinging from the savagery of the sun's glare. And there she was – standing on the bare boards of the open veranda, squinting into the shimmering ugliness of their scorched backyard, full of rock and rubble, where her father, stripped to the waist, all muscle and power, was trying to level a mound of broken shells, some grey and dirty, some porcelain-white and gleaming.

She remembers him dripping with sweat, stopping for a moment and leaning on his sledgehammer. He looks up and, seeing his daughter, gives her a wave and a smile. She can't understand why he's so happy. The only thing that would make her smile right now would be if she and her mum and dad were back in their cosy, one-bedroom flat in Kings Cross, all dark wood and shadows. There was no glare there. Ever.

And on Sundays, each of her parents would take one of her hands, and the three of them would walk together down the big hill, past the stadium to Rushcutters Bay Park, where they'd eat sandwiches on the wooden bench beneath the shade of a giant Moreton Bay fig and watch the sailing boats that were moored at the jetty. Kate loved listening for the clink-clink-clink that the boats made when their masts hit against metal. Afterwards, all three of them would have ice cream and stroll along the pathway that curved around the water's edge to look at all the pretty white sails skating across the sparkling blue rim of the harbour.

But there wouldn't be any water here.

Kate blinked and stared once more at the flinty backyard of her new home, her new view of the world. She told herself she mustn't cry, but then felt the touch of her father's hand on her shoulder.

'So, what do you think?' he asked.

'I don't like it here.'

'You will,' said her father. 'Give it time. You'll see.'

'But there aren't any trees. And where's the water?'

'Is that all you're worried about?' Her father sounded relieved. 'If you go and help your mother unpack, like a good girl, while I finish as much as I can out here today, we'll all go for a little walk when I'm done, and I'll show you the river. How would you like that?'

'There's a river near here?' She could scarcely believe it.

'You bet there is!' came his reply. 'They call it a creek, but it's as wide and as long as a river.'

Kate smiled. Well, there was nothing wrong with her memory. Her long-term memory, that is. All things considered, she'd been happy here in the house made from fibro and love. And she also knew that until her final breath, this small block of suburban history would live within her – the polished linoleum and the neat kitchenette and the singalongs round the pianola and the smell of Sunday lamb roasts and the terrible daylight quiet when her father was asleep after being on night duty and the perfumed marriage of California Poppy Hair Oil and Yardley's April Violets Eau de Toilette and their black Bakelite telephone's unlisted number and the winter morning huddle with her baby brother in front of the kerosene heater and her mother, forever chain-smoking, sitting at the window of her darkened bedroom, watching the street that was waiting for her husband to come home.

*

Just as Kate was about to start the car, she heard the distant, low rumble of a train crossing the railway bridge that spanned the river. How discreet the sound was compared to the clang and clatter of the old red rattlers that rolled their way into the acoustic environment of her childhood. Back then, she'd grown quite fond of the sound. It meant that people were going places, that there was another world beyond her own, which had seemed immense to her as a child. In reality, her neighbourhood really only measured about three square kilometres. Wedged between Belmore Road and the eastern bank of Salt Pan Creek, it stretched from the southern side of the railway station right down to Lugarno, where the waters merge with the Georges River.

She wondered if the local kids nowadays still played in the belt of maze-like bushland that ran along the water's edge. Maybe, in the name of progress and development, it had been obliterated like so much of the natural environment that had once been here. Were kids even allowed to play outside any more? She hadn't seen or heard a child since she got here. Probably too busy swiping iPads and playing *Minecraft* on their phones.

Kate revved the engine. She'd decided to check out the river before going back up the mountains. A few minutes later, she was standing on the shoreline of the river's sleepy waters. She'd been able to drive right down to the river on what had once been a dirt track. She'd parked her car near the first set of pylons of the sewage aqueduct and, before walking to the water's edge, noticed how the bush that had been her childhood playground had all but disappeared, no doubt cut back to expose the backyards of houses that now had water views.

Looking up and down the river, there wasn't a casuarina, or what her father had called a swamp oak, in sight. They'd obviously been swallowed up by the mangroves that seemed to be thriving. With their hopelessly entangled above-ground root systems permanently on display, she'd always considered them to be the ugliest of trees. And she still did. She was sure bottlebrush had grown down here when she was a kid, but there was now no sign of any. Golden wattle too, but it wasn't the right time of year for that.

Kate looked up into the clear, brightness of the sky. A sudden metallic wail from a distant chainsaw pierced the air. A light breeze scudded the dull galvanised grey of the water's surface. She closed her eyes briefly and breathing deeply recognised the dank muddy smell of the river. Her spirits lifted. There was something wonderful, something indefinable about Salt Pan Creek. What stories it could tell of all the lives lived along its shores.

When she phoned Mark later that night, he'd virtually said the same thing. But that had been near the end of their conversation. At first, she told him why she'd gone back there, how since she'd returned from the States, she'd started writing a journal of sorts about her past and how she'd hoped a visit to the old family home might resurrect some buried memories of her childhood. And she told him how she'd driven down to the river and how there's still that lovely dark, wet earthiness of their prohibited playground.

Mark laughed. 'They were the two things I loved most about it – the putrid mud and the fact that it was absolutely *verboten* for most kids in the area to go there. Which made it all the more inviting. Especially in summer.'

He told her then about the boys he'd known, who'd built rafts and canoes, though some had only dinghies. Most of his mates tried fishing from the jetties, but neither he nor Kate could recall ever seeing anyone actually catching a fish. And one thing led to another, and they were soon talking about the families who used to live down by the water's edge in their ramshackle houses – like the Murphys and the Piggots and the Tuckers and the Roaches and how they all had boats, mainly tinnies with small outboard motors.

'You know, Katie, there'd be a lot of material there for a rollicking read. You ought to think about writing a novel instead of a dull, old journal. Introspection is all very well…'

'I know what you're saying,' she said.

And of course, she did. Just like she knew in the darkest chamber of her heart that the place of their childhood no longer existed. Except in reverie. But at that very moment, what she didn't want to tell her brother was how estranged she'd become from her son, Adam, whose bitter resentment towards her hadn't diminished one jot, despite her recent visit to the US to meet his American wife and their baby daughter, Ravenna. What an exercise in utter futility that had been! Which was why writing this journal was so important to her right now. It was her way of learning about herself. By interrogating her past, confronting the truth of it – of the people and places that had shaped her, the choices she'd made and the actions she'd taken – she was hoping to come to understand how she became the person she is. And perhaps she'd then be able to do something about it.

Much later that night, Kate lay awake in bed. She couldn't sleep. Her mind was full of fish and water and mangroves and old, wooden jetties. And yes, the prattle of voices from the past.

'Those families – they're not like us, you know. They're not like normal people – living in hovels down by the river.' Her mother was shaking her head as she spoke. 'They live like gypsies really. They're all intermarried.' Her face grew flushed. She lit a cigarette and took time to draw the smoke into her lungs and then just as slowly, exhaled through her nostrils. 'And not one of them appears to work for a living either.'

'But they're not bothering anybody,' said her father. 'And at least they keep to themselves.'

'Except when they want something from one of us.' Her mother was speaking in that clipped manner of hers, which she often used when challenged or contradicted.

She was right, though. Kate had seen her father on several occasions witnessing the sign of a cross in place of a signature on some official document or other.

It all seemed so long ago. Kate pulled up the bed sheet and rolled onto her right side. In all her years of teaching, she'd never once come across a student who couldn't write his or her name. Her childhood had been another place. Another time. When they'd moved there in the late fifties, most of the roads had not yet been curbed and guttered. Quite a few streets were not even tarred. And as for sewerage – that was to be years off.

But Kate had learned to love it. It became a Meccano and hula-hoop world of yoyos, Malvern Stars, marbles and skipping ropes. The sort of place where, at Christmas time, her father would go to the river with his axe, so he could chop down a small but perfect casuarina tree and then drag it back home for Kate and Mark to decorate with their home-made crêpe paper stars and streamers. Yes, a great deal had changed. She only had to take a look into the mirror to see that. Ready for sleep now, she placed her right hand beneath her pillow and the left between her legs. And was soothed in her dreams by the ancient waters of Salt Pan Creek still flowing south by east down to the Georges River and then onward into Botany Bay and beyond – out, out into the vast blue of the rising Pacific.

Drinking Whisky

Mark poured himself a hefty slug of Scotch, then took it and himself into his study. Tom wasn't home yet. Which was just as well. He needed to calm down after talking to his sister. It was always the same with her. Every time they spoke, it was Kate who set the agenda for the entire conversation. And it rarely had anything to do with anybody other than herself. The phone call just now was a good example: she'd told him she'd visited the old neighbourhood; that she was searching through what she said were the sealed spaces of her soul and then recording her memories and feelings in some kind of journal. Jesus, didn't she have anything better to do than to keep a journal of her tawdry recollections? Was she that fucking narcissistic?

He leant back in his chair, slowed his breathing and savoured a mouthful of whisky. He had to stop getting so het up whenever she called. It was ridiculous how she could get under his skin so easily. Not that she ever noticed his irritation. But then he could hardly blame her for that. After all, it was he who was the expert hypocrite, whose display of interest and enthusiasm for every stupid bloody thing she did or wanted to do was utterly convincing. But the anger and resentment he always felt afterwards was a high price to pay for not wanting to upset her.

Tom maintained that Mark's lack of assertiveness in certain situations was due to the fact that he'd never come out to his parents. And Mark was beginning to see the sense in that idea, because it was certainly not his fault that poor old Milton and Betty had gone to their respective graves not knowing that their only son was gay. Sure, Kate had always known, but she'd agreed that when it came to their parents knowing, it was up to Mark to tell them. And it wasn't as if he'd never tried. It's just that every time he did, there was always something that got in the way.

Like the very last time he'd tried. He'd thoroughly prepared himself for his confession, even rehearsing a little speech about his sexual orientation and then explaining the reasons why he'd chosen to live in Melbourne, so very far away from Salt Pan Creek. But timing was important. He needed to ensure that his disclosure took place during the daytime, in their own home, the family home, and with him and his parents the only people present. He wanted it straightforward, uncluttered. And as luck would have it, his editor at the time suggested he interview the new theatrical sensation, Cate Blanchett, who, fresh out of NIDA, was about to play opposite Geoffrey Rush in a Sydney Theatre Company production of David Mamet's *Oleanna*. So once the interview was arranged, the flights were organised around it and a visit to his parents included in the time frame, as was often the case when he was in Sydney for work.

But this was in 1993, and a lot had been happening outside the bastion of high culture. This was not long after Mabo and Keating's Redfern speech. And there'd been some notable conservative politicians and right-wing shock jocks, who'd been fuelling fear and promoting paranoia about native title. It was in this political climate that Mark came knocking on his parents' front door.

His father was out in the sunroom, listening to the radio at his usual ear-splitting volume. Right from the start, Mark could see that Milton was somewhat agitated but presumed that he'd probably had another row with Betty over his stubborn refusal to wear his hearing aids. But once Mark sat down, the actual cause of his father's agitation became all too clear to him, because Milton suddenly launched into a story about a large oyster shell midden that had been in the backyard when he and Betty had first bought the place, and how he'd levelled the midden to the ground, then covered it with a good layer of top soil and a surface planting of couch.

At this point, Mark very much wanted to know if, at the time, Milton had understood what a midden means to Aboriginal people and whether or not he realised the implications of the deliberate obliteration of that stack of shells. 'Were you aware, Dad, of the significance of what you were doing?' asked Mark.

And so it started.

'I'm not a bloody idiot, you know.' Milton had mounted his high horse. 'I knew that it was some kind of rubbish dump where food scraps are tossed and that the land I'd just signed a mortgage for had probably been some kind of meeting place for feasts and corroborees. Just like thousands of other places in this country, I might add.'

Mark was about to say something, but as far as his father was concerned, there'd be no interruptions until he'd finished his monologue.

'And I'm telling you, there was no way I was going to leave it there either, if that's what you bloody well think! This was my property, my land and still is, and I'll do with it as I see fit, and bugger anyone else who says otherwise.'

Milton paused. He was thinking, remembering. He looked straight ahead towards the river, his eyes as pale grey and watery as the flesh of oysters. 'I can understand, Dad, what you're saying and how you felt,' said Mark.

'And, I'm telling you now, I'd do the same damn thing today. Cause I didn't give it a second bloody thought, back then. All I wanted was a nice bit of lawn for you and your sister to play on, a place where your mother could hang out the washing and a vegie patch for myself. And you've got to remember that when we moved in here, it was only a month or two before you were born. I didn't have a lot of time, and there was no way I was going to let a child of mine crawl all over a backyard of flint and rock and broken oyster shells.'

Betty appeared from the kitchen bearing a tray with tea and cake. 'I agree with everything your father's been saying,' she said, passing around cups and saucers and oversized wedges of sponge cake. 'All this talk about native title and land rights has scared me. And as you can see, it's put the wind up your father. And I don't think we should be worrying at our age about losing our home because of a mound of empty shells.' She sat down then and sipped at her tea.

It was obvious they were spooked. Both of them genuinely believed their property could be taken from them, especially since 'that midden' could be seen as evidence of Aboriginal occupation. Mark did his best to allay their fears by telling them that the chance of them losing the place was extremely unlikely. But Betty would have none of it and accused him of being a know-all. Just like his sister.

Irritated, Mark rolled his eyes. Why did his mother always reduce everything to a personal attack?

'Tell him, Milton,' she urged. 'Tell your son about the Aboriginal camp that used to be down by the river near the end of Ogilvy Street.'

But what his father told him was all rather vague – except for the fact that the Peakhurst camp, back in the thirties, had been a hotbed of dissent.

'So is this camp still there?'

'Not exactly,' said Milton, calmer now. 'Most of the families were moved on, around the time of the Second World War, but there are people around here who reckon that other Aboriginal families replaced them, during and after the war, and I wouldn't be surprised if some were still living along Salt Pan Creek.'

And so it was in this way that Mark's planned confession was thwarted. There was no point in even trying to raise the issue, especially since time had fled and the taxi to take him to the airport was due any moment. As he queued to board his flight back home, Mark felt no animosity towards his parents. They were getting old and insular. The world of their day-to-day lives had shrunk. Fear of the unknown had become their default position. Maybe they didn't need to know that he was gay. As far as he was concerned, it didn't change the way he felt about them.

Still didn't. And he'd always love them. Despite their flaws. Another mouthful of Scotch slid down his throat. Maybe Tom was wrong after all, and what he really needed to do was accept what he couldn't change about the people he loved. He'd done that unconsciously with Milton and Betty. So why couldn't he do that with his sister? Sure, she was self-absorbed. But probably no more than most people in this me-me-me world. And just because he'd assigned some of the people and events in his youth to memory's junk pile, it didn't mean she had to too. And who knows? Reviewing her past in that journal of hers might actually do her some good.

Mark pushed his chair back from the desk and stood up. He hoped Tom wouldn't be too much longer. He was feeling hungry. Back in the kitchen, he rinsed the whisky glass under the tap and suddenly found himself wondering what school all the Koori kids had gone to when he was a kid. He hadn't thought about it before, but if what his parents said was true and there were Aboriginal families living along Salt Pan Creek, then the children would've gone to school somewhere, and the only indigenous kid he ever knew back then was Gary Saunders, Kate's old boyfriend. As far as Mark was aware, there were no Koori kids in his own age group. But perhaps there were, and he was oblivious to them. How awful if that were the case.

He turned and opened the fridge door. He removed two steaks from the meat keeper and placed them on a plate and then onto the benchtop to bring them to room temperature prior to their cooking. He told himself he must remember to ask Kate if she knew whatever happened to Gary Saunders.

Then he poured himself another Scotch and waited for Tom to come home.

Motherhood

Kate Ward hadn't been invited to the wedding. In fact, she hadn't even known about it. Well, not until they'd called her from Vegas, that is. It had been a spur of the moment thing, said Adam. They hadn't wanted any fuss. They'd just taken off to that desert metropolis and, hey presto, they were married.

Thought you'd like to be the first to hear the good news, he said. As he spoke, Kate had a sudden vision of a drive-through ceremony in an Elvis Chapel. But then she heard her new daughter-in-law whispering in the background.

'Hey, I'll put Michelle on,' he said, 'and let you two get to know each other.'

Jesus, thought Kate, I've never even met this woman. What am I supposed to say to her? Then Kate heard her voice, her tinny, cheer-leader's enthusiasm – so cutesy, so phoney, so Ms Peachy Keen.

'So, Mom,' drawled Michelle. 'May I call you Mom?' Kate mumbled a yes. She didn't feel she had a choice. And that was when Michelle informed Kate that she'd soon be a grandmother and that the baby was due in twelve weeks' time.

Kate struggled to stay composed. This was like living in some dreadful TV soap. The rest of the phone conversation was a blur of inanities. Before hanging up, she remembered saying to Adam that if he was happy, she was too.

She was lying.

*

When Adam asked his mother to visit them in the States, the baby was only a month old. Kate was thrilled but thought it best to suggest she stay in a nearby hotel. Adam would have none of it. She was to stay with them, and that was that. But from the minute Kate walked through the front door of the couple's South Berkeley home, she wished she'd never agreed to come.

Perched on Panoramic Hill, the house was large, airy and stylishly decorated, with sweeping views of San Francisco Bay and the Golden Gate and Bay Bridges. In daylight hours, sunshine filled every room, but when Adam went to work, the atmosphere turned glacial. Michelle either wore a frozen smile or a lukewarm sneer. She barely spoke to Kate, for she was always tired or feeling unwell. And every time Kate offered assistance, it was refused and met with a cold shoulder and an icy stare. But each morning when Michelle had her shower, she'd hand over baby Ravenna to her mother-in-law's care. These small snatches of time with her granddaughter gave Kate some joy. Nevertheless, she still felt unwelcome.

One night during the second week of her stay, Kate found herself alone in the kitchen with Adam. She was rinsing the dishes and handing them to him to stack in the dishwasher. Earlier, before they'd even finished eating dinner, Michelle had taken Ravenna off to bed, and had not returned.

'If I'm in the way, Adam, please tell me. I can book into a hotel. I can…'

'For heaven's sake, you're not in the way!'

She heard the irritation in his voice, but still she went on. 'Well, let me put it another way. Perhaps Michelle would rather I wasn't staying here.'

Adam rounded on her. 'Whatever gave you that idea, Mum? Of course, she doesn't think that. Just because she hasn't liked a couple of the meals you've cooked doesn't mean she wishes you weren't here.'

Either he's in denial or he's bloody stupid, thought Kate. At any rate, she was now certain that the antipathy she felt towards her daughter-in-law was reciprocated. The decision to return home as soon as she could organise another flight was not hard to make. She said no more that evening and, as there hadn't been a peep out of the baby for over an hour, and since Michelle clearly intended to remain in her room, Kate followed Adam into the den.

Plonking herself next to him on the sofa, she feigned interest in the program her son had chosen to watch on TV – yet another earnest, but terrifying documentary on the post 9/11 world: a catalogue of wars in the Middle East, suicide bombs, waves and waves of refugees, the tyranny of cyberspace, sexual predators seemingly everywhere, the devastation of the natural world. On and on, thought Kate, when and how would it all end? It didn't bear thinking about.

A few days later over breakfast, she announced she'd be leaving at the end of the week. Kate caught the look of relief that briefly crossed Adam's face.

'Not a problem,' was all he said. He didn't even ask why she'd decided to change her plans.

Kate sat in the kitchen and ate her muesli with all the things she'd wanted to say still left unsaid, unasked and unanswered. Of course, she knew that silence begets silence, that avoidance of problems often creates barriers between people. But she'd never felt so disconnected from her son in her life. It made her frightened – frightened of losing him. She'd never meant it to be like this.

She took a deep breath and could almost smell the heady scent of wattle drifting towards her, sending her back, back…into her past. How many years ago was it now? She and Richard, standing side by side, surveying the beauty of the bush that surrounded the Blue Mountains property they'd just bought.

'You know, Kate,' her young husband said, 'I'm going to create a magnificent garden here for us. Even in winter it will be full of colour. I promise you.'

And he'd been right. She smiled at the memory, just as she had done that day when she'd turned her head to meet Richard's beaming face. She could almost feel his arms around her once again. For that day, they'd held their embrace for some time, gently rocking. Together. Her belly full of baby. Adam, their not-yet-born son, cocooned between them. Safe and loved, even then. How had it all gone so horribly wrong?

It had started so well. They'd met in Canberra in the heady days of the women's movement and the Vietnam moratorium protests. She was an arts student at ANU. Richard was lecturing in pharmacology there. And so it happened that beneath the banners and the placards at an anti-war rally in Civic Square, they fell in love. Two years later, when Richard gained a tenured position at Sydney University, Kate went with him – back to her home state.

She began teaching in the western suburbs. They bought the house in Wentworth Falls. Then she fell pregnant. Marriage and baby followed. Everything had been perfectly fine for years really. Even after the divorce. But when Richard upped and died, that was when the earth suddenly shifted for Adam.

Admittedly, Richard's death had been a shock to everyone, but for Adam, who'd recently turned fifteen, it had been especially difficult. He'd been the one who'd found Richard's body, hunched in the armchair of his study. Pulmonary embolism. No warning. No apparent symptoms. Adam had been living with his father in Sydney since he'd started high school, coming back 'home' to the Blue Mountains most weekends. It was a thoroughly amicable arrangement, but when Richard died, Adam had no alternative but to return full-time to live with Kate, which meant a change of schools. And as far as Adam was concerned, it was all her fault. She was to blame for everything. Not just for his father's death, but for the break-up of the marriage, for the divorce, for all the pain she'd caused his father.

She shuddered now at the thought of that terrible night, not long after Richard's funeral, when Adam stood at her bedroom door and railed at her: 'Do you realise you broke Dad's heart? Do you? Do you?' He was sobbing and wiping at his eyes.

Kate went to comfort him, but he backed away from her.

'I didn't want to believe him when he first told me, but I do now. He was just slowly dying inside. All because of you. And do you know what? Nothing you say or do is going to change my mind about that.'

'For God's sake, Adam, I think you should at least hear my side of things.' Kate spoke quietly, hoping to calm her son. Surely this was the unreason of grief talking. Surely it would pass.

'I don't want to hear any more of your crap,' he yelled. 'You've always cared more about yourself and your fucking job than you did about Dad and me. And you can't tell me otherwise!'

She let him disappear into his room then and after several hours, she went to him and tried to explain that the break-up with Richard hadn't been like that. She and his father had simply grown apart. Like some couples do. Their separation and divorce had been mutually agreed upon. There'd been no real animosity between them. Couldn't he see that they'd remained friends?

Adam would have none of it. Weeks, then months went by and, with gritted teeth, Kate did her best to ignore his sullen silences, his closed bedroom door, the muttered insults under his breath, the occasional angry flare-up. But then in his senior years at school, an unspoken truce came about. Hostilities disappeared. And she took joy in his academic success. Considered gifted in mathematics, he was very much like his father, and this was not altogether unpleasant for Kate. And when Adam was offered the opportunity to complete his PhD in Berkeley, at the University of California, Kate encouraged him to accept the offer. She was proud of him, but she hadn't counted on the possibility of him choosing to remain in the States. Despite the passing of time, there were still moments when Kate suddenly felt a deep, dull, primeval ache at the geographical distance between them. It didn't make for a close relationship.

And now here she was, sitting in her son's kitchen, the two of them as remote and as disconnected as ever. Oh God, thought Kate, was she really such a failure as a mother? And was this to be her post-retirement future: raking over these awful memories — one recollection after another? Constantly lost in reverie until her brain atrophies? It happened to her father, so why not her?

*

On her flight back to Australia, she had plenty of time to think about silences and secrets, families and relationships. About births, marriages and deaths. About parenting and descent, bloodlines and origins, the future and the past. The ties that bind.

While the giant A380 cruised high above the boundless blue of the Pacific, a steward poured wine into her glass. Kate thanked him. He was roughly the same age as Adam, and she wondered if he had a good relationship with his mother. She had to admit that while she'd made a career out of analysing the motivations of fictional characters, she'd always avoided examining the choices she'd made, the actions she'd undertaken. Perhaps if she'd handled his grief differently when Richard had died and given her son the support and demonstrable proof of her love that he'd so desperately needed by taking time off from teaching to be with him, perhaps, just perhaps, things would be different now between them. Instead, she'd opted for empty platitudes, raised voices and indignant denials. And of course, by immersing herself in her work, she'd made sure she had no time for what she used to call self-indulgent navel-gazing.

'Would you like a top-up?' asked the steward, proffering a bottle of wine.

'Yes please,' she said, holding out her glass once again, 'I'd love some more.'

*

The cabin lights were still turned off when Kate woke. She'd slept a whole four hours, which was unusual for her when she flew. And after splashing water on her face and returning to her seat, she raised the blind at her window. A sudden, slim corridor of light fell across her darkened row of seats. Quickly, she lowered the blind.

She tightened her seat belt and closed her eyes. She'd made a decision. She wasn't yet sure how she'd go about it, but she was determined to make amends and heal the rift between herself and her son. For years now, he'd been carrying around the weighty baggage of his past, whereas she'd dumped hers long ago, refusing to look back. It was like she'd been compelled to contain every uncomfortable memory, every painful recollection behind an impenetrable barricade. She'd blocked them at the gates of memory's castle, forbidden them entry. It was an act of deliberate forgetfulness because she'd believed that doing otherwise would've been self-destructive. In this way she'd never taken responsibility for a damn thing.

By the time her plane circled the sprawl of Sydney and began its tilt forward to make its descent, a plan was forming in Kate's head. Delusion had got her nowhere. It was time to come to terms with her personal history.

First Fragment

On the morning of the twentieth day of January, when the last of the First Fleet had arrived safely in Botany Bay, Governor Arthur Phillip knew he had to do something about finding a decent source of drinking water, some relatively flat land for building and a harbour deep enough to moor his ships close to shore. Otherwise, he'd never get this colony started.

Because they'd searched the north side of the bay the day before without result, Phillip ordered Lieutenants King and Dawes to take three marines and explore the two inlets on the south side of the bay as far as possible, while he would follow in a six-oared rowboat with two other officers and three crewmen.

In his journal, Lieutenant Philip Gidley King writes of passing by a long shoal which was quite dry in many places at low tide. He can only be referring to what's now known as Mangrove Island, which is at the mouth of the Woronora River. King and his crew follow this river for about a mile to what is called Bonnet Bay and then row back and cross over to the highest hill in the vicinity. He names it Lance Point, now called Gertrude Point, which is Lugarno's ninety-eight-metre-high headland that stands at the entry of Lime Kiln Bay.

According to King, they land at the base of this point and all but one of them climb the hill and discover excellent black soil and a mighty turpentine forest, the wood of which is borer-proof, and which in the future will provide the timber pylons for Sydney's wharves for well over a century.

Suddenly a red, foxlike dog and a number of Aborigines appear, shouting and gesturing at the British to get right back on their boats and be gone. Undeterred and unarmed, King decides to approach them, offering ribbons and beads. They respond with louder shouting, clearly wanting these uniformed people to clear off and never come back. One of them even hurls a lance as a warning. King begins to retreat but stops at the brow of the hill.

This is met with much louder shouting, and another lance is thrown deliberately close to one of his marines – a clear threat. King gives the order to fire, but with powder only. The Aborigines disappear. Nevertheless, King and his men hurry back onto their rowboat and are joined by Governor Phillip and his crew, who've been exploring the southern side of the bay, where Phillip claims the 'natives' are very friendly and sociable.

It's not hard to imagine how humiliated King would have felt then, when Phillip chooses to disembark alone on the shoreline of Lance Point and demonstrates his superior skills at negotiation by offering the same baubles and trinkets, which are gratefully received by one of the belligerent Aborigines. What happens next is extremely interesting. The natives gather round the two rowboats and make obvious their admiration for the colourful hats and uniforms the British are wearing. And then, in a kind of theatrical performance, they point their spears at the man who threw the previous lance. King's interpretation of this – that they were waiting for the British to give them orders to kill him – is contentious.

The British respond with a little mime show of their own that indicates they want no harm to come to the lance-thrower. A kind of peace is negotiated. Governor Phillip presents more beads and then departs with his crew.

There are questions about this incident that can never be answered – truths that can never be known. Who was this mysterious lance-thrower? This expert marksman? Could it have been Pemulwuy? After all, this encounter took place in Bidjigal country and just around the corner from Salt Pan Creek, where the mighty warrior was later known to have based himself.

Or perhaps in the year before the smallpox epidemic had such a devastating effect on the Eora nation, there were many young and highly skilled warriors who resented the presence of these interlopers. We can only ever presume.

Anyone Who Had a Heart

Everyone knew he'd been born down by the river, but no one knew precisely when or even the exact circumstances of his birth, let alone how or why he'd come to be called Dutchie. Such was the mystery of his past, there were only a few people who knew that his real name was Norman Tucker. And of those who did know, some of them even doubted this to be the truth.

So in the absence of any factual detail, Dutchie became the subject of various local myths, which provided him with a couple of biographical backstories that seemed to explain why he was like he was. One scenario, which accounted for his limited vocabulary, involved him having been dropped on his head as an infant. Another claimed he was never the same after he'd experienced the tangled mire of mud and mortar shells, bodies and barbed wire that was once no-man's-land on the Western Front. And there were stories of Dutchie only having himself to blame. Like the one that was set on a wintry night down by Salt Pan Creek, when he got himself so damn drunk that he passed out and rolled into the campfire, only coming to when he lit up like a Roman candle. Despite all these stories being credible, very few people believed them. But what no one ever disputed was his current situation.

Dutchie lived alone in an old, unpainted, clapboard shack. Its roof was made from various pieces of rusted corrugated-iron sheeting and odd slabs of timber. A path of trampled paspalum led to his makeshift front door, beside which a single window looked out onto the road and beyond. Unlike all the other houses in the street, there was no electricity supply connected to Dutchie's place. A fuel stove and an oil lamp were sufficient for his needs.

Most days, he could be seen unshaven, wandering the neighbourhood, pushing his wheelbarrow wherever he went, and always with his mangy grey dog beside him. He would leave home in the early morning and not return till late afternoon. Day in, day out, he wore the same filthy clothes with a wide brown leather belt wrapped tightly around his middle to keep up his oversized trousers. A ripped and stained singlet substituted for a shirt and, in the winter months, he would add a heavily patched greatcoat. Horn-rimmed spectacles, with one lens a spiderweb of shattered glass, completed the picture, which understandably instilled fear in many of the local kids. If they saw him first on their way to or from school, they'd cross to the other side of the road, especially if he growled his usual greeting: 'I can see ya!'

But Dutchie was harmless, and sensible parents counselled their children to treat him with the same respect they gave to all their elders. Even the Thompson brothers, some local rowdy toughs, left him alone and never mistreated him. But when the Bannons won a considerable sum in the Opera House lottery in 1963, Dutchie's fortunes took a turn for the worse.

*

Henry and Edith Bannon lived directly opposite Dutchie in a white, double-fronted, rendered brick bungalow surrounded by an English garden that Edith had filled with an extravagance of roses, delphiniums, sweet peas and chrysanthemums. She considered it to be her very own oasis, a sacred place of abundant fertility where, at forty years of age, she had felt the first butterfly flutterings of her baby's miraculous movements within her. And so, each day of her pregnancy, when the sun was high in the sky, she'd lie down in her garden and, lifting the skirt of her frock to her neck, she'd reveal her belly to the heavens as a way of giving thanks. And so it came as no surprise when the Bannons called their only child Grace, for she was their joy, their bliss.

Now a young woman in her late twenties, Grace worked in the city as the personal secretary for a prominent divorce lawyer. Every weekday morning, after waving her mother goodbye, she'd walk to the station to catch her train. And if as she did, most mornings, happen to see Dutchie keeping watch by his gate across the road, she'd acknowledge him with a smile and a polite nod of her head.

Everyone acquainted with Grace considered her manners to be impeccable, her disposition charming. Teenage girls thought her the height of elegance and sophistication. Some said she looked like Princess Margaret. Others thought her more like Jackie Kennedy. And there were even some who'd have agreed with Betty Ward, that poor old Grace was being buried alive by her sense of duty and obligation to her parents. 'That girl needs to get out and learn to live a little,' Betty once said.

But in fact, Grace had been learning a great deal about how to live a little, especially when in the arms of Stuart Lang, her boss, who was married with two small children. Their liaison was their well-kept secret. So professional was their conduct while at work that not a single person in chambers ever suspected the pair's relationship was anything other than ethical.

It had started so simply. Stuart had asked her to work back, adding that it would probably be an all-nighter. There was nothing new in that. She'd often stayed back to help him prepare for a case. They'd take a short dinner break and then continue working, stopping around midnight, which was far too late an hour for a young woman such as Grace to catch a train home. Ever considerate of others, Stuart would organise a suitable room for her in a city hotel. It was all very much above board. Until one night, while prepping for quite a nasty divorce case, Stuart had suddenly decided to call it a day.

'Let's celebrate an early finish,' he said. 'Ever been to Beppi's?'

*

After dinner, while walking Grace from the restaurant to her hotel, he'd suddenly kissed her. And oh, it was so lovely to be kissed in such a way by such a man. Like Cary Grant did in all those Hitchcock movies. Just when she thought she might swoon with longing, Stuart abruptly stopped and stepped away from her.

'No, no. We can't be doing this,' he said. 'It isn't right.'

But she thought it was. Yet she said nothing. She only moved towards him. And he knew exactly what to do.

That night was the first time Grace had ever been with a man. She breathed him into her, and he stayed till dawn, kissing every bit of her body with a reverence and tenderness she'd never imagined was possible. She remembered murmuring his name. Over and over. And she knew that she would always love him.

More nights like this followed. A regular pattern evolved. Stuart told her he couldn't get enough of her; that he adored her; that one day they would marry, but she had to understand that he couldn't just up and leave his wife, especially since his young son, Blair had only recently been diagnosed with muscular dystrophy; so she'd have to be patient and accept that they could only be together once a week - just for the time being, of course. Grace sympathised. She appreciated the dreadful predicament he was in. And told him he wasn't to worry about her; that he had enough on his plate; that she would wait an eternity if she had to. Such was her love for him.

As for her parents, they suspected nothing untoward about these weekly overnight stays in fancy hotels. That was just one of the perks of their daughter's job. And besides, she seemed happy enough, particularly now they'd had such a windfall.

For some time, Henry had been in a lottery syndicate with five other milkmen from his depot. They rarely won even a free lottery ticket, so no one was more surprised than they were, when it came to splitting £100,000 by six. It still left each man with a sizeable sum, roughly equivalent to about $500,000 in today's terms. And while it had been Henry who'd bought the winning ticket, it was Edith who did the spending, which was fine by her husband, who intended to retire on a full pension, as soon as their winnings had been spent. To that end, he agreed whole-heartedly with his wife's suggestion to have an in-ground swimming pool installed in their backyard. This soon became the talk of the street, for no one else in the entire neighbourhood had a backyard pool. Grace seemed pleased with it. Most summer evenings she'd swim several laps before dinner. But the Bannons had hoped their daughter would invite all her friends from the city to parties by the pool.

But not a single party eventuated. Henry and Edith put this down to their daughter's natural timidity in all things. But after splurging on such an item for such little return, Edith needed to console herself with the purchase of several dozen garden gnomes, which she believed would contribute to the wonderland ambience of her beloved garden. And it was there, while pruning the roses one afternoon, that she resolved to convince her husband of the need to send their precious daughter on a holiday of a lifetime. One where Grace might even find herself a suitable husband.

'So where did you have in mind?' asked Henry.

'London, of course.'

'That'll cost us a pretty penny.'

'We can afford it,' she replied, patting him lightly on his hand. 'We've still got money left from your winnings.'

'Well, you'd better ask Grace first before you start going buying tickets. She might not want to go.'

'Now never you mind about any of that, Henry,' said Edith, pouring more tea. 'Just you leave it to me.'

*

Dressed in her pink chenille dressing gown and with her hair wrapped in a towel, Grace sat at her dressing table and stared into the mirror. She told her reflection that she would waste no more time weeping silently in the bathtub. Enough was enough. Despite Stuart's protestations to the contrary, he had used her shabbily. He had told a monstrous lie, but at least she'd finally caught him out. Thanks to his wife, Lois, that is, who'd dropped by chambers unannounced yesterday with the children, both of whom appeared to be in the peak of health.

Later that afternoon, well after his family had left, Grace questioned Stuart in his office about his son's magical cure from muscular dystrophy, when there was yet no cure known to science.

'For heaven's sake,' she said, shaking her head, 'you told me he was permanently in a wheelchair, that he was in constant pain and had trouble breathing, but here he was today – walking, talking, laughing like any other healthy nine-year-old kid…' She began to cry. 'You lied to me…and what's more, I realise now, you rat, that you never had any intention of leaving your wife! And I wonder what she'd say if I told her what we've been doing for the past five years.'

Throughout her rant, Stuart stood behind his antique mahogany desk, listening and watching Grace. His face showed no expression. His thoughts were unreadable. But now he went to her. She'd stopped speaking and had dropped herself onto the chesterfield lounge and was quietly sobbing into one of its armrests. He sat down close beside her and tried to console her.

'I do love you, Grace Bannon. Please believe me. I never wanted to hurt you.' A pause. 'And yes, OK, I admit I lied to you… But only about Blair.'

Grace squirmed at this. She stood up and walked to the other side of the room. Dabbing at her eyes with her handkerchief, she turned to face him. Slumped in the seat of the chesterfield, he seemed to her diminished somehow. A weak and paltry version of his former self. And she knew if he hadn't broken her heart, if she hadn't wasted years of her life, she might have forgiven him. But no. She'd have none of it.

'Can't you see?' he pleaded. 'I was stalling for time. I had every intention of leaving Lois. One day. And I still do. I just worry about the kids…the effect a divorce would have on them. If Lois ever got wind of me committing adultery, she'd…she'd…'

'Castrate you?'

Now before her mirror, Grace snorted at the memory of their conversation. Thank God she'd come to her senses. She could see him now for what he really was. A complete and utter bastard, who'd taken advantage of her innocence and trusting nature. Admittedly, she'd been a naive and starry-eyed fool. But no more. She took off the towel from her head and began to rake a comb through her hair. First thing Monday morning, she'd arrange a meeting with the head of chambers to hand in her resignation – effective in one month. Stuart will of course give her a glowing reference. She'll make sure of that. Or else! And tomorrow morning, she'll tell her parents that she's decided to accept their offer of a return trip to England.

Grace slept well that night. And when she woke the next morning, she had such a sense of relief that she almost felt a little light-headed, for she knew for certain that she'd made the right decision.

A mere six weeks later, with a return ticket valid for two years in her suitcase, Grace sailed out of Sydney Harbour on board the Greek ship *Ellinis* heading for Southampton.

*

While her parents missed her, it was Dutchie who felt her absence keenly. He liked seeing her pretty face, her little smiles. There was nothing of beauty to look at now. When he saw Edith Bannon one day in her garden, not long after Grace had gone, he walked across the road and stood at the front gate.

'Oi, missus! Where's you girl? She's gone away, has she?'

'Why yes, Norman, she has,' came the reply. 'As a matter of fact, Grace has gone to London.'

'To visit the Queen,' he chimed, dimly recalling a rhyme he once knew.

On a separate occasion, he plucked up courage to approach Grace's father. 'When will ya girl be back from London town?'

'And what's it to you, eh?' Henry's voice sounded like a dog's growl. 'Why don't you just bugger off and mind your own bloody business?'

Dutchie knew people could be mean, so he was silent and continued on his way.

*

Quite a lot of people raised their eyebrows when the news went round that Grace Bannon had returned to Australia less than six months after she'd sailed away.

'My God,' said Betty Ward, 'what's wrong with the girl? If my parents had given me a free round-the-world trip, you wouldn't have seen me for dust!'

Henry and Edith had quite a different response. Grace had fallen into their open arms, saying that she'd missed them terribly, that the weather over there was always miserable, that the sun hardly ever shone and the English looked down their noses at Australians. 'We're nothing but a pack of convicts to them,' she said.

Her parents were pleased to have her home. Safe and sound. Although somewhat changed. She'd had her hair bobbed by Vidal Sassoon. She'd brought back a suitcase filled with outlandish clothes, including a pair of go-go boots from Carnaby Street. She spoke of seeing the Beatles film *A Hard Day's Night* and having witnessed a riot between the Mods and Rockers when, one weekend, she'd visited Brighton. She filled the house with colour and sparkle. All this they liked. But it was the music they heard her playing late at night in her room that disturbed them. Over and over, the same record, the same song by Cilla Black – 'Anyone Who Had a Heart'.

'You know, Henry,' whispered Edith one night in their bed, 'I think our daughter may have met some English chap over there who's treated her rather badly. Don't you?'

'I reckon she needs to get back to work. And quick smart too.'

As luck would have it, Grace was offered her old position back at the same law firm and, what's more, with her old boss, Stuart Lang. It just so happened that he wasn't able to find anyone as dedicated and professional as their darling girl.

Dutchie was taken by surprise when he first saw Grace again. He'd been in his yard, mending a hole in his wheelbarrow early one morning, when he heard the Bannons' gate swing shut. He'd looked up and caught a glimpse of her leaving for work as usual. He decided he'd stand by his fence the next morning to check he hadn't been dreaming. Perhaps she'd smile and nod to him if she saw him there. And then he remembered the old brooch he'd found down by the railway underpass in Webb Street a month or so ago. It looked like a basket of pretty glass flowers. He'd give it to the mother to give to her daughter. She'd be sure to look for him then and smile and nod. But he'd have to give it a good clean first. He'd better get cracking, he thought, and hurried inside.

That afternoon, he saw Edith Bannon hosing her plants in her front garden and so he shuffled across the road. It wasn't long before she noticed him standing by her fence.

'Oh hello, Norman,' she said. 'Lovely day…'

'Here,' he said, reaching into his pocket, 'I found this a while back. I fought ya daughter might like it.'

'Well, that's very kind of you, I must say.' Using her thumb and forefinger as tweezers, Edith extracted the garish trinket from his filthy outstretched hand. 'Thank you very much. I'll give it to her when she gets back this evening.' And with that, she turned to leave him. As she walked back towards the house, she heard him call out.

'I fink she'll like it, cause it's pretty like her.'

She did not turn round but, by way of a response, she held her hand up and let her fingers wave to him.

'For Christ's sake, Edith, don't tell me you're going to give it to her,' said Henry when she showed him the brooch. 'It belongs in the garbage bin.'

'Oh, he means well. I'm sure Grace will understand.'

'I don't care if she does or doesn't. I'd rather you throw the bloody thing away. I don't want him hanging around our girl. There's something creepy about him…trying to curry favour with our daughter. Who does he think he is?' He took a breath. He knew he had to stop getting so worked up. 'Will you please do what I say, Edith, and just get rid of it?' Then, trying to sound cheery, 'She doesn't need to know anything about it. You know what I always say – out of sight, out of mind.'

*

It was Reg Keller who found him. He'd been walking his dog, Jazza in the pre-dawn light and as he passed by Dutchie's place, he heard a muffled whimper. Not sure of what he'd heard, he stood still in the middle of the road and listened to the quietness. Jazza sat at his master's heels and waited. It was when he was about to continue his walk that he heard the whimpering again and knew then that it was coming from what appeared to be a mound of discarded clothes lying in the long grass by the side of Dutchie's shack.

Reg quickly tied his dog leash to the fence post and as he neared the source of the weeping, he realised it was Dutchie. Kneeling beside him, he placed his hand gently on the old man's back.

'Come on, Norman,' he said, his voice like rustling leaves. 'What's wrong? Are you in pain, mate?'

The mumbled reply was incomprehensible, and Reg had an inkling that the old man's anguish was a personal matter. He managed to get Dutchie to sit up and then he saw it – the cause of Dutchie's distress. In the chaos of his grief, he'd been cradling his scrawny dog in his arms – mourning its death.

'Can ya see?' asked Dutchie. 'Can ya?'

The sun was rising and had lit the yard with a hazy golden glow. Reg looked about him but wasn't sure what exactly he was supposed to be seeing.

'Don't ya see? He's been given a bait, I'm telling ya. Someone round 'ere has given him a bait.'

'Now come on, matey, you can't be going around saying that sort of thing,' said Reg, doubting that would ever be the case. 'How about you let me give you a hand to bury your dog, then?' He didn't wait for a response. He stood up. 'You got a shovel?'

The old man nodded, then wiped the dripping snot from his nose on his coat sleeve. He hauled himself up from the ground and once standing, leant forward and peered at Reg, his eyes two red slits.

'So, what was your dog's name?' asked Reg, pointing vaguely towards the front gate and offering, 'Mine's called Jazza.'

'Faifful,' said Dutchie. 'I called mine Faifful.'

A Little Bit of History

Although never an Aboriginal reserve or a mission, the area to the east of Salt Pan Creek has been a place of refuge for many Aboriginal people in the Sydney basin for a long, long time.

As for Europeans, their first settlement here started with small land grants in 1810. But the area only became known as Herne Bay in the 1880s, when market gardening and logging were its two main industries. However, it wasn't until the railway line from the city to East Hills was opened in 1931 that modernity arrived. The station was, of course, named Herne Bay.

Then in 1942 during the Second World War, the Australian government, at the request of the US army, built a huge military hospital for their war wounded. Called the 118 General Hospital, it cost over a million pounds to build and consisted of almost five hundred barracks-style timber huts that accommodated over 1,700 patients and more than 3,500 staff. Black and white soldiers were segregated into separate huts. Such was the hospital's importance that the first lady, Mrs Eleanor Roosevelt, General MacArthur and quite a few American celebrities paid visits. When the war ended, so did Herne Bay's glory days.

Not long after the military vacated the site, the NSW Housing Commission converted the hospital huts into 'temporary housing units' to ease Sydney's chronic post-war housing shortage. Over time, the Huts or the Camp, as the Herne Bay Housing Settlement came to be known locally, provided shelter for 3,000 families – mainly migrants and refugees from a bombed and battered Europe and of course, our very own relocated, inner-city 'slum dwellers'.

Families shared laundry facilities. Many shared the ablution blocks, and as the huts had no ceilings, the units were not only hot in summer and cold in winter, they also weren't soundproof. Not surprisingly, the powerful combination of poverty, cultural and linguistic misunderstandings, dislocation, despair and disadvantage resulted in frequent acts of violence and other forms of antisocial behaviour. The solid citizens of Sydney in the fifties were outraged, and so it was that Herne Bay developed an unsavoury name for itself.

In a bid to remove the social stigma for those living there, the suburb was officially renamed Riverwood which, by 1958, was in common usage. But few people were fooled. Even when the huts were demolished in the 1960s and replaced by permanent government housing, its negative reputation remained. A cluster of high-rise apartment buildings had been erected on streets with names like Roosevelt and Truman Avenues, Kentucky Road, Idaho Place, Montana Crescent, all reflecting the area's wartime past, but quite bizarre for the socially disadvantaged people housed in these tenements on the north side of the train station.

The railway tracks unwittingly cleaved the suburb in two. All the houses on the southern side of the line were free-standing bungalows. Some were public housing, but most were privately owned or, more correctly, under a mortgage that was being steadily and proudly paid off. What's more, the residents were mainly white, Anglo-Saxon Protestants. The men went to work, and the women stayed at home. An ordered, conformist community.

Not at all like the rabble to the north of the station.

By the Water

When they found out that Old Man Bagley would be spending the entire month of January at his daughter's place on the south coast, the girls didn't take long to convince themselves that he wouldn't mind in the slightest if they used his jetty as their regular meeting place throughout the school holidays. Surely, he'd realise they were doing him a good turn by keeping an eye on his property.

The first time they go there, it's one of those perfect mornings down by the sleepy river – a dreamy, cornflower-blue summer sky; the dull, incessant hum of cicadas; and the occasional, lonely caw of a crow. Kate arrives first. She's early. She hasn't seen Denise since the school year ended, because the entire Reid family took off to Bundeena over the Christmas and New Year period. And Kate had missed her friend.

Lying on her back on the white-painted boards, she flips off her thongs, raises both legs and lets her bare feet rest up against one of the jetty's wooden piers. Reaching for her bag, she is about to pull out her battered paperback copy of *Gone with the Wind*, when a commotion of sulphur-crested cockatoos streaks across the sky. She watches them disappear over the river as the voice of Mick Jagger singing 'Ruby Tuesday' draws closer and closer.

It's Denise with her new transistor radio. 'Got it from Santa,' she says, smirking. 'Are you going to move your bum and let me sit next to you?' She looks down at her friend; her chestnut-brown Mary Quant fringe grazes her kohl-rimmed, hazel eyes. She's wearing a skimpy red T-shirt and a black miniskirt.

Kate wants to tell her she looks fantastic, but instead says, 'Can you turn that thing off?'

'And it's really great to see you too, Mr Magoo.' With a toss of her hair, she switches off the music. 'Sorry, Mick,' she says, as she places the transistor on top of the opposite pier, 'my friend here doesn't like you singing about other girls.'

Denise remains standing and looks down at Kate, who's now grinning.

'You're a laugh a minute, Denise.'

They've been best friends since primary school. Gentle teasing is allowed. Kate sits up and makes room for her friend to sit beside her. With their feet now dangling above the coolness of the water, the pair look out across the river.

'So how have your holidays been so far?' Denise asks.

'Pretty boring. The usual stuff. Tough old turkey and too much plum pudding.' Kate is silent for a moment, then says, 'I went to the beach a couple of times and I've read a few good books…'

'That reminds me,' says Denise, her voice now excited. 'I brought you these.' And she hands her friend a multicoloured string bag full of magazines. 'My cousin Vicky gave them to me, but I've read them all now, so I thought you'd like them. They're all true-life confessions.' She grabs one from the bag. 'Like, listen to this,' and reads from the cover breathlessly, 'Why did I have to be different? The sweet thrill of a kiss… The tender touch of a man's hand on mine… The loving embrace… How I wanted all of these things and yet, deep inside me, I knew that when the time came, I would be in…' She pauses a moment and then theatrically finishes with '…no mood for love!'

'Who writes this shit?' Kate says, laughing.

'I don't know, but I reckon we'd be pretty bloody good at it.'

They spend a few minutes poring over several of the more lurid magazine covers when, without warning, Denise quickly gathers up the magazines, shoves them back with the others into the bag and says, 'You can read them later. I've got something really BIG to tell you.'

'Well, don't beat around the bush.' Kate swivels to face her friend and grabs her hand. 'Out with it.'

'Swear you'll never tell a soul…'

'I swear, I swear…'

'Promise you won't judge me.'

'Why, what've you done?'

'Nothing yet, but oh God, Katie…' She bites her upper lip with her bottom teeth. 'You've gotta promise we'll still be friends no matter what.'

'Of course, you goose. I'll always be your friend. Always.'

'Well, I… I've fallen crazy, crazy in love with someone.' Denise closes her eyes.

Kate releases her friend's hand. 'Oh, come on, will you? Spit it out. Who is he?'

'Graham Ingram.'

'Graham Ingram? The mechanic? The one who lives with his family down on the river at the end of your street?' Kate can't believe it. She doesn't know what to say.

'Yes, that's the one.'

'But…but…'

'I know…you think he's a creep.' She stares straight ahead of her. Her breathing is slow, deliberate. 'But he isn't. In actual fact, he's really nice… I've got to know him, Katie.'

'Really? How? Since when? Don't keep me in suspense.' Kate hopes she sounds carefree, uncritical, supportive.

And so it all comes tumbling out. How Denise's older brother Vince, the panel-beater, who sometimes works with Graham on smash repairs, invited him down to Bundeena for a weekend. At first, he didn't seem to notice Denise, but on the last night of his stay, when everyone was sitting around watching telly, she sees him looking at her – really looking at her – and she starts feeling hot all over, and then he smiles and winks at her, and ever since then she hasn't been able to stop thinking about him.

'And that was it? He didn't speak to you? You were never actually alone together?'

'No, we didn't get a chance.'

Kate is relieved. It's all in her friend's head. 'It might not be anything,' she says, trying not to sound too dismissive.

'Oh, it's something all right! I've never felt like this, Katie. Not ever. And I can't get him out of my mind.'

'But what if he was just being friendly. To his mate's kid sister. I mean, he must be five or six years older than us.'

'You didn't see the way he looked at me, though.' A pause. 'I did and I've replayed that look over and over again in my mind and I tell you, I wasn't imagining it.'

'Have you seen him since you got back from Bundeena?'

'Nah, not yet. But I know I will.'

*

Later, along a treeless street, where bleached grey wooden fences mark out family boundaries, the two friends are walking home past all the sun burnt, crew-cut lawns and the occasional well-pruned rose bush. Denise kicks the odd stone. Kate lets her left hand sweep along the top of a stiffly clipped garden hedge. Unseen, a dog yaps furiously.

'Heard anything from Gary Saunders since I've been away?'

'No, I thought I told you. He has to work during the holidays.'

'I guess you haven't said anything to your parents about him then?'

Kate can't help feeling irritated by this line of questioning. 'What am I supposed to tell them? There's nothing to tell. I'm not allowed to have a boyfriend until I'm sixteen, and they're not going to suddenly change their minds because of Gary...'

'No need to get huffy,' says Denise, 'I was only asking.'

They continue walking in silence, preoccupied with their own thoughts. Denise is glad she didn't tell Kate about the previous night when she was lying in bed, thinking about Graham, imagining him kissing her again and again and how she put her hand between her legs and squeezed and squeezed. And it was hot in her room and it was like he was in bed with her, on top of her and she was breathing fast and feeling hot and clammy, but she liked it. Really liked it. And she's worried now that maybe, just maybe, she won't be able to stay a virgin until she's married like she'd always said she would. And even now she feels wet between her legs just thinking about Graham and she knows it seems crazy because all that's happened between them so far is a smile and a wink. She wonders if there's something wrong with her, if she's oversexed, like one of those girls she's heard her brothers talking about. And it's no good telling Kate about it. She wouldn't understand. She just wouldn't have a clue.

Kate can't stop wondering how on earth Denise thinks Graham Ingram is attractive. The guy's a worm, a slimeball. He makes Kate's flesh crawl just thinking about him. What's wrong with Denise? Can't she see that Ingram's no good? She's always been the smart one about stuff like this, thanks to her having an older sister and three older brothers. What they haven't told her, or wouldn't, she's gleaned from reading the advice columns in magazines like *Playboy* and *Pix* that her brother Doug hides under his mattress. All she knows is that Denise better watch out or she'll end up like her sister Robyn, who had to get married last year and now she hates her husband Keith because she's stuck at home with a baby that cries all day long.

The drone of a lone lawnmower starts up somewhere close by.

'That could be Dad,' says Kate. 'It's his weekend off. I'd better hurry and get on home.'

'Oh, I meant to tell you. Down in Bundeena, I saw your father on TV. He'd arrested some bloke for bashing that Aboriginal man to death on some demolition site in Redfern.'

'Yeah, I saw it too.' Kate starts to turn the corner to head home.

Denise keeps walking along Salt Pan Road. 'See ya!' She gives a cursory wave of the hand. 'I'll ring you tomorrow.'

*

Denise's place isn't far from Kate's – just a short block away and then a few houses up from the corner of Salt Pan Road. Kate stands on the Reid family's backdoor steps and knocks on the door. She can hear the sound of a baby crying somewhere inside the house.

'Robyn's here,' mouths Denise through the fly-screen door. She turns her head to face inside and calls out, 'Hey, Mum, Katie and me are going down the creek for a while.'

'Be back here by noon,' comes the reply.

'Perfect,' says Kate, 'same time I've got to be back home.'

It had been two weeks since the two friends last saw one another. There'd been phone calls, but their conversations had been mechanical.

'I love mornings like these, don't you?' says Denise, 'with these great cotton wool clouds floating in a blue, blue sky.'

And before Kate can respond, the girls grab each other's hand and go racing down the dirt track that leads from the bottom of Clarendon Road to the bushland that borders the creek. The competing perfumes of lantana, mud and pine needles always make the two of them feel happy and safe.

When they reach the water's edge, they bend down almost simultaneously and put their hands in the water to check the temperature. Had they been younger, they would have thrown off their shoes and socks as they once used to do and wade into the dark sludge that was their river and they'd have squealed with delight as the thick black mud squelched between their toes. But they are now far too grown-up for such childishness, so they find a large, dry rock in partial shade, where they can sit and talk and watch the slow, slow flow of the water.

'Guess what?'

'Oh, just tell me,' says Denise, 'you know, I hate dumb guessing games.'

'My parents are letting me go to a birthday party with Gary.'

'You're kidding me. When did this happen?'

'About a week ago. Gary's mum phoned my mum and asked if it'd be OK for me to go with Gary to Paul Cochrane's twenty-first. She explained how the two Cochrane brothers, Paul and Ron, being neighbours and all, have virtually grown up with Gary. Mrs Saunders also said that she and her husband would be going to the party too; that they knew the family very well and that it wouldn't be a late night. Mum just said yes, that'd be fine. I couldn't believe it. She didn't even check to see if Dad agreed.'

'Wow! When is it? The party, I mean.' Denise appears to be genuinely pleased.

'In three weeks' time.'

'That's great. But don't mind me asking…do they know he's Aboriginal?'

'Yeah, I guess so.'

For a little while, neither girl speaks.

Then Kate breaks the silence. 'What do you think I should wear?'

Denise dismisses the question with a casual toss of her hand. 'You've got plenty of time to figure that out, don't you think?'

Kate feels the sting of her friend's words. Perhaps Denise is a little envious. There's been no mention of the ghastly Graham Ingram asking her out on a date. And then, for reasons Kate will never understand, she tells Denise that last night, she hadn't been able to sleep for excitement and she'd kept thinking of Gary and their future together and how they'd be seeing one another not just at school any more, that there'd be times when they'd be together at night, that he'd hold her close and they'd kiss and kiss again and she started to rub herself against the mattress over and over, over and over.

'And you didn't want to stop doing it, did you? Because you liked how it felt.'

'Yes, of course I liked it.'

'That's because it's natural. And when Gary actually does hold you and kisses you just like you imagine, let me tell you, you're going to feel like you're melting, like you never want it to stop…' Her voice trails away for a moment and then she asks, 'So do you reckon you can trust Gary not to go any further?'

'I think so.' It's a pathetic answer, and Denise knows it.

'Well, I bloody well hope so, for your sake, because it sounds to me like you won't want him to stop.'

Kate is stunned. Why the hostility? What is Denise implying? That Kate's too easy or just plain naïve, like some fool waiting to be taken advantage of?

They stay there on the rock for a while in silence, each girl struggling with her own miserable thoughts. Denise fiddles with her hair, picking out split ends, while Kate watches a group of young boys who've gathered by the water's edge and are playing at skimming stones on the river's surface.

Suddenly, Denise grabs her friend's wrist and holds it tightly. 'You've got to look me in the eye right this minute and promise me that you'll never tell a single soul what I'm about to tell you.'

'I promise, I promise. I'll never tell anyone…you should know that by now.' Kate feels afraid. She has no idea what Denise is about to say, but her friend looks tense and serious. Her eyes have become two tiny beads.

And then she speaks, and Kate tries very hard not to look surprised and a little bewildered when Denise tells her that as of yesterday she and Graham Ingram are going steady, and that he's going to buy her a friendship ring, but first they have to keep things quiet, that her parents mightn't understand because of the difference in their ages, and they're going to break the news gently to Vince as well, because he definitely won't want her hanging around with him and his mates.

'How did all this happen?' Kate asks, finding it all too hard to believe. 'When did it start?'

'Only last weekend. He'd dropped by with two other mates of Vince's, and they all started drinking beer and watching the wrestling on TV. I was in the bathroom washing my hair and when I came out, he was standing in the hallway right outside the bathroom door. He said he'd been waiting for me…' She looks away for a moment and when her eyes return to Kate's, she is radiant. 'Then he told me I was beautiful.'

Well, he got something right, Kate thinks, but instead says, 'Where were your mum and dad when all this was going on?'

'At Robyn's.'

'So then what happened? You can't leave it there.'

'He kissed me, and I kissed him back and then he kissed me some more, and I thought I was going to faint, and we couldn't stop kissing, and he was all excited and started kissing my neck, and I let him unbutton the top button of my brunch coat…'

'Oh God, Denise…' Kate tries really hard not to sound disapproving, but her friend straightens her back as if preparing to defend herself, and Kate can't help but notice the icy coolness in her voice when she next speaks.

'Nothing happened. We thought we heard Vince coming, so I ducked back into the bathroom and turned on the tap. When I came out again, only my brothers were left and they were in the kitchen making sandwiches as well as a bloody mess.'

Kate wants to know how kissing in the hallway translates into going steady and when she asks her, Denise slides off the rock to stand and face her friend directly. With feet slightly parted and arms folded beneath her breasts, she proceeds to inform her that since the bathroom incident she and Graham had been secretly meeting most afternoons in his family's old boatshed. 'And what's more, he's already told me he loves me.'

This is Denise at her theatrical best, proudly defiant and daring Kate to pass judgement on her. It's a complex dance, one Kate had seen her present to others over the years, but not one performed especially for her. It's clear that Denise is telling her that she knows that Kate thinks Graham is unworthy of her and that her silence on the matter is cowardly and a betrayal of their friendship.

Sitting there as if she's become part of the landscape, inert upon the rock, still saying nothing, Kate reads the hurt in Denise's eyes. She wants to say sorry, that she was confused, that she should've been honest and open from the beginning, that she never wanted to upset her friend. And now she's frightened, really frightened that their friendship may never recover from her careless deception. How could she have forgotten that she was like a sheet of plate glass to Denise – completely transparent? From the first time she'd mentioned Graham, when they were down on Old Man Bagley's jetty, Denise knew that Kate thought he was a creep and she'd carried that insight within her ever since. Of the two of them, Denise is the better friend; she gives a great deal and demands only honesty in return.

Kate scrambles off the rock and rushes towards Denise. Flinging her arms around her neck, she begs her forgiveness, tells her she loves her, that her happiness is her happiness. The pair cling to one another and rock from side to side, delirious with friendship. Then one of the boys, who'd been skimming stones, turns from the river and seeing the girls, points in their direction and starts to yell to his mates:

'Hey, get a load of the two lesos, will ya?'

'Look, you little shits,' Denise breaks free from Kate's embrace and strides towards the boys and the river. 'Why don't you show us your dicks?' she shrieks. 'Come on, boys, show us how big your dicks are… Come on…give us a look, you little worms!'

They vanish in seconds, and Denise turns back to her friend.

'Ha!' She's grinning with triumph. 'Gets 'em every time!'

They both start to laugh then, and their laughter soon becomes uncontrollable, only ceasing when they squat to pee near the river's shoreline beside a tangled clump of mangrove buttress roots.

Then, together, they walk back home, both girls unaware that by the end of the year their childhoods would be well and truly over.

Second Fragment

Once Governor Phillip clears off, Lieutenant King's party rows up to the head of Lime Kiln Bay which, back in 1788, was an open salt marsh but is now choked with thick and densely packed mangroves. King notices some natives following and once his boat reaches the head of the inlet, even more appear - all armed with spears and what King calls short bludgeons. Some of them even wade up to the boat, which makes King a little apprehensive, for now he and his men are truly outnumbered. More trinkets are given, and King offers two of the 'Indians' some wine, which they try but immediately spit out.

King then writes of how quick these young indigenous men are to learn English. He is impressed by the way they are soon pointing at everything they want and then look at him imploringly, saying 'No?' They accept it when no more gifts are forthcoming and quiz the British by plainly indicating that they think they are women because none of them have beards. Obligingly, King gives an order to one of his crew to unbutton his breeches and reveal what he is made of. Not surprisingly, this is greeted with much yahooing and pointing to a nearby place on the beach, where a number of women and children are gathered. King describes them somewhat demurely, 'All in *puris naturalibus pas meme la feuille de figeur.*' He then records that the young warriors' gestures to him and his crew indicated they were free to have sex with these women.

While claiming he declined their hospitality, he fails to mention what his crew may have said or done with such an offer. Instead, he launches into an extremely odd account of him beckoning one of the women to come to him, and when she does, he places a handkerchief most strategically 'where Eve did ye fig leaf'. Quite the pompous prig, really. Especially when we consider that within twelve months, King had not only set up a convict settlement on Norfolk Island under instructions from Arthur Phillip, but had also taken up with Ann Inett, a female convict, who bore him the first of two illegitimate sons there.

The next thing he reports is that night was fast approaching, and it was time to row the twelve miles back to Botany Bay. He then tells us they boarded the *Supply* around midnight. Based solely on King's journal, several historians believe that the encounter with the local people on the shores of Lime Kiln Bay, lasted about five hours – a lot longer than the fleeting interchange King describes. And perhaps more mutually enjoyable too.

Of course, we're left to wonder just how serious the offer of sex actually was. Was it in fact as Philip Gidley King saw it – an overture of hospitality – or was it an example of the boisterous bravado and macho posturing of young men anywhere, just having a bit of a laugh, however crass and tasteless?

Cold Lamb Chops

Even after it was officially renamed Riverwood, many residents struggled to deal with the suburb's lingering notoriety. Betty Ward was one of them. Whenever she was asked where she lived, she lifted her chin, lowered her eyelids slightly and, with a pout of her lips, whispered Peakhurst, the suburb only two streets further south, but one that had dodged the shameful reputation of Herne Bay. She was able to fool quite a few people, but there were some who suspected her of lying and so they either judged her to be a contemptible snob or felt just plain sorry for her.

Everyone who knew her, however, would have said she was a difficult person and an extremely complex one at that. Her attitude to religion was a case in point. Although raised as a Methodist, she had never been baptised. Not that she told many people about that. At any rate, she was no churchgoer and considered most Protestants who did attend regularly to be hypocrites of the first order.

'You can see them with their noses in the air every Sunday – all righteous and dressed in their finery, as if God could give two hoots how they looked. And off they go to make amends for all the lousy things they've said and done all week.' Then a tiny pause before the sneering summation: 'Fat chance the Lord would be listening to the likes of them, I say!'

As for Roman Catholics, her criticism was caustic and in keeping with the sectarian divide that existed throughout Australia in the fifties and sixties. She maintained that most Catholics were of Irish stock and were therefore shiftless layabouts, not to be trusted. She'd often rail against their belief in the infallibility of the Pope, which formed part of her tirade against the Hogans, one of only two Catholic families in the street. When sixteen-year-old Claire Hogan discovered she was pregnant, her parents Leo and Veronica decided to send her away to have her baby, which would be adopted as soon as it was born.

Betty Ward found this deeply distressing. 'What kind of religion is it, may I ask, that ruins a young girl's life because abortion is forbidden on the grounds that it's murder? Murder of a foetus. What a load of poppycock! How can something the size of a pea be called a foetus? Because that's all it is in the early stages of pregnancy, and that's when you do it. The termination, I mean. No harm's done then. And the girl can go back to having a life. So tell me, what's wrong with that?'

No one dared speak, let alone object.

'But oh no, the Tykes will have none of it. The girl must suffer for her sins. While the boy gets off scot-free and takes no responsibility whatsoever for making the girl pregnant in the first place, the girl must be punished and carry the shame for nine long months with everyone knowing and judging her. And as if that's not enough, she goes through the agony of childbirth to give the baby away and live the rest of her life in a state of perpetual guilt. Do you think that's fair? Do you think that's showing Christian mercy? All that suffering because some pipsqueak Italian male way over in Rome says that's what must be done. And all the bead-clicking idiots say he's right!'

Betty's audience was always spellbound. And this occasion was no different. She had Kate pouring more tea while her two closest friends, both devout Catholics, smiled and nodded as if they approved of every word she'd said. Maria was an Italian, originally from Calabria, and Erika was from Hungary. Each of them was married to one of Milton's two best friends and fellow detectives – Maria to Ted Mercer and Erika to Trevor Clunes.

Much later that night, long after the visitors had left, Betty went to check on Kate, who was in bed reading. 'Lights out,' said Betty, who'd poked her head round the bedroom door.

'OK, but Mum…' she said, closing her book and placing it on top of her bedside table.

'Yes, Katie.' Betty sounded tired, but she entered the room and approached her daughter's bed. 'What is it?'

'I've been thinking about what you were saying about Claire Hogan and Roman Catholics, and I agree with what you were saying, but I did kind of feel sorry for Aunty Erika and Aunty Maria.'

'What do you mean, you felt sorry for them?'

'Well, you were saying some terrible things about Catholics, Mum, and they're supposed to be your best friends and all. Don't you think you were being a bit disrespectful of them and their beliefs?'

'What nonsense!' came the reply. 'Maria and Erika are nothing like the Hogans. They're different. I know them, and let me tell you, they agree with me.' She turned to go and then, as an afterthought, added, 'If you hadn't been there, they'd have said plenty about abortion. And contraception too. You mark my words, my girl. There are just some things you don't yet understand.' And with two of her fingers, she tapped her daughter on the forehead, switched off the reading lamp and was gone.

Kate lay on her back in the darkness of her room and thought about her mother. She wasn't one bit like any of the other mothers she knew. And she certainly wasn't what you'd call affectionate. Well, not to Kate, she wasn't. Mark, of course, was quite a different matter. She always fussed over him, but then he was her pet. Her favourite. Her baby. And Kate accepted that. Without rancour. After all, she had her dad. She'd never doubted his love. He would've kissed her goodnight – that is, after he'd asked her about the book she was reading. Milton was a reader, just like she was. Whereas Kate couldn't remember the last time she'd seen her mother with her head in a book. She just wasn't that sort.

Not that she had any idea what sort her mother actually was. Although she wished she wasn't so critical of other people. Betty always seemed to have some bee in her bonnet about somebody or something. Like at the Kellers' barbecue a few weeks back. Most of the neighbours had been invited, and people were scattered about the backyard in little animated clusters. Milton was over near the keg and makeshift bar, helping Reg Keller serve drinks. Kate looked uncomfortable in a deckchair next to her mother, who was sitting in a plastic folding picnic chair beneath a colourful beach umbrella.

'Will you get a load of June Morrison over there?' Betty said to her daughter between puffs on her cigarette, then tilted her head in her victim's direction. 'Just look at her – nodding in agreement with every stupid bloody thing her husband says. You'd think she didn't have any views of her own. Hasn't she got a tongue in her head?'

Kate stared across the yard at Mrs Morrison, wondering if she'd overheard her mother, who couldn't have cared less even if she had. Betty often bragged to anyone who'd listen that she didn't mince her words for anybody. Her daughter had no reason to disbelieve her. About anything really. Including Betty's frequent claim that the happiest time of her life was when she was single and training to be a nurse.

She'd said it again only last week when Milton failed to come home at his usual time of six p.m., which was sometimes the case if he had to work back, or if there was a cause for celebration, such as the solving of a murder or a conviction being secured. And that's what had happened eight days ago. Kate had answered the phone when Milton rang in the late afternoon. As soon as she heard the rowdy pub laughter in the background, she knew her father wouldn't be home for dinner.

'Tell your mother I'll be a little bit late. OK?'

'What's happened, Dad?' She knew he'd been at court all day.

'McKnight changed his mind and decided to plead guilty this afternoon. So we're having a few quiet ales. Tell your mum I won't be too long.' And then he hung up the phone.

Betty wasn't pleased. As she always did on such occasions, she put Mark to bed straight after the evening meal, which Kate took as a signal that being so much older than her brother, she was free to do as she pleased. This usually meant she could go to her room and read to her heart's content and she did just that, after she'd eaten and helped her mother do the dishes. Of course, she knew exactly where her mother would be. She would go to her bedroom and sit on the edge of her bed by the window. Smoking one cigarette after another in the darkness, she would stare out through the slats of the Venetian blinds into the loneliness of the street and wait for the headlights of a Ford Falcon to slash the road's black night that would announce her husband's return to her.

Hours passed. Kate finished her library book but she wasn't tired. She went into the kitchenette and put on the electric kettle. Time for a cup of tea. Perhaps her mum would like one too.

'Why don't you watch TV, instead of sitting here in the dark?' she asked as she entered her parents' bedroom.

Betty didn't even flinch. 'Why don't you mind your own business for a change?'

Kate didn't respond at first. She sat down beside her mother and after a while said, 'You can't blame Dad for wanting to celebrate the end of a pretty terrible case.'

'Yes, I can. I gave up the happiest years of my life for that man. I can do whatever I like.' She stubbed out her cigarette into the almost filled ashtray. 'But anyway, I don't wish to discuss it, Katie. With you or anyone else for that matter.' Betty spoke slowly, trying to control her fury. 'Now, if you want to remain here, you can do so, but there'll be no talking. Not a word. Understood?'

'Yes, but would you like some tea?'

'I'd love some. Thank you.'

When Kate returned with the mugs of tea, she handed her mother one, then sat down beside her.

Silence.

Kate started thinking about Pauline Sykes, the murdered girl, who was only a year younger than she was. She'd gone missing on her way home from school back in November. Police searched for days while Pauline's face smiled out from the front page of every daily newspaper in the state. 'Disappeared Without a Trace!' shrieked the headlines, when, in fact, she'd been strangled and stabbed to death with a broken milk bottle before being dumped into an old, disused water tank. Her water-swollen body was found by a couple of young boys on the lookout for tadpoles. Pauline Sykes was no teenage runaway. The suburbs of Sydney became fearful. Milton was one of the more senior detectives put on the case and, without any real leads, he began to despair of ever finding Pauline's killer.

Then, the breakthrough.

Another girl came forward, reporting she'd been attacked by some hoodlum who'd tried to push her into the boot of his clapped-out Holden sedan. Thankfully, she managed to struggle free and, what's more, she remembered most of the car's registration number, as well as its colour and make. This information led to a house in Dural, where nineteen-year-old Stephen McKnight lived.

'He's not home yet,' said his mother to Milton and his junior partner. 'But you're welcome to come in and wait for him. He shouldn't be too long.'

Once inside and seated at the Laminex kitchen table, Milton spoke first. 'Mrs McKnight, we'd like to speak to your son in relation to the suspected rape and murder of Pauline Sykes.'

'What? What did you say?' The woman's face looked incredulous.

Milton repeated what he'd said and waited to hear the mother's protests, her disbelief, the denials.

But instead, she turned pale and clutching at the stainless-steel edge of the table, began to cry, 'Oh, no…oh my God no…this can't be happening.'

When Milton told his wife and daughter about Mrs McKnight's despair that day, Kate had visualised the entire scene, how the poor woman had lost her husband in a mining accident and was left to raise her three children alone and what a handful her son had become, how she'd had to have locks fitted on the windows and door of her daughters' bedroom to keep her son from molesting them. 'I'm at my wits' end,' she'd said, 'at my wits' end.'

Two slender beams of golden saffron light split the road outside.

Betty stands up. 'Here,' she says to her daughter, handing over her empty mug, 'put them in the sink.'

Just as Kate finishes washing and drying the mugs, Milton comes stumbling through the front door. She can tell by the racket he's making that he's as drunk as an Irish priest on St Patrick's Day.

'Hello, darling,' he says, trying to lean towards Betty for a kiss.

She slips behind him to shut the front door and so avoids his lips. Milton kisses the air instead. He doesn't seem to mind and totters backwards, almost falling. Somehow, he steadies himself and makes for the dinner table.

'Sit down, before you fall down,' Betty snarls, 'and I'll get you your dinner.'

Milton obeys then grins. He's spied Kate standing at the other end of the table. His eyes tell her that he wants her to stay, that there'll be less trouble for him that way.

'Here it is!' And with that, Betty slams down a plate of cold lamb chops and vegetables. 'It was good and hot five hours ago. What a pity you weren't here then.' Betty's face is ablaze with the smirk of victory.

Expressionless, Milton looks down at the plate in front of him and begins to cut the meat. Forking a piece into his mouth, he looks up at Kate and begins to chew. He gives her a wink. She smiles in return. Having seen this silent conspiracy between father and daughter, Betty sweeps out of the room, which appears to shudder when she slams her bedroom door.

Milton pushes his plate aside. Some peas roll unnoticed onto the tablecloth. 'Don't worry, love,' he says, 'she'll come round.'

But she doesn't. The following morning, a Saturday, Betty fills the house with her sulking. It's fierce, and the silence screams her rage.

'Do you think they might get a divorce?'

'Nah, I don't think so, Mark,' answers Kate, placing her arm loosely around her young brother's shoulders.

They're taking their dachshund, Otto down to the river. Anything to get out of the house.

'It's not the first row they've ever had. And it won't be their last. You'll see.' But she's not so sure. She fears the worst. She doesn't want to end up like Susan Underwood. When her parents divorced, Susan was the talk of the school and she didn't stop crying for a week. Then she moved away and had to change schools. More tears.

Kate and Mark walk on in silence. As they near the river, Otto pulls on his lead.

*

Three days later, Kate comes home from school and finds her parents standing by the sink in their tiny kitchen. Folded tightly together, they are unaware of their daughter's presence. She is taking in the scene: Milton's hands are cupping his wife's buttocks; the hem of Betty's dress is halfway up the back of her thighs.

She's seen enough. She goes straight to her room, determined never to grow up to be like her mother.

Third Fragment

Within days of the exploration of the Georges River, Governor Arthur Phillip deems Botany Bay unsuitable for the first English convict settlement in Australia and chooses instead Sydney Cove.

Phillip nobly follows King George III's official instructions that he should 'endeavour by every possible means to open an Intercourse with the ~~Savages~~ [sic] Natives and to conciliate their affections, enjoining all Our Subjects to live in amity and kindness with them'.

Understandably, this doesn't mean much to the Eora people – at first. But as time progresses, things begin to get very grim. For everyone. There are no supply ships for almost two years, and while the colony starves, desperation sets in. Meanwhile, the Eora not only see their food and tools stolen, but they also see trees being cut down, bush being cleared and, as more and more of their land is being taken, sacred sites are being violated.

Finally, in December 1790, a hunting party, consisting of a sergeant of marines and three convicts, sets off to Botany Bay in search of food. One of these convicts is Phillip's gamekeeper, John McIntyre, a man despised by many Eora people, including Bennelong. Allowed to roam the bush freely, McIntyre poaches game from Aboriginal land and, what's more, he uses a gun to do so, proof to the Eora nation that he's not only a pathetic stalker of game, but by firing a weapon he drives the animals away. Not at all sporting of him. But even some notable British have little time for the man. The well-respected officer Watkin Tench and David Collins, judge advocate and the governor's secretary, suspect the gamekeeper of killing Aboriginal people.

The small hunting party heads south away from the British

settlement towards Botany Bay. Near the Cooks River the party is ambushed, and McIntyre is wounded by a spear that is barbed with small pieces of red stone, designed to shatter inside the body. The spear pierces his lung. Once back at the settlement, the gamekeeper admits to having committed terrible crimes. He lingers for weeks then recants and protests his innocence just prior to his death on 20 January 1791.

The spear is identified by many in the colony as belonging to Pemulwuy, clever man, Dreamtime warrior, and leader of the Bidjigal (River Flat) clan, known for being hunters and woodsmen. Evidence suggests that Bidjigal country stretched west from Botany Bay to Salt Pan Creek, where Pemulwuy was said to have a camp.

Incensed by his gamekeeper's death, Phillip abandons his commitment to forge an agreeable alliance with the Eora and punish only individuals. Now he decides to make an example of the entire tribe. Retaliatory expeditions are organised under the leadership of Captain Watkin Tench, who is able to persuade Phillip to reduce the number of captives to be taken, as well as the number of indigenous heads to be brought back to the settlement for public display. But the entire scheme is a failure of almost farcical proportions, with uniformed marines crashing through the bush, men, including Tench, almost drowning in mud, swarms of sandflies attacking the troops and not one Aboriginal warrior in sight.

This military bungle may have established Pemulwuy's reputation as an elusive resistance fighter, but it is the ever-increasing attacks on settlers' properties – on their crops and livestock – that cements his notoriety. Many of the attacks are payback for atrocities. But it is his 1797 raid on a government farm at Toongabbie with a force of over one hundred Aboriginal people that makes Pemulwuy legendary. Critically wounded, he is taken to hospital and, in leg irons, escapes and survives. This incredible feat gives substance to the Eora's belief that he could change into a crow at will. Like all stories of heroes, his became a potent tangle of myth and fact.

When British settlers begin to farm around the previously safe

Georges River, a series of successful raids led by Pemulwuy result. In the hope of destroying the invaders' houses, fences, crops, stock and supplies, fires are lit. These are guerrilla tactics used by increasingly desperate people, many of whom have died from European diseases such as smallpox, as well as in battles with the settlers. And so in 1801, Governor Philip Gidley King decides to offer rewards of free pardons for convicts and twenty gallons of spirits for Pemulwuy's capture, dead or alive. In June the following year, Pemulwuy is shot dead, decapitated and his head immersed in spirits and sent to England. In the nineteenth century, his head was known to be in the Hunterian Museum at the Royal College of Surgeons in London.

In 1809, William Bond and Frederick Meredith are each granted considerable parcels of land along Salt Pan Creek, which they intend to clear and cultivate. Pemulwuy's son, Tedbury, continuing his father's campaign of resistance, embarks upon a battle for possession and drives them away. He is killed the following year.

It should be noted that despite numerous recent requests to have Pemulwuy's remains repatriated, the location of his head in England is now unknown.

Traces

The most unusual thing about the Cochrane brothers was their mother. Cherie Bassani wasn't like any of the other mums in the district. She'd been married three times. And rumour had it that she'd had more than a few lovers in her time. Cherie never appeared to care too hoots that she was the subject of salacious gossip. She believed such talk was driven by envy and so she basked in the backhanded compliments from those she considered were discontented, bitter people.

As a young woman, Cherie had been a nightclub singer, and her first husband, Sam Cochrane, had been both her manager and piano accompanist. When Cherie was pregnant with Ron, the younger of the two brothers, her nightclub work dried up somewhat, so Sam took a job in the entertainment section of a P&O ship that was headed for Southampton. He never came back. According to Paul and Ron, their dad was now some big-time music director and record producer in London. They might not have had much to do with him, but that didn't stop them from feeling proud of his success.

As for Cherie, she was forced to raise her two sons on her own. At least until she met husband number two, or Uncle Dave, as the boys called him. He was a bookmaker and an extremely good provider, but he didn't last long. Dave dropped dead in 1960, two days after Hi Jinx won the Melbourne Cup at 50 to 1, leaving Cherie financially secure for the rest of her life. The first thing she did was to buy herself a brand-new EK Holden, as well as the Elwin Street house, where she now lived.

A year later, Mario Bassani, a tall and handsome Italian, moved in.

In search of a future, he'd come to Australia in 1952 as an assisted migrant by working on the Snowy Mountains hydroelectric scheme. Cherie was soon pregnant again and in due course gave birth to Benito or, as Paul and Ron preferred to call him, *il piccolo bastardo*.

*

On the night of her eldest son's twenty-first birthday party, Cherie took to her bed. She professed she was suffering from a severe migraine and needed a darkened room and a good dose of solitude. The guests understood. They were her friends. They knew her well. She was just one of those artistic types – unpredictable in an amusing, theatrical way. And that's precisely what they liked about her. And though they were familiar with her dying swan routine, they knew it wouldn't last long. Starved for attention in her room, she'd make a dramatic appearance soon enough.

Out in the backyard, despite the heat of a late February evening, a fire raged inside a forty-four-gallon drum. Strings of festive coloured lights had been draped along the wooden paling fences. Two long trellis tables covered in butchers paper supported piles of plates and an assortment of cutlery. A third table had an enormous keg of beer at one end, while the rest of it was covered with bowls of nuts and potato crisps, various glasses, flagons of wine and several bottles of spirits. Nearby, an old concrete laundry tub was filled with ice and a good variety of soft drinks. From a speaker perched on the veranda, Jose Feliciano's faultless diction pleaded for his baby to light his fire. Some people were dancing. Others stood around or sat in nests of chairs, drinking and talking and laughing. Mario played the consummate host, making introductions and keeping glasses topped up, while Paul and Ron were left to welcome guests and apologise for their mother's absence.

Although the night was still young, the party was well underway when Gary Saunders arrived holding the hand of his girlfriend, Kate. Paul rushed to greet them. As he opened the front screen door, he flashed what would one day become his trademark grin. It was warm, reassuring, open. You can trust me, it said. In years to come, well after he'd completed his economics degree and saved enough money to go to England to reunite with his father, he would find his grin extremely useful when he began to make his fortune as the UK's most successful punk rock impresario.

'You must be Kate,' he said. 'Glad you could make it. Ron and Gary have told me all about you.'

Of course, they have, thought Kate, the colour rising in her cheeks. So who else knew how strict her parents were?

Gary handed Paul what could only be a record album. 'Here, this is for you. It's Cream's *Disraeli Gears*. Heard you didn't have it. Happy birthday!'

Then suddenly, there was Ron, tugging at Kate's sleeve. 'Hey, my mum wants to meet you.'

She started to follow him through the lounge room, while over his shoulder Ron said to Gary, 'Not you, Gaz. She's met you. This is Kate's private audience with her majesty. Everyone's out the back. I'll join you in a sec.'

Kate noted the lounge room's muted lighting. Thinking about it later, she realised that it prepared her for Cherie's bedroom, which was doused in a scarlet glow, thanks to the strategic placement of red chiffon over all the lights and lampshades. Dominating the room was a big brass double bed with Cherie reclining in its centre. Rubens and Renoir would have loved her. She wore a diaphanous white negligée that, with its plunging neckline, revealed more than just the swell of her ample breasts. A shock of lustrous dark hair brushed the top of her shoulders. Kate couldn't help thinking of Elizabeth Taylor in *Cat on a Hot Tin Roof.*

'Come in, come in, Katie.' There'd been no introduction. 'Come and sit down beside me.' Cherie patted a space on the bed to her right, and Kate obliged. 'You can run along now, Ronnie,' said with a dismissive wave, 'and let us two girls get acquainted.' She smiled as she turned her head to face Kate. 'I simply have to tell you, sweetheart, that you look like something straight out of Carnaby Street. I adore miniskirts, and I reckon this current craze for psychedelic print is fantastic. I'd be wearing it just like you, if I could, but I'm afraid I'm just a little too old for it. Nothing looks more ridiculous than mutton dressed up as lamb. Though, mind you, if I was still in the business, I would have to keep up with the times in the costume department. But then I've always been fashion's fool.' A slight pause. 'Did you know I was once a professional cabaret singer?' And before Kate could respond, Cherie had rebooted her soliloquy. 'Be a sweetie and grab me that fresh pack of ciggies over there.' She pointed with one long red varnished fingernail at her dressing table by the window. Again, Kate obliged. 'I can see why Gary's fallen for you. You're an absolute darling. A free spirit. Just like me.' She paused to light a cigarette. 'Now, where were we?'

And off she went again, but Kate was not at all bored. She'd never met anyone like her and wished her mother was more of a free spirit. Or at least painted her nails red like Cherie did.

A tentative tap on the open door. It was Ron and Gary. They were both smiling.

'We've come to rescue Kate,' said Ron. 'You've had her long enough. And maybe it's time for you, Mum, to say hello to our guests.'

'Oh, all right,' she said, grudgingly. 'But I'll have to slip into something more appropriate, don't you think?'

'Whatever you say, Mum. Whatever you say. I'll be back in ten minutes, so you'd better be ready by then.'

The three young ones went outside. Ron said he needed to take care of the music and excused himself. Gary grabbed Kate gently by the arm and led her to the trellis table, where his parents were seated. The sky was almost night dark. But the air was filled with music and laughter, colour and movement. Kate's pulse was racing. She was floating, feather-light. Les and Hazel Saunders had kept two places for them. They ate and talked and Kate was introduced to all the neighbours and some of Paul's friends from Sydney Uni. Kate thought they were all incredibly nice. Not the least bit stuck-up.

Everyone mingled. Everyone danced. But an ear-splitting metallic screech from a microphone attached to the speaker changed all that.

'Give that to me, you little bastard!' Ron's voice boomed across the yard.

'Let me go, you dick! Let me go!'

The party looked up towards the veranda to see Ron struggling to prise the microphone from Benito's fingers. Meanwhile, the five-year-old *piccolo bastardo* was kicking at Ron's shins. And Ron was getting a bruising.

'*Abbastanza!* Enough!' And it was too. Mario had spoken.

Benito let go his grip on the microphone.

'Go and play on the highway, you little shit!' Ron snarled. He might have had his property back, but his pride had fled.

A supportive cheer went up from the uni students. Benito, who *was* a little shit, was at that moment being carried screaming into the house by his father.

People resumed their conversations, but when Cherie was seen floating across the veranda, her stage for the evening, there was a sudden communal intake of breath.

'Good evening, everyone.' She had taken control and was purring into the microphone.

Some of the older male guests looked as if they'd sensed her heat, her carnality. There was certainly no doubt in anyone's mind that she would've once been considered quite a beauty. Traces of her loveliness still remained, despite the way her crow-black hair had tonight been piled high upon her head and its beehive shape fixed rigid by enough lacquer to polish a table.

Her face too was powdered almost white, her mouth a blood-red slash and her voice was breathless and smoky when she said, 'This is for you, Paul, my darling son. My firstborn. Happy birthday, sweetheart!' With that, she launched into her song, a sultry number that was part of Eartha Kitt's repertoire.

Kate looked around her and saw the polite expressions on the guests' faces. Like her, some of the audience recognised Cherie's neediness, her vulnerability. Kate's eyes searched in the crowd for Paul and Ron. Were they embarrassed by their mother's performance? If they were, they never showed it. In fact, they seemed proud of her. When her song finished, Ron led the enthusiastic applause as Paul mounted the stairs of the veranda, two steps at a time, and embraced Cherie with obvious affection. After that, there was the cutting of the birthday cake, more eating, more dancing, and time telescoped. Everyone agreed it had been a wonderful party.

*

It was almost midnight when Gary walked Kate back home, which was only a few blocks away. Above them, the high, black sky was dusted with hundreds and thousands of stars, and hanging in the air was the rich, earthy smell of the river. Just before they rounded the bend into Salt Pan Road, they stopped beneath the darkness of a massive old tree. The pair embraced, and Gary gently pulled Kate close to him. Their mouths met, and they began to kiss. And kiss and kiss again.

He held her tightly and as he pressed his body against hers, she took a few steps backwards until she was leaning up against the tree. He nuzzled into her neck, one hand fondling her breasts. She felt his tongue in her ear. Her neck and ear – all wet. He was breathing heavily, both his hands all over her now. Her legs were turning to jelly, and then she felt it – the bulge in his jeans pushing, pushing, pushing hard against her. He was drinking in her mouth and just as she was about to say stop, stop, he took a step back and lifted up her dress. His fingers glided between her legs into the wetness inside her panties and somehow, she found the words – no, no…

She heard him groan, and he pulled away, muttering groggy apologies. 'I didn't want it to be like this.'

'Me neither,' she whispered. 'Me neither.'

Somehow, they continued to walk in silence to Kate's house, unaware that their actions beneath the blanket of darkness that night would become an irresistible pattern of behaviour for every date they ever had.

The Rat

Over the long summer vacation, Denise and Kate had taken sales assistant jobs in Grace Bros department store in nearby Roselands shopping centre. Although Kate worked in the ladies shoe department and Denise was in children's wear, they still managed to see a great deal of one another. Each Monday through to noon Saturday, the pair travelled together to and from work and spent every lunch break together as well, often complaining bitterly about their customers, or clients as their floor managers would have them say.

On particularly hot days, Kate detested having to help swollen, foul-smelling feet squeeze into shoes and slippers, while Denise insisted that her job was far worse, because Kate didn't have to deal with brats and bloody little monsters.

'I tell ya', Katie, it's turns me right off ever having kids of my own,' she says one afternoon walking back home from the bus stop.

'You'll change your mind, when the right bloke comes along.'

'What do you mean, when the right bloke comes along? He already has. What do ya think Graham is? A flash in the pan or something?'

Her words hover in the air around them, like wasps poised over water.

Oh, God, here she goes again, thinks Kate, accusing me of being critical of her choice of boyfriend.

Denise moves closer to her friend. 'Come on then, tell me what you really think, you coward!' She's sneering, her face full of threat, daring her to tell the truth. 'Come on, out with it!'

Oh, bugger it, thinks Kate, she's asked for it, and so she launches in. 'Well, I'm sorry, Denise, but I hardly think he's the right bloke for you. I mean, it's been months now since you started going steady with him, but you're still seeing him on the sly. And your parents still know nothing about it, and Vince is none the wiser.' She doesn't want to hurt her friend, but there's no stopping her now. Fury is guiding her. 'And I hate to say it, but where's the friendship ring he promised to give you? You can't blame me for thinking maybe Graham Ingram is just not that serious about you…'

Denise's shoulders slump as she turns away and starts to walk in the direction of home. Kate pulls at her arm, forcing her friend to face her again and now she sees that her eyes are two black smudges of kohl, mascara and tears.

'You don't understand,' she says. 'I don't want to love him, but I do. I can't help it and I don't know why. I just do.'

Kate squeezes her friend's hand. 'Come on,' she says. 'I guess we need to talk. Properly.'

Denise lets Kate guide her towards the treeless rectangle of green that's called a park in Webb Street. They stop at the play equipment and sit down on the bare boards of the merry-go-round. When she begins to speak, she seems almost calm. She tells Kate she was right, that Graham had been using her.

'I've been an idiot. I guess I've known it all along, deep down, but didn't want to admit it to myself. But now, Katie…' She lowers her head and looks down into her lap. 'Now, I can't bear it. I'm so ashamed of myself.'

Her anger takes over then and out it all pours in great waves of weeping. She tells her friend that she's gone all the way with him; that she never should've agreed to meet the bastard down in the boatshed – that that had been her first mistake. But in the beginning, he'd been all lovey-dovey. It had been nice to kiss and cuddle, but one afternoon, they'd shared a bottle of beer, and he suggested they'd be more comfortable if they were lying on the old, stained mattress of the rusted-up, wrought-iron bed that the Ingrams kept down there. And then every time she went to the boatshed after that, no matter how determined she was not to get on that bed, she'd give a little more of herself to Graham. And before she knew it, they were having sex all the time. She hadn't wanted it to happen, but it did and it hurt, especially the first time, and later he swore he loved her but he wanted to keep things a bit low-key, keep things quiet…until the time was right, he said, and when it was, they'd tell the world.

'So I waited cause I trusted him, but the right time never came. And yesterday, I got angry. Really angry, and I started nagging him and I refused to lie down on the bed with him. And he said I was blackmailing him and he grabbed hold of me and he shook me so hard, I got frightened and that's when he told me I was nothing but a slut and to clear out and never come back. And now I just want to die.'

'No way!' says Kate, with her arm firm around Denise's shoulders. 'No way am I going to let you die because of that creep! He's a louse of the first order. And let's get one thing straight – you're not a slut and never will be.'

They hug one another and Kate holds her friend until she's stopped crying. She smells of hairspray, and Kate tells her everything's going to be all right. Yes, she wants to reassure her, but more than anything, she wants the old Denise back, the tough, outspoken girl, her brave and confident friend.

'And this is what you're going to do,' says Kate with absolute conviction. 'There are only three people in this world who know about this, and you and I are not going to say a word to anyone, because it's no one else's business, right?'

Denise nods. So far, so good.

'And if that rat decides to tell people because he wants to brag that he's some big-time Casanova or something, do you reckon anyone's going to believe him?'

This time, Denise doesn't move her head. She stares straight in front of her, across the park, over the road and to the houses opposite, her expression blank.

'I'm telling you, Denise, no one's ever going to take him seriously, because you're going to hold your head up high, very high. You'll deny it and call him a liar. You'll say he's got tickets on himself, because you wouldn't go to bed with him for all the tea in China.'

A flicker of a smile crosses Denise's face. Hope on the horizon.

'And if I get wind of anything myself – rumours, gossip – I'll laugh them off. Deny it all. Say it's ridiculous, how I'd surely know if it was true, being her best friend and everything.'

A few seconds pass, then Denise says, 'But what if I'm pregnant?'

Kate hadn't thought of that. 'Why? Is it possible?'

'My periods are way overdue.'

'But he used protection, didn't he?'

'He promised me he'd always get off at Redfern, but I reckon it would be just my luck if he didn't one time.'

Kate thinks so too, but she doesn't say that. Instead she tells her not to be so negative, that she's sure her periods will come any day, that they were probably late because she'd been upset, what with the way she'd been treated and all by the Rat.

Denise almost laughs then. 'That's a good name for him,' she says. 'It suits him.'

'You mean because of his beady little eyes?'

'Yeah, that'll do for starters.'

Kate wonders what Denise will do if her periods don't come. But she's frightened of her answer, so she doesn't ask her.

They start walking home. The red-hot sun, still visible on the horizon, warms their faces. Neither girl speaks until they turn the corner into Salt Pan Road and they are no longer looking directly into the setting sun's fiery rays.

Denise breaks the silence. 'I swear I'll never see the Rat alone again.'

Kate smiles. She believes her.

'And I tell you what, if I am pregnant, I'll be getting an abortion. There's no way I'm going to get stuck with a baby. And I know Robyn will help me because she's said millions of times that she wished she'd taken the advice of a friend of hers who knows this doctor in Melbourne, and no one will ever know a thing about it.'

Kate's pleased. She's got her old friend back.

*

When the summer holidays come to an end, Denise and Kate go back to school. This is their HSC year, and both girls want to do as well as they possibly can. Becoming full-time shop assistants is now not a career option either of them wants to contemplate. At the end of February, Denise takes a couple of weeks off school to go to Melbourne. Officially, an aunt has died, so she's accompanying her mother to the funeral. Kate is the only person outside the immediate Reid family who knows differently.

Around the same time, a rumour circulates that Graham Ingram had been set upon by an unknown group of thugs one night as he was getting out of his car.

'Gee, I hope it's true,' Denise says to Kate, 'and not just idle gossip.'

The two girls look at one another and collapse into convulsions of laughter. They never speak of him again.

Blood Ties

The elation people felt when Neil Armstrong took those first few steps on the moon was short-lived for many people living in the district surrounding Salt Pan Creek. For not long after that giant lunar achievement, a well-respected local businessman was viciously murdered.

The road that still runs north of Riverwood Station was at that time lined with a variety of shops – a delicatessen, a men's clothing store, a haberdashery, a couple of milk bars, a Chinese restaurant, a pharmacy, a post office, a bank, a cake shop and a newsagency. Among them was a small independent supermarket, owned and operated by Alfred Carmelo Attard.

It was a Friday night. Alf had failed to come home at the usual hour, and when the supermarket's phone repeatedly rang out, his wife, Tereza became concerned. It was not like her Alfie to be so late, so she sent Rocco, their twenty-four-year-old son, to see if his father's car was still in the lane at the rear of the store. Sure enough, it was. What's more, the light from the manager's office was shining out of the half-opened roller doors. Rocco didn't hesitate. He entered the premises and went straight to the office at the back of the supermarket. The last thing he expected to find was his father, propped up against the far wall beneath the sink.

The young man was distraught when he phoned the police.

*

Four CIB detectives were assigned to the investigation and, as he lived close by, Milton Ward was the first of the four to arrive at the scene. It wasn't pretty. Someone had taken to Alf's head with a hammer that was lying between his outstretched legs. The place was a mess – blood-spattered files and bits of invoices and torn receipts everywhere. Milton was briefed by the uniformed cops, who'd cordoned off the area – all were stunned by the banal brutality of the murder. Not content with merely smashing the man's head in, his killer had also punctured his cheeks over and over again with an ordinary old dinner fork and then poured a bottle of caustic oven cleaner over his entire face.

'You might want to take a close look at the poor bastard's left ear, sergeant,' suggested one of the uniformed cops. 'I don't know what it is, but there's some kind of circular metal object rammed against his head. It looks pretty bizarre to me.'

Milton squatted down by Alf's side and peered into the bloodied mess of flesh and matted hair. He wasn't sure what the damn thing was either. 'I think we'd better wait until the scientific blokes get here. They'll know what it is.'

He stood up and, moving away from the body, surveyed the scene. His pale blue eyes narrowed as he took it all in. He needed to record what he saw in his head and store it there for later reference. He knew from experience that he'd want to reconstruct it in his mind's eye, so that he could scour it again and again for clues that he may have missed, for signs left by a careless killer, and for all the mute secrets carried by the corpse. Even before the forensic pathologists reported that the metal object up against the victim's head was the round iron base of a steel spike, the kind that's used to file receipts and dockets, Milton felt sickened by the ferocity of the attack. In the last war, he'd witnessed brutality in the jungles of Borneo and, as a cop, he'd seen the hurt and damage that violence could do, but to thrust a filing spike in someone's ear took cruelty to another level. There was no doubt about it. This murder was personal. It was all about inflicting pain – the obscenity of evil.

There'd been no disturbance in the supermarket itself. The day's takings were still in the victim's briefcase. The safe was intact. No cash had been stolen. All four detectives ruled out robbery as a motive, and when the post-mortem report stated that the cause of death was due to massive physical damage to the brain, they all agreed – Alfred Carmelo Attard had known his murderer.

The problem was that Alf seemed to have been liked by everyone who knew him.

*

Milton was well aware that the pressure was on to solve the case. He didn't need to be reminded by his wife that the entire community wanted the killer found. And quickly. Alf had lived a faultless life. Devoted to his family, he didn't drink or gamble. At sixty-seven years of age, he'd known he should've retired, but he'd loved his job, especially his customers, who all spoke highly of him.

As is the norm in such cases, the deceased's family and supermarket staff were among the first to be interviewed, and the name of a former twenty-year-old employee, Kenneth Michael Stanton, who'd been recently sacked by Attard, was repeatedly mentioned. Milton and his young offsider decided to pay him a visit.

The Stantons lived in nearby Narwee. The house was a typically small, dark brick Housing Commission structure in a cul-de-sac, intriguing by its lack of trees and ill-kept front yards.

Mrs Stanton, Kenneth's mother, answered the door and invited the detectives inside after Milton explained that they were investigating the death of her son's former boss. She took them through to the kitchen and introduced them to her son, who preferred to be called Ken, and his father.

Later, Milton would describe the suspect as 'a pretty cool customer', who, when asked, was able to account for his movements at the time of the murder the day before. His girlfriend, Karen, had paid him a visit in the late afternoon and then stayed for tea. After that, he'd driven her back to her place in Riverwood and then, like a good boy, he'd returned straight home. His parents corroborated his story.

'What clothes were you wearing yesterday?' asked Milton, and Ken produced from the clothes basket a long-sleeved shirt that had no visible bloodstains.

'What about your trousers?'

'I took them to the dry cleaners at Hurstville with other stuff earlier this morning,' said Ken's mum. 'And I can assure you, sergeant, if I'd seen any blood on them, I would have contacted you lot immediately.'

Milton didn't believe a word of it. Not all parents covered up the sins of their children, but Milton had met some who did. He asked for the whereabouts of the dry cleaners. Mrs Stanton told him and showed him the ticket.

*

Back in 1969, all shops, including dry cleaning businesses, shut from noon on Saturdays, and as this was late Saturday afternoon, the cops had to wait until Monday morning to retrieve the trousers so that they could be scientifically tested for the presence of bloodstains.

Milton spent all day Sunday worrying that Ken's trousers were soaking in dry cleaning fluid at that very moment. 'I know the bastard's guilty, Betty,' he told his wife, that night. 'And you can call it what you like – a hunch, a sixth sense, I don't really care. I just know he did it.'

Early next morning, Milton Ward put his photographic memory to good use when he recited to the dry cleaner the details from the docket Mrs Stanton had shown him. Ken's trousers were immediately spread out over the counter, and hey presto! There they were – a splatter of little black spots across the front of both trouser legs. Ken's mother was in need of new glasses, and forensic tests confirmed the spots were human blood, which was enough to formally interview Stanton and put to him that he'd killed Mr Alfred Carmelo Attard in a fit of rage because he hated him for giving him the sack. But that wasn't going to be easy.

Stanton wasn't there when the four CIB detectives got to his place later that day. His father greeted them on the doorstep and informed them that he wasn't expecting his son home until sometime in the evening. According to him, he and his wife had no knowledge of his son's whereabouts. One of the detectives then asked him if he knew where Karen lived. The answer was no, but Mr Stanton suggested that as her surname was Ingram, perhaps they might find the address in the phone book. Milton smiled and said he didn't think that would be necessary, that he and the three other officers would return later to interview his son.

'It takes a fox to catch a fox,' said Milton, 'and there's four of us here in this car and only one of him, and I've already got a fair idea where Ken Stanton might just be.'

It was Graham Ingram who answered the knock on the door of his parents' place just off Salt Pan Road. Two plain clothes cops greeted him, then one of them asked if Ken Stanton happened to be visiting that day.

'He's not here, mate,' came the reply. 'Haven't seen him for a while.'

'Is that so?' said one of the detectives. 'Well then, I suppose you wouldn't mind us taking a look around.'

'Sure thing. Come on in,' said Graham, grinning.

While the two detectives checked out the house, six other men ever so quietly surrounded the boathouse at the bottom of the Ingrams' property. They were fairly certain that Stanton was inside. And of course, he was.

*

In the record of interview tended before the court much later that year, Stanton, having broken down, confessed to the murder.

'See, I had money problems. Me and Karen wanted to get married. I thought if I could rob the store, my problems would be over. I could buy an engagement ring. It'd all be sweet. I'd been visiting Karen at her place and when I was driving back home I saw some lights on in the shop. I knew it must've been old Alfie, stayin' back. I started getting really angry and so I parked the car in Coleridge Street and walked down the lane to the back of the shop. I came through the rear gate and grabbed an empty bottle out of one of the crates in the yard and the next thing I'm in the office and there's old Alfie and he sees me and starts to back away from me and so I hit him on the head and he fell down, saying, "Oh God, oh God," and he kept on sayin' it, over and over, and I picked up a tin of beetroot and hit him again and then some more. And he was groanin' and he wouldn't bloody shut up, so I jabbed a fork into his face and poured some stuff all over him. Then I went through his pockets looking for the keys to the safe but I couldn't find them.'

When asked about the spike that had been pushed into his head, Stanton said, 'I knew he recognised me, so I had to make sure he was dead.'

Milton then asked him why he hadn't taken the twenty-dollar note that had been lying on the office floor.

'Because it had blood on it,' was the response. 'I'm not stupid, you know.'

After the interview, he was charged with the murder and agreed to return to the supermarket with police to re-enact what he had done. The re-enactment was filmed. Despite the blood evidence, the signed confession and the filmed re-enactment, Stanton pleaded not guilty in Central Criminal Court.

During the trial, Stanton's father said in evidence that he believed his son had been terrified of the police officers who had interviewed him.

Stanton himself claimed from the dock, 'Detective Sergeant Ward struck me and that is why I wrote out a statement that the police dictated to me and then they told me to sign it, which I did.'

But when the Crown Prosecutor tendered a letter written by the accused to his fiancée, Karen Ingram, while he'd been in custody, the courtroom was shocked. In the letter, he had twice used the phrase 'I did it for us'.

The trial lasted only three and a half days, with the jury retiring at noon and returning in less than an hour. They found Stanton guilty, and the judge sentenced him to life imprisonment.

*

Ultimately, the murder of poor Alfred Attard affected the entire community. Initially, the brutality and the grisly circumstances of his death shocked and outraged everybody. But those feelings soon gave way to disgust as people followed the court proceedings in the daily press. In time, the intensity of the tragedy diminished for many, but there were some who grew to understand that the potential for evil is in us all.

Admiration for the Attards, though, was universal. Many of Alf's immediate family attended the trial every day. There was a quiet dignity about them, even though their faces were studies of pain and their anguish was immeasurable. Two days after the sentencing hearing, a beribboned basket containing traditional sweets, pastries and a bottle of Maltese liqueur appeared unannounced on the Ward family's front porch. It came without a note. But as far as Milton was concerned, words were unnecessary.

Besides, he was glad this particular case was over. It had been impossible to disregard the publicity that was generated by the intense public interest in the trial. And while his wife and kids understood that from time to time his photo would appear in the papers regarding some crime or other, he'd been taken aback by the number of times he'd appeared on television.

'It must've affected the kids,' he said to Betty one night.

'They haven't said anything to me about it,' she said, patting his hand. 'So I wouldn't be losing any sleep, if I were you.'

But Milton was right to be concerned. For he'd seen the terror in his daughter's eyes when, one evening, the seven o'clock news reported Stanton's allegation that Milton had hit him. And yes, Kate was frightened – frightened of going to school the next day. What might her classmates say? Would there be accusing looks and whisperings behind her back about police brutality and forced confessions? And what if she defended her father? Would there be the predictable taunts: 'But of course she would say that, wouldn't she?'

But she needn't have worried about that. Nothing was said. No allusions to newspaper or TV reports were made at all. Not until after school, that is.

Kate caught the later of the two school buses that took her close to home. Denise was with her and although the bus was packed, the girls managed to get the last free seat. Quite a few students had to stand in the aisle. One of them, a boy about fifteen, was holding onto the seat in front of the one Denise and Kate were sharing. He was wearing grey gaberdine Bermuda shorts that looked tight around his expanding thighs and backside, which lurched threateningly towards Kate's face whenever the overcrowded bus came to an abrupt halt.

Suddenly the boy reeled around, steadied his feet, peered down at Kate and said, 'Is your dad that copper? The one who solved that murder of the man in the supermarket?'

Kate turned to Denise. 'Here we go,' she said, nodding towards the boy. 'What's it to you?' she asked.

'Ugh, no reason.' He was grinning. 'Just wondering, that's all.' And still grinning, he raised his arms up in the air and, as the bus went round a corner, he started to sway, like some crazy Disney cartoon character, all arms and legs and utterly harmless.

Kate felt a sudden relief. She'd been on edge all day, but there'd been no scorn or sneering. No ridicule or insinuation. And it was at that moment she realised, but could barely articulate, that being a copper's daughter moderated the way people saw her, and that in turn affected the way she saw herself. That accident of birth had come to define her: it bound her to family; it restricted her behaviour; it mapped the geography of what she could and could not say. She was hemmed in, locked up, restrained by the love and loyalty she had for her father – her much-adored father, who, she feared, might well have feet of clay.

A Right To Justice

The moon was full the night Joe Anderson allowed his rowboat to drift with the river's current. He'd always loved being alone out on the water in the darkness and the silence, with all the mysteries of the sky and stars above him. This was his place for contemplation and on this night that was what he needed to do.

He'd always known that the white man's notion of progress was suspect. He'd learnt that at the feet of his elders over many years as they talked around the campfire. It seemed to him that white fellas were never satisfied. They always wanted more of this, more of that. And never gave a thought to what the black fella wanted. The fact was, they just didn't like sharing. And despite the way they always preached forgiveness and brotherly love, Joe hadn't seen much evidence of any of that in what they ever did. Sharing was just foreign to them.

But what they liked doing most was starting up progress associations, which were all about making progress for the white fella and making sure the black fella progressed himself as far away from them as possible. What worried Joe most was the number of these little progress groups popping up all over the place, planning for the kind of future that was good for white fellas, but not so good for anyone else.

What happened to his parents was a good example. Hugh and Ellen, with their friends, the Rowleys, had bought two adjoining blocks of land in Ogilvy Street. They were happy times living and working there, with the river providing them with oysters to collect, fish and prawns to catch, swamp wallabies to hunt and wild flowers to gather and sell at Paddy's Market in the city. Their place became known as the Salt Pan Creek camp – a perfect refuge for many Aboriginal people in the Sydney basin, especially for people desperately wanting to escape the control of the Protection Board. For them, Salt Pan Creek symbolised freedom – a kind of hub for them to air their views, to share ideas and to dream better futures for their people. It was a vibrant place to be and provided many young indigenous people, like Jack Patten and Bert Groves, who often visited there, with the perfect breeding ground for what would be their political activism in the future.

And even though Hugh and Ellen owned their own land, the land that had always been black fellas' country, they still had to fight to remain on it. Some local white fellas had complained to Hurstville Council that the Aboriginal community in Ogilvy Street was disturbing the peace and tranquillity of the area. Too much noise, they said. Filthy and unsanitary living conditions, said others. Thankfully, the health inspector begged to differ.

But Hugh died in 1928 and, when the Depression hit, Ellen was forced to sell the property, and so their community of around forty-odd people moved closer to the river into the relative security of the bush that lined it. They were tough times. But things got even tougher. The Herne Bay Progress Association upped the ante. The group wanted 'the blacks' camp' gone. They argued that the district was growing; that such a community was out of place; that the people should be 'removed to the compound at La Perouse, where they could be supervised and protected'.

In the name of progress, the railway line from the city to East Hills was opened in 1931. And in that same year Ellen died, leaving Joe the senior member of the Anderson family. He wasn't afraid of opposing evictions. He'd had plenty of practice doing just that. Most Friday nights for the last decade, he'd been stepping up onto his soapbox in Paddy's Market and spruiking his ideas about Aboriginal land rights and the forced removal of children from families to anyone who'd listen.

The world was changing, which made it all the more urgent for Joe to find new ways of conveying his message and of saving his community. He looked up at Warrawul. He'd always found inspiration there in its rivers of stars that spread across the night sky. It was like sitting in the dark of a picture theatre. It had a magic about it. And its name – Warrawul sounded mighty and strong. So much better than the Milky Way. Yes, white fellas could sure learn a thing or two.

He took back control of the oars. He would row back home now. He knew what he wanted to do. But first, he had to talk to his brother Jack, who was good-looking and had scored jobs as an extra in a number of home-grown movies. He had connections in the flourishing Australian film industry at the time, and if Jack would help him court these connections maybe, just maybe, he could use this new-found power of cinema to demand recognition for his people.

*

On a windy September day in 1933, Cinesound Movietone News came to Salt Pan Creek and set up their equipment within a clearing in the bush. Joe felt calmly confident as he faced the camera. He'd not underestimated the significance of this opportunity, so he'd taken time to prepare the speech he'd give.

His decision to refer to himself as King Burraga was a master stroke. He knew that in this way he'd be asserting his pride in being the grandson of his maternal grandfather, Burragalang or King Burraga, and grandmother, Bi-yar-rung or Biddy Giles, from the north Dharawal country at Kurnell, whose uncle witnessed Cook's landing there. But more than that, Joe would be making clear the long-standing presence his ancestral line had on the area surrounding Salt Pan Creek.

When he heard the word 'Action!', Joe began to speak. 'Before the white man set foot in Australia, my ancestors had kings in their own right, and I, Aboriginal King Burraga, am a direct descendant of the royal line…

'The black man sticks to his brothers and always keeps their rules,

90

which were laid down before the white man set foot upon these shores. One of the greatest laws among the Aboriginals was to love one another, and he always kept to this law. Where will you find a white man or a white woman today who will say I love my neighbour… It quite amuses me to hear people say they don't like the black man…but he's damn glad to live in a black man's country all the same!

'I am calling a corroboree of all the natives in New South Wales to send a petition to the King, in an endeavour to improve our conditions. All the black man wants is representation in federal parliament. There is also plenty fish in the river for us all, and land to grow all we want.

'One hundred and fifty years ago, the Aboriginal owned Australia and, today, he demands more than the white man's charity. He wants the right to live!'

*

Like most newsreels of that time, this one was shown across the nation in large cinemas preceding a feature film, as well as in dedicated newsreel theatrettes. And while this audio-visual record has become an important historical document, the white audience's immediate response to Joe's plea for justice is unknown. However, what is known is that Joe's struggle didn't end there.

Throughout the thirties, he was often featured in newspapers and magazines, fighting eviction from the public land at Salt Pan Creek for some spurious reason or other. The complaints of some local white residents had never gone away. They'd just developed in number and in style and were becoming increasingly more difficult to combat. Of course, Joe knew only too well that to observe the sesquicentenary commemorations on 26 January 1938 was impossible for his people; to do so would be to rejoice in 150 years of misery and degradation for indigenous Australians by the white invaders. And so it was, that Joe Anderson was one of the hundred Aboriginal men and women who participated in that first Day of Mourning and Protest, organised by many of the same activists who'd felt the warmth of friendship and the stimulation of debate around the Andersons' campfire.

But within the first few months of the following year, Joe was forced to withstand further calls for the wholesale removal of the Salt Pan Creek camp on the grounds that the residents were spoiling the beauty of the bush. As if that wasn't enough, there was then a complaint that the population of local swamp wallabies was under threat due to Aboriginal hunting in the area. Not long after this accusation, Joe died. The courageous spirit of King Burraga was now peacefully dreaming in the sky world, within Warrawul's rivers of light.

By the end of 1939, the remaining residents of the Salt Pan Creek camp had been forcibly removed to La Perouse. And although the natural environment was beginning to show signs of some river degradation, the culprit was certainly not the Aboriginal people. Instead, it was, as Joe had predicted, the fault of progress itself. And with more, much more of that progress yet to come, with Sydney's post-war urbanisation creeping westward, the Georges River system would soon be under a great deal of stress.

In His Bed

He moves towards her. She doesn't back away. He circles her in his arms, and she lets him kiss her lips, her cheeks, her eyes, her neck. He nuzzles her ear. She whispers his name. He presses his body against hers and walks her backwards, one…three…five steps and lifts her up and lets her gently fall onto the divan. She feels his breath on her face as he extends his right arm and flicks a switch. Lamplight. Soft illumination. She smiles up at him and, moving her legs apart, he kneels between them. She tries to sit up and reach for the zipper in his jeans. But he shakes his head.

'What's the rush?' Ron says, leaning down over her.

His kisses are long, lush and open-mouthed. Her tongue plays with his until he pulls up her dress, and she helps him raise it over her head. She tosses it onto the floor. His mouth returns to hers, and his hand is at her back, unhooking her bra. As she yanks it off, he stands up and looks back down at her.

His eyes survey her body. She knows he wants to see everything. She lifts her bottom and removes her panties. Now naked, she closes her eyes and waits. He's drinking her in: her red-brown hair, her face as round as the moon, her slender neck, the warmth and silky grandness of her breasts, the very curve and shape of her.

And then she feels him. He's lying naked beside her, caressing one breast, then the other. Her nipples are pebble-hard. He murmurs something in her ear, but she can't make out what he's saying. And suddenly he's there, kneeling again between her legs, and his fingers and tongue are everywhere. He bites a nipple and fingers the lips of her vulva.

She lets out a little moan. 'Oh God, oh God…'

And now his tongue is there and it finds the spot, the little nub of pleasure, the quick of her. She's as wet as the river bed. She feels delirious with wanting. Wanting him and only him. Now, yes now. She wants him to cover her body with his. Please. She wants him pressing against her breasts. She wants to feel him inside her. Yes. Yes. She tries to sit up as her hands reach for him. She opens her eyes and starts to stroke his hair.

But he pulls away from her. Suddenly. He stands up. There's a moment of panic. Her breath is jagged. She asks him what's the matter.

He's smiling, his mouth, his chin, his nose – all wet with her. 'Nothing. I'll be right back.'

And he is. He gently drags her down to the end of the divan, so her feet touch the floor. He raises her buttocks and places cushions beneath them. He stands above her. She can see his eagerness. Raising her legs off the floor, she places her feet on the edge of the divan, inviting him in. He's standing back, peering down at her – into her. She's so bloody beautiful. He can't believe his luck and he knows for sure that one day she'll be his wife. And he doesn't care what his mother thinks about her. She's wrong. Dead wrong.

Even this morning, before she'd left, she'd started up again, reminding him to be careful. 'I didn't come down in the last shower, Ronnie. I know about these things,' Cherie had said. 'And I've got a really funny feeling about that girl.'

'Oh Mum, please…give me a break. I know you don't like her.'

'You're wrong about that.' She clutched his hand and squeezed it gently. 'In actual fact, I do like her. But like I've told you before, she's not the one for you.'

Ron had closed his eyes with exasperation then. He and his mother had had this conversation before. She was scared Denise would somehow jeopardise his future career. Or derail it, before it'd even begun.

He'd looked at his watch, then at Cherie. 'You'd better get going,' he'd said. 'I reckon right about now Mario would be finding it pretty damn hard keeping Benito in the car, don't you?'

A car horn beeped outside.

Cherie walked over to the front door then turned back to face her son. 'I'm no idiot, Ronnie, and I know she'll be staying here this weekend while we're away. So I've put some Frenchies in your sock drawer. Don't forget to use them, son.' She opened the door and was gone.

And now, being here with Denise, he would tell his mother as soon as he could that she had nothing to fear. He and Denise were in love, and she must never speak to him like that again. Yes, he'd talk to her as soon as she got back home tomorrow night. Meanwhile, he had better things to think about.

*

Ron moves towards the divan, towards Denise. She's admiring his glistening chest, which seems more tanned, more muscular than the way she'd remembered it. He grips her knees and holds them apart. Wide. The tip of his penis touches her there where his mouth had been, but then it withdraws, just for a moment. Then it's back. Then it's not. He's teasing her, and it's too much. Too much. Words are beyond her.

She reaches for his penis and slides her fingers down its shaft. Up and down. Up and down. With her other hand, she grips his balls and lightly squeezes. His eyes are closed. His mouth hangs open. His breathing is heavy.

'Don't, Denise. I'll come. I'll come.'

But it's too late, because he has. And it's everywhere: in her hair, on her breasts. She hears him groan, and her arms go round his neck. She brings him down on top of her and clings to him. They rock together, and when his breathing subsides, he tells her he's sorry. Denise laughs and asks what for. His weight is heavy on top of her, but she doesn't mind. She doesn't care. She likes that she can feel the slippery wetness between them. But he rolls off her and lies on his side, his right arm holding her close. From time to time, he nuzzles into her ear or kisses her cheek.

'It's not over yet,' he says.

*

Denise can't believe how uninhibited she feels with Ron. She is completely at ease in her nakedness. She'd never ever felt this way with Graham. He'd always made her feel cheap and grubby. But with Ron, she feels beautiful and adored and shameless. But then, he's an expert, considerate lover. And she starts to think about the ways she might please him.

Ron can't believe how he's just lost control of himself. He hadn't wanted it to happen, but there was some kind of force, some primeval unreasoning that'd been working against him. He had to face facts: there was no escaping from Denise's strange magic. It'd been like this ever since he'd kissed her on their first date that Gary and Kate had organised. And she gets more beautiful every day. So what chance has he got? She's been his constant fantasy long before they went out together, jerking himself off when there was no one else, or sometimes even when there was.

And now the reality of her, here in this house, her flesh against his. They'd planned this for a while. After a few desperate and fumbled fucks in the back of his car, they knew what they both wanted and that involved a decent bed, an entire night and no condoms. Denise would go on the pill.

So here they are, six weeks later, and not a shred of disappointment. Not on his part, at any rate – just joy and love and carnal desire.

*

The bathroom is small and it's blue and white like the sea. Denise and Ron are standing together beneath the circular shower head, letting the water rain down on them. First, he soaps her down, and then she rubs her body against his until there are no suds clinging to them. Ron turns off the taps and reaches for a towel. He pats her dry.

'I need a towel for my hair,' she says.

He hands her one, and she wraps it round her head while he dries himself.

'Sleepy?' he asks her.

She smiles and shakes her head.

'Are you thirsty then?'

'For you, I am. I'm thirsty for you.'

He kisses her and feels the fire in her touch as she moves her hand to take hold of his penis. This time, he doesn't stop her but he pulls back his head and says, 'How about we make love in my bed?'

*

His fingertips are light. They circle her navel – once, twice, and then move on, down through her pubic hair and then between her legs. Denise doubts she can cope with much more of this, and then, as if in silent agreement, he's above her. She parts her legs and feels his stiffness enter her. It fills her up, and he hears her moan. It's a wild and intense call to him and only him, coaxing him forward. And then she feels the strength and power of him moving inside her. She rises to meet him, and they move together like the waves of an ocean, gathering and rolling and receding and falling together as one into the fathomless depths of feeling.

Afterwards, they lie side by side in silence. Like innocent children, they hold each other's hand. They listen to the room. The outside world is incomprehensible. It means nothing. It's only here, in this bed, where there's any meaning.

They sleep and dream of savage seas and space and eternity.

Poems for Denise

by Ron Cochrane

Without You

I'd be a ship without an anchor
I'd be a bird without a song
I'd be a car without a battery
A mallet without a gong.

I'd be a chef without a menu
I'd be a fish that cannot swim
I'd be a shower without water
A light that's always dim.

I'd be night without the sunrise
I'd be a flower that didn't bloom
I'd be a bee that made no honey
I'd be Shakespeare's nibless plume.

Without you I'd be nothing
Like a judge without a crime.
But if you love me, tell me
And I'll love you for all time.

1969

Endlessly

I press my flesh
            upon your flesh
I orbit round your sun
I place my lips
            upon your lips
and trail your neck with tongue
I finger every part of you
I lick
     I kiss
          I come.

You smile at me
You drink me dry
You sing me songs
            of bliss
but then you cry -
You love me not
But darling
          please know this -

that I will love you
            endlessly
till angels cease to kiss

1969

The Split

Summer had started early. By November, it's the main topic of conversation with most people predicting a prolonged drought, though that doesn't deter them from using their sprinklers willy-nilly. By the end of the month, tempers are beginning to fray, for there's not been a single drop of rain, despite several congregations of prayers for a downpour.

Kate Ward has also been praying. But not for rain. Her periods are overdue, and she's frightened. Very frightened.

'You've been late before,' says Gary. 'Stop worrying. They'll come. It's because of exam stress, that's all.'

His reasoning seems logical. It's true she's been anxious about the exams. But the stakes are high. She wants a scholarship to go to university. She wants to do well…very well.

She takes her fears to Denise. 'What if I'm pregnant? What will I do?'

'Look, there's no need to panic,' says Denise, throwing open her tiny bedroom window in the hope of some fresh air. She sits back down on the edge of her bed and looks at her friend sitting opposite on her satin-covered dressing table stool. 'I reckon Gary's right. It's very early days and you're getting your knickers in an absolute knot over nothing.' A sudden breeze assaults the stillness of the room. It feels hot, almost tropical. 'But I do understand how you might be anxious. I mean, it'd be pretty terrible if God decided to punish you in this way for saying you were an atheist.'

'That's not one bit funny, Denise. And you know it! It's not very kind either.'

'Lighten up, will you… I was trying to make you laugh. That's all.'

But Kate knows that that isn't all. Her friend's needling her. There's no doubting that. It has only been a couple of days now since Kate happened to tell Denise that she no longer believed in God. Her friend's response had startled her.

'You only think you're an atheist because you've been reading all those stupid French writers for your HSC.'

'No, no, it's not because of that…'

'Yes, it is… What's his name again?' she'd asked, pronouncing the t and the s: 'Albert Camus?'

Stupidly Kate had corrected her.

'Ooh la la! Look who can parley like a Frog!' Denise's face was scrunched in a sneer.

Kate was stung, then and now, by the venom of her friend's words. How and why had she become so mean and spiteful? They were obviously growing apart, but Kate didn't want to admit it. Not even to herself. Not yet. Besides, she's been too busy of late, what with all her spare time being spent studying. Meanwhile, Denise has been seeing an awful lot of Ron, but she hardly ever speaks about him or their relationship, and when she does, it feels like she's drip-feeding only very superficial information, like what movie they've recently seen, never anything to do with feelings. All this has made Kate suspicious. Naturally, she suspects them of having sex. And lots of it. She guesses it would be protected sex too. Denise would be very careful this time round.

Unlike her and Gary. When it comes to having sex – real sex, what Kate calls intercourse – has only happened twice, and both times it was virtually over before it had even properly started! She thinks it would be extremely unfair if she's actually pregnant. And she tells herself she must stop thinking about it. She really has to try to push to the back of her mind the fact that her periods are late.

And that's what she does, until just before Christmas, when the HSC results are published. She'd matriculated and has been offered a number of scholarships. Her family is thrilled.

'Which one will you take?' asks Milton. 'The world's your oyster now.'

And so it is. But she has to talk to Gary. Seriously.

*

'What am I going to do? What am I going to do?' She's pacing up and down the old wooden jetty that pokes out into the river at the back of Gary's parents' place. 'I'm so scared, Gary. I really am…'

He takes hold of her, and his voice is gentle and as comforting as his arms. 'I think you should be asking what are we going to do, don't you? We're in this together, you know.'

Kate nods and closes her eyes. She's facing the sun, that's already fierce that morning, but when a sudden goose-like call echoes across the water, they both lift their heads skywards to watch a giant bird glide in an arc high above them.

'It's a white-bellied sea eagle,' says Gary. 'There's a little family of them that live on the other side of the river.' He nuzzles her neck and whispers in her ear, 'They mate for life, you know.'

He's being romantic. She knows that, but all her senses are dulled. She wants answers. She wants a plan. Frank and straightforward, not sentimental rubbish.

'We'll be OK, no matter what happens,' says Gary. 'I promise you that.'

His lips lightly brush her forehead, and she knows he means every tender word, every caress, but it's all wrong.

She pulls back and steps out of his embrace. 'What do you mean, "no matter what happens"? Do you think there's more than one possibility here? Like maybe I'm not pregnant? Is that what you mean? Is it?'

'Don't do this, Katie. Please.' He remains still, staring at her. 'You know damn well what I mean.'

'Well, I hope you understand this – I'm pretty sure that I am pregnant. I know it hasn't been scientifically confirmed and all that, and I know my periods can be erratic, but I've never been this late before. And yesterday, I was on the verge of vomiting all day long.' Kate wants to close her eyes. She wants this to be a dream – a terrible dream that she'll soon wake up from. 'So what do you think of that, eh? What do you think of that?'

Calmly he says, 'I'll tell you what I think of tha–'

And he does. He tells her that if she's carrying his child, he'll not only share the responsibility, but he'll also love and protect and provide for that baby like no other child has ever been before; that he's sure his folks would be delighted to have her move in with them there in Elwin Street; that they would all live happily together; that he'd have finished his apprenticeship in two years and if he managed to get a job with a construction company, which he's pretty sure he would do, he'd be earning plenty of money so that the three of them could live independently of his parents. And yes, he also mentions that they'll get married.

'But what will I be doing all day in this cosy little plan of yours?'

Kate sees the surprised look on Gary's face. He hasn't expected this response. He'd imagined her sighing with contentment and falling into his out-stretched arms.

'You'd be looking after the baby, of course.' There's a definite hint of exasperation in his voice.

What's wrong with everyone, Kate wonders. First Denise, now Gary. Is there something peculiar about them? Or is it her? They've all grown up in the same place, in roughly the same time, but they have vastly different ways of viewing the world. And each other.

'I don't think you understand what I'm trying to say. I don't want a baby. Not right now. I'm too young. I want to live a little. I'm not ready for nappies and puke and potties.' She can feel her eyes filling with tears. This is indeed a nightmare. 'And if I'm perfectly honest, I may not ever be ready.'

She pauses, waiting for a response. When there is none, she flees –

down the jetty and along the path that Gary's dad had cleared between the mangroves, and into the open grassed space that is the Saunders' backyard and out, out onto the street and onward home. Home. Then straight to her room to lie on her bed and wallow in her misery.

*

When Gary phones later that morning, Kate refuses to take his call.

'What's the matter with you?' Betty asks, opening her daughter's door without knocking. 'Do you mind telling me what's going on?'

'I've had a fight with him, that's all.' No lying there. 'Plus, I don't feel well and I really don't want to talk about it, if you don't mind.'

'Is it your periods?'

Kate nods in reply but is astounded by her mother's uncanny prescience. Had Betty's voice not sounded so routine and unconcerned, she might have wondered if her mum knew more than she was letting on.

'I'll make you a nice cup of tea then. It'll make you feel better.'

Tea has always been her mother's remedy for any minor ailment. Kate smiles and thanks her as she turns to go, but she suddenly pokes her head again around the door.

'And next time that boy rings here, you'll get up from that bed and answer the phone. And you'll be quick about it too, my girl. Just because you've got your periods, doesn't mean you're dying.'

She returns a little later with a tray bearing a cup of milky tea and three buttered Sao biscuits with cheese on top. 'Sit up now. You'll feel so much better after you've eaten something,' she says, then places the tray on Kate's lap.

Once Kate finishes eating, she does feel better, so much so that when Gary arrives unannounced in the early afternoon, she agrees to go for a drive with him.

'It'll do you good to get some fresh air,' says her mother, waving them goodbye.

If she only knew, thinks Kate. She wouldn't be so bright and breezy then. She can imagine her mother berating her, telling her how she's disgraced the family, then she turns to Gary and lashing out at him, demands to know why he can't keep his penis in his pants. Kate shudders at the thought.

'Where would you like to go?'

'I don't mind,' she says, 'as long as it's not too far away.'

They drive in awkward silence, but Kate has a fair idea where Gary is heading when they pass Lugarno's nest of shops and service station. Soon they come to a stop behind three other cars at the end of Forest Road. Kate gazes out through the open window. She can see the old cable-hauled ferry making its way across the Georges River towards them.

'I thought we'd take the punt across to Menai,' Gary says. 'It's easier to park the car somewhere close to the water over there. And we can talk in peace. What do you reckon?'

'Fine by me.' Smiling, she turns to look at him and knows the moment their eyes meet that he loves her and that he knows she loves him.

But once Gary parks the car near the ferry's off-ramp on the southern side of the river, a casual observer would have thought otherwise. There they sit, facing one another – his back against the driver's door, hers against the passenger's, a canyon of air between them.

From the beginning, Gary tries to control the conversation. 'I'm really hoping we can stay calm and rational while we talk about this.'

'Sure,' she says, swallowing an urge to challenge his use of the word 'this'. What was 'this' supposed to mean? The baby? The situation? Kate's wishes? His?

'I reckon we should each have our say without any interruptions.'

'Agreed.'

'Then is it OK if I go first?'

'Fine.'

And then he says, 'I'm sorry about this morning. I really am. I should've grabbed hold of you there and then and kissed you and told you how crazy-happy I am. That I never want to be with anyone else, that this baby, our baby, is a part of us. All perfectly natural – we made love, and our love made this baby.' There's a pause, then, 'Do you still love me?'

Kate feels as trapped as a matchstick ship in a bottle. 'Yes,' she says.

'Well, say it then. Tell me you love me.'

'I love you.' Her voice is drained of all feeling.

'Really?'

'Oh, for heaven's sake. You know I do.' She thinks he's being ridiculous.

'Well, that's it then.' He moves closer towards her and takes her hands in his. 'We'll move in together and get married if you want. We'll make love every single day. We'll be happy. I know we will. And if you want, you can still…'

'Whoa, hang on a minute. I…'

He pleads with her to let him finish. 'Please,' he says again and, proud of her self-control, she gives in to him. 'You see, I've been thinking and I reckon if you really want to, you'll still be able to go to uni. You could start next year like you planned and then after the baby comes, when you're ready, you could go back. I'm pretty sure Mum'd be happy to look after the baby while you go to uni. If we love one another, we can do this.'

It's Kate's turn now. She sees the tears and desperation in his eyes and knows that she is about to hurt and disappoint him. She waits a few seconds then speaks softly, gently. 'It's not going to work. And if you really think about it, you'll know I'm right.'

Gary shakes his head. He is having none of it. She reminds him to hear her out before he objects and then she launches headlong into her argument. Firstly, she asks him a string of rhetorical questions like when would Hazel, his mother, get a break from child-minding when she, Kate, had essays, assignments and exams that had to be done; what would happen if his mum fell ill; what if the baby was born with some defect or disability; did he really believe their lives wouldn't change forever; what if he became resentful that his freedom had been curtailed and that his dream of going to the Munich Olympics and competing in the 200 and 400 metre sprints was impossible because he couldn't maintain his training regime; did he really believe he was ready and well-prepared for the responsibilities of parenthood and so on…

She stops to breathe, and Gary says, 'I can't believe you're so negative and pessimistic about this.'

'And I can't believe you're being so naïve.' She wants to scream. 'But I do know that I can't be responsible for what you think or what you want. I just want you to understand that I'm not ready for motherhood and I'd like you to help me get an abortion.'

Gary lets go of her hands and throws himself back into his car seat. 'So how come you're the only one who gets to decide here?' He's raised his voice. 'Don't I have any say in the matter? Is that what you mean? Or is this your way of telling me I'm not the father?'

'I beg your pardon!' She hates him now. She stares at him. She can't believe what he just said. She holds back her tears. She's glad she's seeing this side of him. 'You bastard.'

She pauses. Her last two words hang in the air between them. He looks away – across to the other side of the river.

'You know bloody well there's no one else, and there's never been anyone else!'

'Okay, okay.' He turns his head back to look at her squarely. 'I know…I know, and I'm sorry I said that… I didn't mean it… It's just that you want it all your own way, and I can see another way…a way we can keep this baby…but…but you're not listening.'

'Oh, I'm listening to you, Gary. It's just that I don't think your way is going to work. I reckon your way would be a disaster, because you don't respect me, or my wishes. I'm the one whose body is affected here. I'm the one who has to go through the pain of childbirth, not to mention the neighbourhood gossip.' Kate is starting to cry. 'Please Gary, please can't you see? I just don't want this baby.'

He's about to speak, but he looks at her instead, his face contorted, then hammers the steering wheel with both fists several times. The two of them stare out through the windscreen, back towards Lugarno's shoreline with its couple of ramshackle boat sheds and an assortment of sailboats and motorised tinnies buoyant near their moorings. It is a picturesque scene, but there is fury in their silence. They are lost for a moment in their own self-interest.

It's Gary who breaks the silence. 'Don't worry,' he says, 'I can see very well what you want. I also know exactly what you don't want, and that's a black baby. I reckon the very thought of giving birth to a kid that might look like me scares the living daylights out of you. You'd rather murder it before it took its first breath!'

'I can't believe what you just said. Do you really think that about me? Do you really believe that I'm like that?'

'If the shoe fits…'

His sneer is arctic cold, and with those four words, if the shoe fits, he's set her adrift. She feels like she's drowning. She doesn't know him any more. And it's clear to Kate that he doesn't know her at all. Where's the affection, the so-called love? This boy, this man, is vile. He's an ogre, and she wants nothing to do with him.

For the second time that day, she wants to flee and get as far away from him as possible. This time the grey-green murkiness of the river bars her way.

She waits till she's composed herself before she speaks. 'Take me home, please.'

'Anything you say, your majesty,' his words now pure acid.

He turns the keys in the ignition and pumps the accelerator. She tells herself once, twice, to stay calm and not tell him what she thinks of him. By remaining quiet, by not making matters worse, she'll get home without any more drama. The day's been emotionally draining and she's exhausted. She's not sure what she'll end up doing, because she isn't sure of anything any more. But right now, all she wants is to be rid of Gary Saunders.

*

Spare Saturday afternoons are always good for reruns of old movies, especially classic weepies. Kate spends the rest of the day in front of the television. There is no competition for what programs to watch. Her brother Mark is staying at a friend's place overnight, and her father is interstate on some police business, so it's only Kate and Betty at home this weekend. A situation for which Kate will later be grateful.

In the middle of the night, her mother, who had often claimed she had a sixth sense, comes to her bedroom and asks what's wrong, saying she'd heard her crying. Kate knows this is a lie because she'd made sure her tears had been silent that night. And for her mother to have heard her, Betty would've needed to have more than one ear pressed to her door. But as far as Kate's concerned, one way or another, it's of little consequence.

Betty sits down on the edge of her daughter's bed. It means she's going nowhere.

'A problem shared is a problem halved, you know.'

Yes, her mother is the queen of clichés, but it's the loving gentleness of her tone that loosens the floodgates of Kate's emotions. In a rare display of maternal protectiveness, Betty puts her arms around her sobbing daughter, and Kate surrenders. She tells her everything.

'I wish you'd been as sensible about avoiding pregnancy as you're being about terminating it,' she says. 'But I won't harp on about that.'

'Oh, please don't, Mum.'

'I said I wouldn't and I won't. Now, first things first. You needn't worry about a thing. I'll organise it all. And what I'd like you to do is to do what you'd normally do. Though I'd prefer you not to spend too much time with that Gary Saunders...'

'Mum, believe me, I never want to see him again. I promise you, it's all over between us. We're finished.'

'Well, that's good. I'm relieved to hear it. But I'll tell you this,' and she leans in closer to Kate, 'you mightn't have minded having a coloured kid, but I'm not so sure I'd be happy with a grandchild being –'

'Oh, Mum, please…'

She closes her eyes. This is all too much. She's had more than enough racial prejudice for one day. But this time it's coming from her own mother, who often declared to anyone who'd listen that Sidney Poitier, her favourite actor, could put his slippers under her bed any time he liked. Was that what her mother enjoyed doing? Playing at the fringes of old taboos? Always being deliberately provocative?

Thankfully, Betty somehow knows that now is not the time and so changes tack. 'Now, as for your father, you must promise me never to breathe a word of any of this to him. He thinks you're perfect, so why shatter the illusion? And besides, what with all that kerfuffle with Bertram Wainer about backyard abortion rackets, I think your dad's had his fill of this sort of thing, don't you?'

'Yes, yes, of course.' Kate would've agreed to anything.

'Good. That's settled then. We'll just keep this entire business to ourselves. And love, I'm including Denise here too. I wouldn't be telling her either. Loose lips sink ships.' Her mother straightens her back and looks hard at Kate. 'But that doesn't mean that you're going to any fly-by-night backyard abortionist's either, my girl. Not on your Nelly! We'll be doing things properly.'

When in matron mode, Betty is magnificent, and Kate feels only sweet relief.

'First thing Monday morning, we'll get this pregnancy confirmed with a urine test and by New Year, all this will be behind you, a little nightmare not worthy of thought.'

At this, Kate cries again and grabs at her mother, hugging her and telling her how grateful she is and when she tells her how much she loves her, Betty cries too.

*

Next morning, Kate is woken early. The pain in her lower abdomen is excruciating. The cramps come in waves. It feels like her insides are being twisted and tortured. She throws off the sheet and sees that she's lying in a pool of blood. She calls out to her mother, who comes running. When she sees the state her daughter is in, she claps her hands and gives Kate a hasty kiss on the forehead.

'Well, what a good morning this is,' she says. 'It was a false alarm after all.' And while remaining magnificent, she organises everything – the running of a bath, the washing and changing of sheets, the hot-water bottle, some pain relief and of course, a cup of tea.

Some time later, Kate will consider herself lucky. On several counts. She will also be proud of the decision she made as a mere eighteen-year-old girl, when she recognised that the timing for becoming a parent was not right. And although in the end she had no need of a termination, she will see that she had the strength and courage of her convictions and had determined the direction she wanted her life to take.

In some ways, she'd set herself free.

Rivers

There's something pretty special about rivers. Always has been. Ancient civilisations knew a great deal about them. They drew sustenance from their ever-moving waters. They built their mightiness along their river's shores. Think the Euphrates. Think the Nile. And old Huang He – that yellow muddy mother river of China has been a blessing and a curse. These great watercourses, symbols of fertility, were in continual motion. As they headed ceaselessly towards the sea, their waters irrigated the soil, sometimes even flooding their banks.

Rivers represent different things to different people. For some, rivers correspond to the creative powers of nature and the irreversible passage of time. Because of this, they can denote a sense of loss and oblivion. For others, freedom, salvation and possibility – the very drift of life.

Rivers are the stuff of myths and legends, of tall tales and truths. They are the silent witnesses to human foibles. As sources of serenity, they are places for quiet reflection. Meditation. Contemplation. Some rivers are even holy. They are the great connectors – linking the past to the present and one place to another. They are a place for play and adventure, for new beginnings, for memories. They are repositories of sensual delights. To look at, to wade in, to row down, or to float upon a river, while trailing your hand in its waters, is to feel at one with the natural world.

Some say a river represents life itself and is a path to enlightenment.

Irma and the Rock Star

Irma Keller can hardly wait to tell Mark about who she's met that morning. But waiting is what she has to do, because Mark has to clean the Ward family car before he can go anywhere. He promises he'll only be an hour at most, then he'll be able to join her while she walks her dog in the afternoon. So she goes back next door to her place through the gap in the old wooden fence that has separated their families' yards for as long as she can remember.

Part of Irma's daily routine is to walk Jazza. Normally, she takes him down to the river and back. But this is no normal day, and a walk to the river and back is too short a trip for all the things she wants to tell Mark about. And she can't decide where they'll walk to this afternoon because she can't think straight. All she wants to think about is life's glamorous possibilities that have revealed themselves to her that morning beside the Raindrop Fountain at Roselands, when Peter Wallace kissed her with promises of a thousand more.

'You mean *the* Peter Wallace, the lead singer of Dark Daze?' Mark asks when she tells him.

'Yep,' she says, hoping she doesn't sound too pleased with herself. 'He writes most of the band's songs too, you know.'

Mark is aware that the music industry considers Wallace the most talented member of the group. What he wants to know now are the details of how Irma got to meet him. 'I thought you went to Roselands to buy your mum a birthday present,' he says. 'Did you know he was going to be there? How did you actually get to meet him?'

'I didn't have a clue he'd be there and even if I had, I wouldn't have expected to meet him like I did.'

'Oh, come on, Irma. Stop being coy and tell me everything, will ya?'

She laughs. This is why Mark is her best friend. He loves a good story. Always has. When they were little, they used to read fairy tales aloud together, though it was Mark who read most of the characters' voices. She wonders if he can still cackle like an evil crone. But she doesn't ask him. Instead, she tells him how she'd not been at the shopping centre five minutes, when she bought a glass vase that she thought her mother would like.

'I had about forty minutes to wait for the next bus home, so I went down to the food court to get myself a milkshake, and this gorgeous guy walks up and sits next to me. I thought he looked familiar but even when he told me who he was, I didn't really believe him. Anyway, we talked for a while about all sorts of things, and I kept thinking how really, really nice he was…you know how you can tell just by looking into someone's eyes…and there was just this fantastic connection between us…'

She pauses to brush back her hair from her eyes with her fingers. 'After a little while, he starts looking at his watch and saying he has to go soon and then he pulls out a piece of paper from his jacket pocket and gives it to me. It was an entry form for a competition, and he said if I filled it out quickly, he'd make sure it was placed in the barrel before a winner is chosen…maybe I'll be lucky and win a prize, he says.'

Irma suddenly stops walking and falls silent as they turn into Ogilvy Street. Her world has never looked so splendid as it does at this moment. The entire street is awash with purple blooms from the jacarandas lining both sides of the road. Gazing into the amethyst wonder of it, she leans up against somebody's brown brick fence, while Jazza cocks his right hind leg to water a nearby wooden garden gate.

Mark stands still and drinks in the scene. 'Don't worry,' he says, observing how her dog has finished his job and is raring to go again, 'he won't be straining on his lead much longer. Once we start walking up that hill,' and he flicks his thumb in the direction of their old primary school at the top of the street, 'he won't be so eager… I'll take him for a while if you like.'

Irma hands Mark the lead. 'Ta,' she says. 'Now, where was I?' Then remembering, 'Oh yeah, I know, the entry form...so I fill it out and hand it back. Then Peter asks me to come and see the band perform their latest single at the Raindrop Fountain. They're scheduled to appear at eleven o'clock – he calls it a "promotional gig", that it won't take long and that we can meet again after it's all over.'

'Where were the rest of Dark Daze while all this was going on?'

'No idea, but they were all there at the fountain when the show started. So was the DJ, Ward Austin. He revved up the crowd and introduced them. A lot of girls were pushing and shoving – trying to get closer to the stage.'

'You mean, closer to him...'

Irma ignores Mark's comment. 'But I had a great possie on the next floor up. From the balcony, I could look directly down onto the stage. Peter spotted me and he kept looking up and winking and stuff. Then his manager came out and announced the winner of the competition and guess what? It was me.'

'Surprise! Surprise!' As soon as Mark speaks, he regrets his cynical tone. But if Irma is offended, she doesn't let on.

'Yes, it was a surprise.'

And Mark can see from the light in her eyes how thrilled she is. 'So what did you win?'

'A date with Peter, of course,' says Irma, imagining candlelight, linen tablecloths and hovering waiters.

'And I suppose you haven't told your folks yet.'

Irma looks at her friend and shakes her head.

'So, what do you think they're going to say? I mean how old is he?'

'He's still only nineteen.'

'Sure,' says Mark unconvinced. 'Even if that's true, it still makes him a good four years older than you. Do you honestly think they'll let you go out with him?'

'Anything's possible,' she says.

They aren't far from the Henry Lawson Drive Bridge that crosses

Salt Pan Creek, when a sudden swooping magpie appears from behind. Mark waves his arms and yells at the bird to piss off. Convinced the bird's target is Jazza, Irma tugs at the dog's leash and veers right to take her little party along the dirt track that cuts through a great clump of bush. They'll soon be in Elwin Street. Almost home.

*

Peter promised he'd ring her that evening, and Irma has no reason to disbelieve him. Over dinner with her parents, there hasn't been an opportunity for her to divulge the circumstances of her morning, what with her mother consumed by what choice of dessert she should make for tomorrow's lunch. Cheesecake or trifle? Pavlova or Black Forest cake? Whenever her brother Warren and his wife Sandra come for Sunday lunch, it's always the same – Yvonne frets about the menu, which drives Reg to the television set and their daughter into her room. But on this occasion, Irma remains and does the dishes without complaint. She even offers to help her mother make the trifle.

That's when the phone rings.

Irma answers the call. 'Hello?'

'Hi there, beautiful. Whatcha been doing?'

'Walking the dog…listening to the radio…'

'And thinking about me, I hope?'

Irma is smiling. 'A bit.'

'I can't wait to see you again… I've got some free time Monday afternoon. I can pick you up from school, and then we could go for a drive somewhere and talk, if you like.'

'Look, um… I don't know… I've…'

'Oh, come on, Irma. Stop stalling and give me a chance, will ya? We'd be so good together… I know you think so too, so how about the pictures then on Friday night?'

'I'll have to check with my parents first.'

'Yeah, sure… I'll wait on while you ask them.'

'Look…um, how about you ring back tomorrow night? And we can talk about it then, OK?'

'Sure. Fair enough… Just remember I'm serious about you, Irma. Really serious. I want you to know that.' A pause. 'Until tomorrow, then…'

Irma says goodbye and replaces the receiver.

'So who was that?' asks Yvonne, who's suddenly appeared in the doorway.

'His name's Peter.' She turns to face her mother.

'I've never heard you talk about a Peter before. Is he new to your school?'

Oh God, here we go, thinks Irma, following her mother into the dining room. 'No,' she says, 'I met him at Roselands today when I went to get you a present for your birthday.'

Yvonne has already taken up a position at the table. Irma follows her mother's example and sits down. Indistinct television noises waft from the lounge room.

'You what?' is her mother's response.

'I told you. I met him at –'

'And you gave him your phone number? A perfect stranger? Do you know anything about this boy?'

'Of course I do. He's famous.'

'Famous? What do you mean famous?'

'He's Peter Wallace, the lead singer of Dark Daze, the rock band.'

'Good God, girl. What were you thinking giving him our number? He's far too old for you. What did he want…ringing here?'

'He wants to know if I'd be allowed to go out to the pictures with him.'

'And you said?'

'I said I'd have to ask my parents.'

'But Irma, you know full well what our answer is, so why lead him on this merry chase?'

'I was hoping that you'd…'

'You can hope all you like, young lady. You know what our rules are. For God's sake, girl, you're barely fifteen!'

'But Mum…' Irma doesn't stand a chance.

'But Mum nothing! You're still a child and while you live under my roof, you'll do as I say. Am I making myself clear?'

Furious, Irma stands up and the back of her chair hits the sideboard, making her mother's prized Bohemia crystal decanter and wine glasses tinkle their displeasure. 'VERY clear! You think you're always right! You never make any exceptions, do you?'

Yvonne's eerily composed. She rises and placing her hands on her hips, hisses: 'Now listen here, my girl, don't you raise your voice at me.'

'Ha, but it's OK for you to raise yours whenever you feel like it.'

'I'm telling you, Irma. Calm down.' Her voice throbs with control. 'You're just being hysterical, as usual.'

'Yeah, that's right, any time I disagree with what you say, it's me being hysterical. Well, I'm not going to calm down. Not ever. You never let me do a thing. I've got no freedom. You don't trust me. You think I'm some kind of baby who…'

And why should I trust you? Just look at yourself. You're acting like a little brat.'

'Well, get used to it, cos I'm going to continue to act like this till I've got a job and enough money to leave this hole!'

Irma is crying and turns to go to her room, but her mother grabs hold of her right arm and brings her face close to her daughter's. 'Very well.' Yvonne has lowered her voice to a rasping whisper. 'One day, when you're a wife and have children of your own, you'll appreciate why your dad and I have these rules…'

'Oh, I don't think so…because I'm never going to be like you. I don't plan on ever getting married, let alone have any children. Cos this is the seventies. The world has changed. Women can do whatever they want now.'

'But you're not a woman yet, so you can get to your room, young lady and stay there until I tell you otherwise!'

*

The distant drone of the TV is switched off. Irma knows she's crossed the line and turns to go as Reg reappears at the entrance to the hallway door. The sleeves of his shirt have been rolled up, ready for action in front of the television screen.

'What's all this racket about?' he says. 'They can hear you two yelling at the end of the bloody street.'

Irma wants to run next door and talk to Mark, but she goes to her room instead and so doesn't see her father putting his arms around her teary mother, who finds comfort for her head on her husband's shoulder. Speaking softly, she tells Reg about Peter Wallace, the rock star, who wants to take out their daughter.

'I'll talk to her,' says Reg.

Not for the first time, he goes to Irma's room and taps lightly on her door before opening it. She is sobbing into her pillows.

'Now look, luv,' he says and sits on the edge of the bed. 'This is not the end of the world, you know. And this Peter Wallace…he must be in his twenties…'

'Dad, he's nineteen.' She sits up. She's stopped crying and is alert and ready to plead her case.

'So he says, luv.' Irma's about to protest, but Reg takes both her hands in his and says, 'And even if he is, you're only just fifteen. You're too young for him, darlin'.'

'Even if he was twelve, Mum wouldn't let me go out with him.'

'Now you're being silly. You're supposed to be an intelligent girl. For heaven's sake, start acting like one. Your mother's only trying to do what's best, and I agree with her. I know what boys are like at his age and I'm telling you, he's too old for you, Irma.

She wrenches her hands from his. 'But Dad, he's not like that…' She can see bunches and bunches of burgundy-coloured roses being delivered to their front door. 'He's really, really nice. I know you'd like him.'

'Well, if he's as decent as you say he is, he won't mind waiting a bit till you're older, then.'

Knowing it would make no difference to her parents if she mentioned she'd won a date with Peter, Irma tries another tack. 'But Dad, he'll be going away soon. The band's going to England. They've been offered a recording contract there and I might never get to see –'

'What did you just say? Off to England, is he?' Reg can barely hide his delight and relief. 'Geez, luv, use your brains. Why bother starting something that'll only end in tears? You'll never see him again… He's off on his wild goose chase. But you…you, Irma, you're going to get yourself an education. Mark my words, you'll do a lot better than him, I can tell ya.'

'But I might never meet anybody else like him ever again.'

Assured of victory, Reg hugs his daughter. 'I doubt that very much,' he says. 'You're a wonderful girl, luv, and I'm telling you, there's plenty of bigger and better fish in the Pacific than the likes of this Peter Wallace character. He's just a flash in the pan. You'll see.'

*

There is no phone call from Peter Wallace the following night. Irma blames herself at first. She should have been more enthusiastic, more encouraging when he rang yesterday. What if she never sees him again? It'll be her parents' fault if that happens. If only they were more flexible about things, less old-fashioned. There are girls in her class who sleep with their boyfriends, whereas she's not even allowed to have a boy-friend. It's so unfair.

Next day she goes to school. Miserable. Mark tries to jolly her out of her mood. But he can't. Her only smile is when the bell rings at the end of the school day and she is walking out the gate and hears the beep-beep of a car horn.

It's him. And he's wound his window down and is calling her name. 'Irma! Irma! Over here!'

She's the centre of attention. Several students are openly gawping as she crosses the road to greet the driver. She hears someone say his name. Peter Wallace. That's Peter Wallace. She pecks him on the cheek, then gets in the car. Vroom vroom. He drives away.

A little later, he pulls up beneath a shady tree not far from Irma's place. The street appears deserted, quiet.

'We can talk here,' he says. He's already apologised for not ringing last night. He'd spent the entire day in the recording studio in Hurstville. Got caught up. But couldn't let another day go by without seeing her.

He moves across the front seat and begins to kiss Irma. She thinks she's melting. The kiss keeps going. On and on. His tongue is moving in and out of her mouth. He's squeezing her left breast. He's gentle. It's nice. He's kissing her neck and steering her hand to the zipper of his jeans.

'Hold me…hold me.' His voice husky. Urgent.

She feels his hurried breath. His fingers beneath her uniform claw at the legs of her knickers. She grabs his hand. Moves it away. A little struggle. 'No no…' she says, 'no…'

And he slowly sits up. Back behind the steering wheel. His eyes are shut. He murmurs something.

She's hears him say, 'Jesus!' She tells him it's too soon. They don't know one another. Not really. She tells him she likes him. Very much. But it's all too fast. She's not like that. They haven't even been out together on a date.

He smiles and says, 'Fair enough. I'll ring you later.'

'OK,' says Irma and leans across to him to kiss him on the cheek.

As soon as she's out of the car, it takes off. She turns and runs up a nearby laneway. She's hoping Mark will be home.

*

The two friends are sitting on the Kellers' back porch steps. Still in her school uniform with her school case at her feet, Irma looks up towards

Mark, who's sitting on the upper step. He's been listening intently to Irma's description of her eventful afternoon.

'So, do you think he'll call you tonight?'

'Pretty sure,' says Irma. 'He reckons he can turn Mum around. Have her eating out of his hand.'

Mark finds this hilarious. When he finishes laughing, he asks her how she feels. About him. Peter.

'I'm not so sure any more.'

'Well, keep me posted,' says Mark.

*

Following Peter's instructions, Irma places the receiver on the phone table and leaves the room to fetch her mother. When Yvonne returns, Irma stands at the doorway to observe and listen to her mother, whose back is now ramrod straight as she picks up the telephone receiver.

'Yvonne Keller here, Peter. What can I do for you?'

Embarrassed by her mother's expression, Irma closes her eyes.

Then she hears, 'That's all very well, but there's far too big an age difference between you, I'm afraid.'

There's a weighty pause. Irma is feeling ill. She wishes she could hear what Peter is saying. What she can hear, though, is Yvonne's hard line beginning to soften.

'But I'm sure you can appreciate my point of view as well.' A pause. 'I can assure you, my daughter won't be going out with anybody else either. For some time yet.'

Irma groans and covers her face with her hands as she hears her mother. 'Well, that's very nice of you to say, Peter, but it's only words.' Another pause. 'Look, I'm sorry. Really, I am. But my husband's quite adamant about this.' Yvonne is smiling as she listens. Then, 'Yes, I understand and I wish you all the very, very best in your future endeavours… Bye bye.' She is still smiling when she hangs up.

'Oh, Mum…did you have to speak to him like you were flirting with him or something?' Irma follows her mother back into the kitchen, where they continue putting dishes away – a task that had been interrupted by the phone call.

'I wasn't doing any such thing… Anyway, he took it well and, I have to admit, he's extremely polite and courteous.'

'And incredibly talented. You know, he'll probably be a millionaire one day.'

'He's got as much chance of that happening as me winning the lottery. And you, my girl, are a hopeless romantic, with your head in the clouds, and I really don't know what's to become of you.'

*

Several months pass. It's now late January. Irma, wearing a bikini, is sunning herself in the backyard.

Reg in shorts and an Hawaiian-print shirt rounds the side of the house, and brandishing mail, approaches his daughter. 'Look what's arrived for you… A postcard from Lover Boy himself!'

Irma takes the postcard from her father. She looks at its front – an image of Thursday Island. Puzzled, she flips it over and sees,

DEAR IRMA,
FIRST STOP ON THE CANBERRA ON OUR WAY TO ENGLAND. HOPE YOU HAVEN'T FORGOTTEN ME. I'VE WRITTEN A FEW SONGS FOR YOU.
PETER

Reg shakes his head. 'Honestly,' he says. 'I can't believe that fella. He's got such tickets on himself.'

*

Some years later, Yvonne and Reg were to eat their words. As a member of Dark Daze, Peter Wallace went on to sell in excess of 250 million records and singles worldwide. His success and his music became a bit of a joke within the Keller family. Many of the lyrics of his hit songs concerned 'the girl I left behind' and 'the one that got away'. There were times when Irma wondered what she'd lost. Until of course it was revealed that Wallace, before his departure from Australia, had secretly married a long-time girlfriend who'd accompanied him to the UK. The marriage did not last.

It's currently rumoured that Netflix is investigating the possibilities of producing a television series based on the rags-to-riches story of Dark Daze. As for Irma, she's now a newsreader for a commercial television station and, while she's never seen Peter Wallace again, she and Mark Ward are regularly in touch.

Losing Hope

On Monday 14 August 1944, a posse of press reporters and photographers transformed the reception room of Mascot aerodrome into a small film studio. Cameras, lights and a bank of microphones had been installed which created a patient, static display. And despite the plane's lateness, the crowd of fans and onlookers, who'd been standing outside in the cold for several hours, still appeared eager and orderly.

But then the news arrived. The US navy's Catalina flying boat would not be coming. Earlier that day about 400 kilometres north of Sydney, there'd been trouble with the plane's starboard engine. It started losing altitude and that's when Gary Ferguson, the pilot, decided to make an emergency landing.

'Open the hatches and throw out whatever you don't need,' he ordered. 'We've got to lighten this thing!'

The crew and some of the passengers obeyed. While Ferguson searched for a suitable place to land, several crates of whisky went flying, as did some articles of clothing.

'Now hit the floor!' he yelled, and the Catalina began to skim over the Camden Haven River near the small fishing village of Laurieton.

The plane made a sudden lurch, then hit a narrow sand spit and almost somersaulted as it ran aground, finally stopping near a bend in the river between Dunbogan boat shed and what locals called Bunny's Corner. No one was injured, but some of the passengers were a little shaken. A couple of them had managed to crawl out onto one of the flying boat's wings and were hollering at the local fishermen, who'd rowed out to see how they could help the poor unfortunates who'd been inside that Catalina. Their American accents were unmistakeable, but it was the sight of Bob Hope's face that completely amazed them.

The good townsfolk couldn't believe their luck when word went round that Hope and his entourage – that included the singer Frances Langford, the comedian Jerry Colonna and the dancer Patsy Thomas – were in town. This was the first time a famous American movie star had done Laurieton the honour of literally dropping by. The place came to a standstill. Even the local sawmill stopped work early that day.

Hope made his way to the post office to send telegrams and make the necessary phone calls to their organisers. Laurieton's entire population of 600 people soon learned that their very own American celebrities had been entertaining troops, who'd been fighting the Japanese in the steaming jungles of the South Pacific. They'd been heading to Sydney for a short break before flying back to New Guinea to complete this particular USO tour.

This was a cause for celebration. An impromptu dance was quickly organised for that very evening and, to the delight of the township, Hope agreed to put on one of his shows in the School of Arts hall. Five hundred people turned up. The next day, six American cars came from Newcastle to take the entertainers to Sydney, where they were mobbed almost everywhere they went.

The day Hope came to Laurieton has become a part of that town's history. An autograph book takes pride of place in the display case commemorating the comedian's unexpected stopover in the Camden Haven Historical Society Museum, that was once the School of Arts building where the film star danced the hokey-pokey until the early hours of the morning.

While in Sydney, Bob Hope stayed at the Hotel Australia. Newspapers of the time report that he was received at Government House; that he watched a show at the Tivoli; that he accompanied several Tivoli chorus girls to Romano's one night; and that he attended a luncheon given by Cinesound Studios. They also mention that he gave concerts to patients in US military hospitals. But no specific mention is made of the 118th General Hospital, the largest military hospital for wounded American servicemen built in Australia during

World War Two. Yet he did go and give a concert for some of the 1,700 patients there. And no item of memorabilia of that time is known to exist. Not a single souvenir, not even a lousy photograph remains of Hope's visit to Herne Bay. And there's absolutely no evidence that he ever went near Salt Pan Creek.

The only Australian river he ever spoke about was Laurieton's Camden Haven.

All Sorts

Many years ago, when Mark permanently moved to Melbourne to live with Tom, Irma made Mark promise that no matter what happened in their individual lives, the two of them would do everything in their power to meet together at least once a year for a boozy lunch in Sydney. Despite the geographical distance at times making such a commitment difficult for Mark, they managed to keep their pledge. As far as the choice of venue was concerned, the only stipulation they agreed upon was that the restaurant had to have water views. Usually this has meant somewhere on the harbour, though they had ventured as far north as Palm Beach and as south as Cronulla. But never to Salt Pan Creek, because there are no restaurants there.

'That's because it's not a real place,' said Mark at their most recent lunch together. 'According to Kate, it's just a state of mind.'

'Maybe she's right,' said Irma, with a gentle shake of her head. 'Because what it's become is nothing like what it once was. It's changed beyond recognition. God, you should see it now.'

'I saw enough when Kate and I were selling our old place.'

'Of course, I forgot about that.' She scooped up some of the chocolate confection in front of her and spooned it into her mouth. 'How about as soon as we finish these overpriced desserts, we take off and find a nice pub somewhere and get well and truly plastered?'

And that became their intention for the remainder of the day.

Once they'd found a table in the outdoor bistro area of the Watsons Bay Hotel, they settled into a steady afternoon of gentle inebriation. Inevitably, the conversation meandered from the state of politics in Australia to the catastrophic ecological disaster of the planet. But returned to Salt Pan Creek. As it always did.

'You have to admit, it was a funny place to grow up. In a lot of respects, it was just an ordinary, post-war Sydney suburban neighbourhood, almost bland really,' said Mark.

Irma shook her head. 'Yes, but as kids we had the river and all that natural bush. That's what made it so special for us.'

'You'll get no argument from me there. But lots of people grow up living near rivers. What I reckon, though, is that our childhood was quite different to other people's. It was unique precisely because our river was different.' Mark drained his glass and placed it firmly on the table. 'I mean, when you think about it, there were a lot of eccentric people living in our neighbourhood. In fact, I'd go so far as saying there was a disproportionate number of misfits and nonconformists who washed up on the shores of our river.'

'And there were a couple of dodgy ones as well, like Silas Avery, for example.'

'Oh God, he was really creepy...' Mark signalled to the waiter. 'I'm going to order a coffee,' he said. 'Do you want one?'

Irma nodded. 'But Dutchie wasn't like that...'

'Yeah, I think everybody felt sorry for him.' Mark ordered two espressos. 'Do you remember *The Merry Widow*? Now there was a free spirit. A bit unconventional, but no one would bat an eyelid these days.'

'Reminds me of the Kendricks kid. What was his name again?'

'Barry, wasn't it? I'd forgotten about him. He was quite the trailblazer – though we didn't know it then. Do you know what happened to him?'

Irma shook her head, then sipped at her coffee.

Mark seemed lost in thought, then spoke again. 'It was considered to be a bit of a backwater – Salt Pan Creek, I mean – and I think a lot of the people who lived there back then were looking for a place to hide, somewhere benign where they could feel secure...'

'You mean a safe haven for fish out of water?'

Mark laughed, savouring the joke. Irma was still the most quick-witted person he knew. 'You know what we should do before we destroy all our brain cells?' A pause. 'We should make a list…a kind of inventory of all those odd bods we can remember.'

'For posterity's sake?' Irma's tone was deliberately ironic.

'No time like the present. Let's just do it!'

And with that, she reached into her handbag and retrieved a pen and a slender A5 journal. Mark watched her print the title in capital letters across the top of an open double page.

'OK,' she said. 'Who'll be the first one on our list?'

It was in this way that the two childhood friends spent what was left of the afternoon, both happily immersed in a stream of remembering, itemising and recording. When Irma finally stuffed her journal back in her bag, she promised Mark that she'd type it up and email it to him so he could make any revisions he thought were necessary.

What neither of them knew then was that, in the distant future, Irma's adult children will uncover a moss-green leather Moleskine notebook in a drawer among their deceased mother's personal papers. Rose, her only daughter, will take it home to read. In it, she will find within her mother's handwritten notes several seemingly random newspaper clippings that include various reviews of films she'd seen and books she'd read, a couple of recipes for elaborate desserts, quotations from a number of famous writers and philosophers, as well as pages upon pages of her mother's rambling thoughts on an assortment of topics such as religion, sex, leadership, raising children, ethical behaviour, feminism and the importance of friends.

As she reads her mother's words, she will shed tears of joy and laughter. But when, towards the end of the journal, she comes across a number of pages devoted to what her mother called *Fish out of Water*, which was some kind of catalogue of people's names with descriptions of some wildly unorthodox behaviours, Rose will question whether she'd really known her mother at all.

Back to School

If school reunions were meant to be celebrations of the past, Kate wasn't sure she wanted to rejoice about anything that happened so long ago, especially with people she could barely remember in any real detail. But she was curious nonetheless about who would turn up and who wouldn't. Would the bullies have the nerve to show their miserable faces? Would the bullied not attend, choosing to remain cowering at home? Of course, there were a few people she'd love to see again. Denise, for instance. She hadn't set eyes on her since leaving school and had often wondered what became of her. How marvellous it would be if she appeared today from nowhere, haughty and magnificent as ever. But if that were not possible, surely there'd be someone there who knew what had happened to her – where she now lived, what she was doing.

By design, Kate arrived late. She knew how these things worked: early birds stood about, engulfed in the menace of semi-empty space, prey to the prospect of judgement. But as she was determined to avoid the scrutiny of others, Kate made an unobtrusive entrance a half an hour after the starting time, and simply mingled in with the hordes at the back of the hall. Based upon the invitation, she'd calculated that in all probability there'd be a lot of people in attendance. And once at the door, she saw she'd been right.

The old school hall was full of laughter and light and conversation and music. As Kate looked around the crowd, searching for a face she remembered, someone tugged at her arm, gushed a welcome and asked her name. She was given a name tag and advised not to miss the large display to her left.

May as well start there, she thought, so as suggested she turned left. What she noticed first was a large, semicircular rosewood table placed against the back wall. It held a huge, black felt board that was covered in neatly pinned photographs. Candles of various sizes, all lit, had been placed on the table itself. And when she realised she was staring at a memorial to the dead, some of whom, might well have been her classmates, she shuddered. This wasn't what she'd been expecting at all.

She turned away and walked back towards the living throng of people in the body of the hall. She let her eyes search around her for a familiar face, but to Kate it seemed that the entire gathering was somehow contrived and artificial, like a grand masquerade. Only the removal of masks was forbidden. She saw awkwardness disguised as bravado. She saw how time had been cruel to some faces that no amount of Botox or make-up could hide. Kate failed to recognise anyone. She wanted to flee.

There was a sudden tap on her shoulder, and she heard from behind her, 'You've got to be Kate Ward. I'd recognise you anywhere!'

Kate turned around to greet the voice. 'Oh, hello,' she said. 'I remember you too.' What a relief! She knew someone. 'You're Faye…Faye MacDonald. We were in the same French class together, weren't we?'

'Yes, we were. And isn't it wonderful? We've passed the memory test and won't be needing these hideous name tags.' Faye waved hers about, then shoved it into her jacket pocket.

They laughed together then, and Kate asked her what she'd been doing since she left school.

'Well…' Faye began, rolling her eyes dramatically, 'since you've asked…' And off she went, summarizing, without a note of false modesty or boasting, an event-filled life: some tertiary study, overseas trips, career, marriage to a businessman, a couple of kids, a husband who ran off with his secretary, an acrimonious divorce, kids all grown up, then via an online dating site, she meets a farmer, marries him, moves to Forbes and only now has come to appreciate just how Eva Gabor felt in *Green Acres*.

Kate was almost doubled-over with laughter. 'You missed your calling, Faye,' she said. 'You'd have made a brilliant stand-up comedian.' She hadn't known Faye all that well at school and now almost regretted that they hadn't been closer.

A few other people soon joined them due, no doubt, to the hilarity Faye generated. Kate relaxed. She was starting to enjoy herself.

'Excuse me. I'm very sorry.' The voice sounded breathless and wounded like a lost, small child's. 'I can't recall your name, but I never forget a face and I'm sure you were best friends with Denise Reid. Am I right?'

'Yes, you are.' Kate was looking at a scrubbed-clean, fresh-faced woman with a blaze of red waist-length wavy hair. It badly needed a comb. Dressed in faded paisley-printed loose-fitting trousers, a grey-white caftan top, chunky bangles and enormous, colourful dangly earrings, she smelt vaguely of patchouli oil.

'My name's Ariel... Ariel Wildflower. It used to be Sharon Powell.' She made a strangled giggle. 'I was two years below you and Denise at school, but I'll never forget her...because she came to my rescue once...when I was being bullied.'

'That'd be Denise...' said Kate.

'She was a wonderful person. Just wonderful.' Ariel's eyes blinked rapidly. 'I hoped she might be here.'

'Me too.' Kate felt suddenly protective of this strange childlike woman.

'I don't suppose you know where she lives, do you?'

'No, unfortunately, I don't.'

'I bumped into her once...a few years back now, but...'

'Really? Where? What was she doing with herself?'

'It was in the street. In Byron.' Ariel locked eyes with Kate, then blinked again and said, 'You see, I was busking in the main drag where all the boutiques and cafés are. I'd been living off-grid and I needed some money fast.' She took a breath and blinked again. 'Anyway, this woman, dressed like she'd just walked out of *Vogue* or something, comes striding along and she stops, takes a real good look at me and says, well, if it isn't Sharon Bloody Powell – just like that.' Ariel shook her head – still in amazement at the unpredictable synchronicity of life. 'And so we got talking, and she bought me a coffee and then gave me fifty bucks.'

'How wonderful. Did she tell you anything? About herself, I mean? Like what she was doing in Byron?'

'Same thing most loaded people do when they get to Byron – she was looking at real estate. Said she'd married some rich old bloke and was now living in Queensland. She said she preferred living in a tropical climate up there.'

'Ladies and gentlemen, good afternoon. Could I please have your attention for just a moment?' A woman on the stage was speaking into a microphone. The hall was almost silent. 'My name's Janet Nicholson. I'm the current principal of this, your old high school, and I'd very much like to welcome you all back here today. I know this informal gathering time is most important to you so I won't hold you up for very much longer. I just wanted to say…'

Ariel mouthed a few silent and indecipherable words to Kate in the middle of the principal's welcome address before sliding away into the crowd. And it really wasn't very long at all before the hall erupted once more in noisy chatter. But Ariel was nowhere to be seen.

Someone in the group that Faye and Kate had been standing with suggested they take a walk outside – get some fresh air, check out the old playground, the canteen area and the sporting field.

'Yes, why not?' Faye said, and they all began to move off, forming a group that then narrowed to become a single file so it could weave a path to the hall's exit through all the little clusters of people.

Finding herself at the rear of the line, Kate was suddenly swung around and there before her stood Ron Cochrane, looking sprightly with his still boyish face, despite the addition of a bushy but greying moustache.

'Well, well, well, if it isn't Kate Ward. Am I glad to see you! I was hoping to find you here.'

'It's fantastic to see you too!' And Kate meant it.

The two old friends hugged one another and when they broke off their embrace, their eyes met and both felt again the affinity they once had.

'I wasn't really expecting you'd be here. A while back I was told you lived abroad – had done for years. So I hardly expected you to return for some lousy little school reunion.'

'Actually,' he said, 'I've been back home – in Australia, that is – for quite some time now.'

'Really? The last I'd heard was that you'd travelled the world, picking up degrees everywhere, including Cambridge, and that you had a couple of kids – daughters, I think – and you were lecturing or something in the Faculty of Engineering and Design at the University of Bath.' Kate thought she'd done well not to mention Denise. Thanks to what Ariel had told her, she'd surmised there'd been a divorce, because there was no way Ron could be described as 'a rich old bloke'.

'Yes, you're right, I was living in Bath, but that was some time ago now – we moved back in the early nineties, to Melbourne, in fact, when I took up an appointment at Monash. They'd wanted someone who specialised in bridge engineering, who could develop some postgrad courses in structural design, so for me it was a position made in heaven.'

He beamed with such obvious pleasure as he spoke that Kate couldn't help thinking how inspirational his enthusiasm would be for his university students.

'I went there with high hopes and while I loved the work I was doing at Monash, it was while I was there that my so-called charmed personal life began to implode.'

'I'm sorry to hear that. I used to get news of you via Mum, who used to get regular updates from your mum when they ran into each other in the supermarket. But I vaguely recall Mum telling me that Cherie and Mario had moved down the south coast.'

'All true. They bought a place in Ulladulla. There's quite a little community of Italians down there. Mario loved the place, loved the fishing, and he and Mum got Benito to move down there too. Now he owns a pizzeria in Mollymook. And, what's more, does a roaring trade…' Ron started to laugh and Kate followed. 'Yeah, can you believe it? *Il piccolo bastardo* turned out OK in the end.'

When they'd both stopped laughing, Kate asked how his mother Cherie was going.

'She and Mario have both passed on.' There was a little pause then. 'I'd heard your parents had died too. I suppose there's not many of that vintage still left now.'

'Probably not. But tell me, did you come up from Melbourne especially for this reunion or for some other reason?' Kate wanted to know more. She wanted to know more about Denise. And dare she even mention Gary Saunders?

'Well, not exactly. The reunion was one of the reasons I came to Sydney, but I came down from Newcastle. That's where I live now.'

Both of them fell silent for a moment, then Kate noticed that Ron was scanning the room.

He leant forward, the tip of his nose almost touching her and said, 'It's a long story… I don't suppose you'd fancy a drink?' He straightened and tipped his head slightly to the side, waiting for her response.

She smiled and said, 'Actually, yes I would. It's pretty thirsty weather.'

'You sure you don't mind leaving here?'

'Not in the slightest.'

'Great! Then follow me.' He grabbed her hand and steered her towards the door.

She heard someone call out, 'Hey, Ronnie!' And Kate saw him respond by raising his free hand in a friendly salute, but he didn't stop moving until they stepped from the doorway into the light of that February afternoon.

*

They'd taken a table in the corner of what had once been a milk bar, now converted into a light and airy café. Colourful folk art graced its walls and a whimsical display of strangely shaped teapots helped to create an atmosphere of homespun cheeriness. But the longer Ron stayed outside on the footpath, having excused himself to take an important mobile phone call, the less cheery Kate felt. She thought it rude of him, especially since it was taking far too long.

She glanced out the window that gave a partial view of an old and elephantine concrete water tank that stood across the road from the café and wished she'd stayed at the reunion. She remembered how her father had never attended a police function of any kind after his retirement from the CIB.

'You can never go back,' was one of Milton's favourite maxims, often delivered in declamatory fashion with slow, rhythmic shakes of the head. 'For you soon discover that nothing's ever really the same as you'd remembered it.'

But Kate now wondered what was wrong with that. Why was her father so fearful of the one true thing about life? That time did not stand still. That change was inevitable.

'I'm really sorry about that.' Ron had returned. 'Have you had coffee yet?'

Kate shook her head. 'No, I was waiting for you.'

Ron sat opposite his old friend and ordered two flat whites. 'I should explain,' he said. 'That was actually Gary on the phone. He had every intention of coming to the reunion with me, but then his daughter was so distraught having been informed only last night that her mother had been diagnosed with pancreatic cancer, he bailed out. He felt he ought to be with Claudia – that's his daughter – to support her. And he was just explaining to me on the phone how grim the prognosis was looking, and how he'd been trying gently all day to convince Claudia that she should visit her mum without too much delay, that this form of cancer was not only indiscriminate, but it was also swift.'

'Oh God, that's awful... I didn't even know he was married, let alone him having a daughter. How many kids has he got?'

'Just the one, and she's thirty. Gary never married... But I'm sure you would've known Margot Henshaw. She's Claudia's mum.'

But of course! One of the bitches from Lugarno. 'Yes, I do remember the name very well,' said Kate.

Margot was one of a group of unpleasant, vicious girls in her high school year group, who'd enjoyed inflicting emotional and psychological pain on particular fellow students. Their cruelty was only matched by their unshakeable belief that they were superior to most of their peers. A belief, no doubt, that had been fostered by their parents' sense of entitlement, since they, after all, had purchased property in what Kate's mother, full of envy, referred to as 'the Vaucluse end of Salt Pan Creek' – namely Lugarno.

Kate thought it unlikely that any of this miserable set of bullies would have changed much in the intervening years since secondary school. They probably hadn't even strayed far from their childhood homes either. For they were the types who needed their status continually confirmed. And who better than their neighbours to fulfil this mutually rewarding task? But no, she still wouldn't wish pancreatic cancer on any one of those girls.

'Yes, the sad thing is, Margot lives in London – has done for years now. That was where she raised Claudia while Gary lived here.'

So much for my theory on the girls from Lugarno, thought Kate. Then asked, 'Did he see much of his daughter then while she was growing up?'

'He did his best. He tried to visit at least once a year. It was all pretty civilised until Claudia turned eighteen and decided she wanted to live with her father. Up until then, Gary and Margot had been on friendly terms.'

'Oh dear, it all sounds very difficult.' Kate wasn't sure what to say. She couldn't help thinking that Gary might not like her knowing the details of his personal life.

Then Ron said, 'By the way, he just asked me to send you his regards.'

'That's nice,' she said, now really not knowing what to say.

'Yeah, except for his trips to the UK, Gary's never roamed too far from home. Did you know he still lives in Elwin Street?'

'No, I didn't.' She said no more as the coffees appeared.

'What about you? Where are you living these days?'

'I've got a place in the mountains, at Wentworth Falls.' She stirred her coffee that had just arrived. 'I'd been living there alone for quite some time but then my son Adam returned from the States six weeks ago, after a very nasty divorce from his American wife, and so I guess he'll be staying with me until he gets back on his feet, which is absolutely fine by me. And what about you? What have you been up to since last we met?'

As they drank their coffees and ordered more, Ron gave an outline of his life since his return from England: that Kate had been right about him and Denise having two daughters – Alice and Camilla – but once they'd settled in Melbourne, things started going awry. Basically, Denise left him and took the kids, but when she later wanted to move to Adelaide, the girls demanded to remain with their dad. In the end, he and Mira, a GP who became his second wife, raised them. His daughters now both live in Sydney. Alice is married with two children, Max, who's five and Cleo, who's two.

'And you and Mira live in Newcastle and visit Sydney often, I suppose.'

'Exactly,' said Ron. 'We love living there. It's just the perfect distance from Sydney – not too far away, but not too close either. And I love being the Dean of Engineering there. I work with some great people...'

'I'm so pleased for you, Ron.' And Kate meant it. Ron was one of the world's nicest people. He deserved to be happy.

'Yes, life's pretty good really. Mira still works two days a week in a nearby medical practice, and we manage to get down to Sydney quite often. To be honest, I can't keep Mira away from our two grandchildren…' He reached into his jacket pocket then and pulled out his phone.

As he scrolled through his photo collection, proudly showing Kate dozens of shots of Max and little Cleo, she noticed how naturally Ron used the plural pronouns 'we' and 'our' when referring to his grandchildren. He was obviously in no doubt that Mira had well and truly earned the status of grandmother, which made Kate think about her own grandmotherly role. She had very few photos of Ravenna and, while she hadn't been the least bit fond of her American daughter-in-law, she couldn't help but think she might have had the opportunity of getting to know her only grandchild if only Michelle and Adam had remained together.

But that was foolish thinking. Selfish too. And what about Adam? What must he be feeling so far, far away from his daughter? When he'd first returned to Australia, he'd been profoundly unhappy. He'd told her he was a failure as a husband and a father. And with a wave of her hand, she'd dismissed the very idea. She'd hugged him and told him how much she loved him, that she was proud of all his achievements and that he'd never be a failure in her eyes. Never. But now she wondered if that had been the kind of comfort he'd been seeking. Her response had been from her own perspective of her relationship with her son. Her comments had very little to do with the way he saw himself as a man. Oh dear, she thought. Life could be so complicated. Especially when couples broke up. There was always collateral damage created by divorce. It was never just about two people. Her own divorce was a case in point.

And what of Denise? What had made her flee from Ron? Did she have regrets about giving up her children? Did she even know about the existence of Max and Cleo?

*

Kate was grateful for the silence as the convertible swept down Henry Lawson Drive and onto the bridge that spanned Salt Pan Creek. She had to admit she rather liked the wind playing havoc with her hair. Always had. There was something liberating and carefree about it. Like being on the back of a Harley Davidson. So when Ron pulled up behind her unremarkable but reliable sedan and switched off the ignition, she knew she probably looked a mess, but she didn't care. And she knew Ron wouldn't either. She unclipped her seat belt.

'Now, you're not going anywhere until we've exchanged contact numbers and all that. I'd love you to meet Mira some time and I really don't want to lose touch with you, Kate.'

'So you're not going back inside to the reunion?'

'No, I'd say it's probably nearing the end, judging by all the car spaces there are in the street now. Besides, I've caught up with you,' said Ron, 'so as far as I'm concerned that's all that matters.'

'And you're still the same sweetie I remember,' said Kate and, as an afterthought, 'I suppose I'd better give you my numbers.'

She rattled them off as Ron typed the information into his phone. He then sent a smiling emoji in a text message back to Kate.

'We both now know how to find one another,' he said. 'And next time, we'll have a real drink. What do you say?'

'Sounds great to me. I thought you must've been a teetotaller.'

'You've got to be kidding!'

Kate grinned, leant across to Ron and pecked him on the cheek. 'I almost didn't come today, but I'm so pleased I did.' She got out of the car and closed the passenger door. 'Send my regards to Gary, won't you?' It was a throwaway line, and she wasn't sure why she'd said it.

'As a matter of fact,' said Ron, 'before I head on to Leichhardt to pick up Mira from Alice's place, I thought I'd drop in to see Gary and check on how Claudia's going.'

'I'm sure he'd appreciate that.' She took a step back from the car and she was still smiling and waving as Ron pulled away from the curb.

Fish out of Water

Dutchie

But of course.

Silas Avery

Silas was a loner and rarely spoke to anyone. His only form of greeting was a high-pitched giggle that made people wary of him. He lived on the western side of Salt Pan Road in a tin-roofed, unpainted fibro cottage that had a simple wooden veranda looking out onto a narrow front yard which was filled with an assortment of rusted metal machinery. For many years, a low, cement brick fence and a gateless driveway was the only indication of his property's boundary line.

Silas walked everywhere. He didn't own a car. Around the time of the Cuban missile crisis, he built himself a bomb shelter down by the river and commissioned the construction of an imposing four-metre-high rectangular archway at his driveway's entrance. Engraved on the lintel of this impressive portal were the words 'The Avery Estate'. Neighbours sniggered, shook their heads and went about their business.

A few years later, there was a period of heavy rain. Severe flooding occurred around Milperra on the Georges River. For many people, verandas provided an undercover outdoor solution for drying clothes. Even Silas erected a makeshift clothesline. It was said that June Morrison, not at the time an experienced driver, had been about to turn left, when she witnessed Silas fondling and sniffing the crotch of a pair of ladies cotton briefs that were pegged on his clothesline. To avoid crashing into the bus stop, she applied the brakes of her car and almost hit her head on the steering wheel. She steadied herself and all

she could hear above the purr of the engine was the unmistakeably
shrill, falsetto giggle of Silas Avery.

Old Mother Roach

No one knew her age, but she was as wrinkled as an oven-dried plum.
She lived next door to Silas Avery and appeared to live alone, except for
a scrawny grey goat and a squawk of chooks that she was on occasion
seen to shoo out of her house. Always dressed in black and only ever
seen clutching an old straw broom, she often visited the midnight
dreams of local children as a wizened hag and sorceress. And so they
confused her with the wicked witch of fairy tales.

The Merry Widow

Mrs Audrey Hart lived four houses up from the Wards' place. Although
a little plump, she was an attractive-looking woman with short blonde
hair in the style of Doris Day. Never seen without make-up or a smile,
she was universally liked. And Audrey liked being liked.

When her husband passed away early in their marriage, she took to
the kitchen, finding solace in baking. Her lemon meringue pies and
chocolate cream horns won ribbons at the Royal Easter Show, as well
as compliments from the baker, the dry-cleaner and the milkman.
Each of them paid Audrey a visit once a week to collect what she owed
them – Harry, the baker on Mondays; Lance, the dry-cleaner on
Wednesdays; and George, the milkman on Fridays. This arrangement
suited all four of them and gave her neighbours food for talk.

'Can you believe it, my dear? She's at it again,' breathed Owen
Fitzgibbon to his God-fearing wife.'

'I can believe it,' came her reply. 'I can believe it.'

Mitchell Yates

Mitchell was an only child, who came to live in the area as a
twelve-year-old in one of the tiny brick Housing Commission boxes

towards the end of Weemala Avenue. The family didn't stay long, leaving a year before Mitchell finished high school. His father had returned from the war not right in the head. That's what people said. And no one refuted it. His mother was the breadwinner of the family. She was a cleaner at one of the local schools.

Mitchell made few friends, but those he had were loyal and true. They predicted that one day he'd be famous as a writer, that all we had to do was wait and see. So everybody waited, and see they did.

At twenty-five, he published a slender volume of impenetrable verse. Critics, whose speciality was poetry in all its forms, called it a work of genius. But three months later, he was found dead from a heroin overdose beneath a park bench near Central Station. Sydney's literati still mourn his loss.

The Sheehans

At the bottom of old Mr Bagley's property, there was a weatherboard boatshed that had been converted into simple living quarters offered rent free to Ray Sheehan, provided he and his wife, Enid took care of all Mr Bagley's household needs and personal requirements. The pair moved in with their two small children, Matthew and Beverley, who never seemed to play with other children. But when walking to and from school, they were universally admired for their perfect manners, their good grooming and immaculate uniforms.

The Sheehans kept to themselves. No one knew much about them at all. Ray always appeared surly and uncommunicative when seen chauffeuring Mr Bagley about or maintaining his grounds. As for Enid, she was rarely seen by anyone, but when she was, she was always wearing large black square-framed sunglasses. Some people saw this as clear proof that Ray was a drunken brute who knocked his wife around. Others insisted Enid was visually impaired.

No one ever learnt the truth, for on the day that Mr Bagley died, the Sheehans cleared out of the boatshed and literally disappeared.

Mr & Mrs Dodwell

Samuel and Cora Dodwell lived close to Belmore Road. Their children were adults and had moved away from home. Samuel was of small stature and suffered greatly from curvature of the spine. Cora was a tall, straight-backed woman who wore clothes considered fashionable in the 1930s.

Every Thursday, they walked, with Cora leading the way, to the Riverwood shops to purchase their weekly grocery needs. Every Thursday, on their return, Cora would walk behind Samuel. And every Thursday, as they made their slow approach towards their house, Cora would urge her husband on by beating him with a carton of cornflakes, its contents falling like confetti over his back and shoulders.

Clayton Thompson

The four Thompson brothers were known as thugs and bullies, who were always looking for a bit of bother wherever they went. All of them left school early. All of them, at one time or other, were in trouble with the police.

The most intelligent of the four was Clayton, the eldest. He had the bright idea of robbing a bank. 'How hard can it be?' he was heard to say. He and two mates, each with a shotgun, pulled stockings over their faces and walked into a busy Hurstville bank late one afternoon.

Just like in the movies, one of them called out, 'Everyone down on the floor! This is a stick-up.'

And within what seemed like seconds, they were out the door and into their getaway vehicle with their bag full of cash. Nothing could have been easier.

High on adrenalin, Clayton couldn't wait to open the bag. He and the car's entire interior were sprayed with hot, red dye. Whether or not this was a case of divine justice, the driver, in shock and unable to see, drove the car headlong into a semi-trailer, killing him instantly. Clayton and the other armed robber sustained critical spinal injuries.

Barry Kendricks

Barry's father had been a fireman until he was severely burnt in a factory fire. He rarely left the house. With a pair of toddler twin girls and a husband who frequently demanded her attention, Mrs Kendricks was a harried woman, who was happy to leave her adolescent son to his own devices.

Somehow, young Barry had free rein over his mother's wardrobe. Most afternoons, he would dress himself in a flutter of fuchsia taffeta and organza and, wearing satin-covered high-heeled shoes, he'd hold court to nobody in the Kendricks' backyard. Sometimes, he'd be seen collecting mail from the letterbox with a chiffon scarf wrapped loosely around his neck and sporting one of his mother's aprons and her red velvet slippers.

Nobody teased him, bullied him or judged him. Other kids stared, then looked away. They didn't understand why at his age he'd want to play dress-ups in his mother's clothes. And no adult explained why.

The Vissers

Dirk and Margret Visser emigrated from the Netherlands after the war. They had three Australian-born children – Wilhelm, Lucie and Astrid. No one ever talked about the German occupation of their country during the Second World War.

Except in private moments when Dirk and Margret spoke Dutch, the family always spoke English. Unlike Margret, Dirk's Dutch accent was strong and when he was angered, which was often, he sounded to the ears of his neighbours very German, just like Hitler sounded in the newsreels of the Nazi rallies in Nuremberg.

For several years, the family seemed happy enough living where they were. That was until Margret Visser knocked on Betty Ward's door to say they were packing up everything and would be leaving the very next day. They were moving elsewhere. Precisely where, she wouldn't say.

Betty was astounded. She wanted to know why, and a tearful Margret told her that they were being persecuted; that on certain mornings Dirk had discovered swastikas chalked on their driveway; that they'd received several anonymous letters accusing Dirk of being a Nazi; that there were telephone calls in the middle of the night when all the caller would say was '*Sieg Heil*' and then hang up; that it was sending Dirk crazy; that he felt like a hunted man. Betty asked whether they'd referred the matter to the police.

'Of course not,' Margret said. 'Do you think we're stupid?'

At the tennis club several months later, Betty was told that the Vissers hadn't gone far. They'd only moved down the river to Lugarno.

Mending

She'd taken a break from her writing and had started to clean out the wardrobe in the spare bedroom when she found it – the Ward family's old photograph album. Sitting on the floor, Kate opened it and within seconds she was nostalgia's prisoner. All the tiny, monochromatic snapshots catapulted her back into the gossamer haze of her formative years.

There are two particular photos that capture her close attention. Both are of her parents. One is the size of a postcard and has been hand-coloured. In it, her parents stand side by side. Betty is wearing pale green satin, with a low scalloped neckline, while Milton sports a jaunty black bow tie, and with his arm firm around her mother's waist, Kate could almost hear the first eight bars of Glen Miller's 'Moonlight Serenade'.

The other is a sepia photograph of a youthful bride and groom at a church door. They are both smiling into their rainbowed future, and the sweet seductive scent of frangipani from Betty's bouquet seems to drift in the air.

Kate snapped the album shut. Like everybody else's childhood, hers had cast its shadow over her adult life in ways she would probably never fully understand. Nor did she realise, as she looked at these photographs of her parents, that the feelings she was experiencing about them that morning were of the glib and cheaply sentimental kind. They failed to take into account the vital complexity of Milton and Betty's relationship, the mess and wonder of it.

But she knew that it had been their powerful attachment to each other that had forged her emotional identity and taught her the basics in how to love. She had been an eager student, but she'd also witnessed the negative impact their love had on her mother's autonomy. And such was the sense of Kate's own uniqueness and personal power, she'd actually believed, for far too many years, that had her mother exercised some firmness of purpose, her suffering would've been completely avoided. Or, at the very least, minimised.

Ever since her return from that terrible visit to her son's place in California, when she'd begun to take some responsibility for Adam's troubled state of mind, she'd been forced to question the wisdom of her fierce adherence to self-governance. It had certainly helped to undermine the two major relationships of her life, which in turn affected the happiness of other people. And since she'd been reflecting on her past, she'd discerned a recurring pattern in her behaviour towards those she'd loved.

In the case of her marriage to Richard, once the initial passion waned, so did the loving behaviours. Some rare moments of selfless give and take remained, but mostly they consisted of Richard doing all the selfless giving, while she the selfish taking. And Kate knew that she wasn't being too hard on herself. In fact, she found the very act of reviewing her marriage with more clarity and light utterly liberating.

As for her earlier relationship with Gary, she'd come to believe that they were both too young to deal effectively with their emotional barometers. They were bereft of the necessary tidal sensors that measure the push and pull of one's feelings, those subterranean needs of our individual souls. They'd both walked away from the other with their precious egos intact. And when you're young, perhaps that's for the best. She only had to look at Adam's situation for that.

Michelle had walked away from that marriage with her cutesy ego whole and unscathed. She was living the high life now in New York with her new husband, big-time stockbroker Hank Becker, and while Adam's ego may have been battered and bruised by the ugliness of the divorce, it wasn't entirely destroyed. Thanks to the Mathematics Department of Macquarie University virtually pleading with him to be part of their academic team, his ego looked as if it would make a complete recovery. It was as if he'd drawn a thick, black line beneath what he now referred to as his 'American experience'. He'd moved on, crossed the bridge, turned the page. Trite but true and, in her son's case, probably a very good thing. The alternative was far too dark to contemplate.

It was little Ravenna's ego that Kate now worried about. Only last week, there'd been one night when she'd had difficulty sleeping because she couldn't stop thinking about her granddaughter, wondering if she'd ever get to really know the child, or she her. And that led to thoughts of her own grandparents which were all haphazard and fragmented like a jigsaw puzzle with half its pieces missing. And then uninvited came a flash of words from a poem she'd studied so very long ago.

When her brother phoned her the next morning for their weekly chat, she told him about the family album and that what with all the writing and the introspection she'd been doing of late, she was becoming increasingly intrigued by the way memories work.

'I looked at the album first, which was full of pictures of Mum and Dad from their early courtship days up until you were born and I recognised the locations and every person in these photos, but then when I got to the end of the album, right there at the back was a large yellow envelope containing lots of those miniature box Brownie snaps of yesteryear and I hardly recognised a soul.'

'I don't suppose there were any names or dates on the back of them either.'

'Not even a pencil mark,' answered Kate, 'so of course all these nameless people have little meaning for any of us now. It's as if they've been wiped from our family memory, yet they were important enough and special enough for our parents to have kept the photos. It's like they intended to put them in the album…'

'But never got around to it, leaving us with all these unidentified, mysterious faces.'

'They may as well have never existed – which is not a very pleasant thought.'

'So you've come to realise just how fragile the past is,' said Mark. 'Can you understand the existential horror that historians must experience? They have to confront this sort of thing every day. No one journal, letter or any other type of primary source tells the whole truth and nothing but the truth. It's all about gathering as much evidence as you can, then cross-checking it and analysing...'

'I suppose a certain amount of empathy or emotional intelligence helps.'

'Precisely. Especially when we know that history is littered with silences, and the voices we do have are not only subjective but are often based on an individual's unreliable store of memories.'

'Well, you've certainly done a lot of thinking about all this.'

'I hate to remind you, dear sister, but I do have a first class honours degree in history. Remember?'

'Ah yes,' said Kate, laughing, 'I do have a vague recollection of that.' Then added, 'You know what makes me really scared about all this memory stuff, though?'

'No, tell me.' Mark wasn't sure where his sister was headed.

'Well, what frightens me, little brother, is that I'm getting older, and I'm well aware that, at any moment, my memories could suddenly become – from age, accident or lack of use – irretrievable, like some ghastly computer program failure.'

'Yeah, I must admit that thought has crossed my mind more than once as well.' Mark had often wondered about Milton and that famous photographic memory of his. What must it have been like for him - the homicide detective reduced to singing nursery rhymes in the lavatory when the fog of dementia tangled so cruelly with his brain? How had that come about? Had a switch been turned off in his head or had there been slow, incremental stages that no one had noticed or wanted to notice?

'It's pretty scary, isn't it? The idea that it might be hereditary, that you could go the same way yourself – caught between the light and perpetual darkness.'

'Yeah, well…' Mark wondered how he could adequately respond. He'd heard the fear in Kate's voice, but she needed to lighten up. 'So are you telling me, in a roundabout way, that the real reason you're writing this book of yours is to keep geriatric amnesia at bay and stave off the inevitability of decay and death?'

'Oh, you know me too well…' And he did. He really did, for she was smiling. She could always rely on him to lift her mood. 'It may not have been the original reason, but it's sure been the by-product of all this contemplation I've been doing.'

Kate could never lie to Mark, but she didn't tell him that it had been a line of Eliot's in *The Waste Land* that for some reason she'd recalled out of the blue, which in itself was another example of the magic of memory. Just eight little words: 'These fragments I have shored against my ruins…' and a switch in her brain was tripped. She'd made the connection. For that was what she'd been doing – piecing together the shards of memory, gathering them up so she could locate her place in the world by examining all the little moments in her life, trying to make sense of it. Before it was too late.

She wasn't sure why, but that simple realisation made her feel a whole lot better.

Fearing Death

When British philosopher Bertrand Russell was eighty years old, he wrote that the best way to overcome one's fear of death 'is to make your interests gradually wider and more impersonal, until bit by bit the walls of the ego recede, and your life becomes increasingly merged in the universal life. An individual human existence should be like a river – small at first, narrowly contained within its banks, and rushing passionately past boulders and over waterfalls. Gradually the river grows wider, the banks recede, the waters flow more quietly, and in the end, without any visible break, they become merged in the sea, and painlessly lose their individual being. The man who, in old age, can see his life in this way, will not suffer from the fear of death, since the things he cares for will continue.'

Two Phone Calls

The phone's shrill ring perforated the early morning's silence. He grabbed at the receiver beside his bed and was relieved to hear the gentleness of his daughter's voice.

'It's all over, Dad. She's gone. She passed away in her sleep about an hour ago.'

'I'm sorry, love. I really am.' He knew he sounded pathetic, that he was hopeless at this sort of thing, but Claudia didn't seem to mind.

'It's OK, Dad,' was all she said, but he heard her sadness.

'And what about you? How are you?'

'I'm fine. A bit tired. But Mum's in no more pain. And that's a good thing.' There was a pause and then she said, 'I'm so glad you convinced me to come over here, Dad, to be with Mum. She was really happy to see me. But I'll be coming home as soon as I can, do you hear?' The tears came then.

'Cry them all out,' he said. 'I mean it. It's good to cry. Don't let anyone tell you otherwise.' And he listened as she cried, and soon enough the laughter came.

'I love you, Dad,' she said before she ended the call.

'And I love you too, my darling girl. With all my heart.'

*

After speaking with his daughter, Gary sat on the edge of his bed and looked blankly out the wall of glass that was his bedroom window. For a good five minutes, he saw nothing of the outside world, not even the silent flow of his beloved river that formed the background of his view.

All he saw was Margot bathed in Chelsea sunlight. She was waiting for him outside St Luke's Church, where they often met after one of her shifts at the Royal Brompton Hospital a block away. They liked meeting there on Sydney Street. Especially when either one of them felt a bit homesick. It was their private little joke. They didn't even share it with Ron and Denise. But then, their relationship hadn't lasted all that long, based as it was on mutual convenience rather than any grand passion. When Denise introduced them in Cambridge, each of them recognised a mutual need in the other. They'd both been badly wounded, both were starved of affection and were longing for any form of physical contact with another human being.

And that first night they spent together, they'd almost ripped each other's clothes off in their haste. There'd been no mucking about. And no emotional expenditure either. But there was respect. Of sorts.

'The shagging's magnificent,' Margot announced to friends a few weeks later.

She'd already affected an English accent and vocabulary after only being in London several months. Gary had been impressed by that and also by the way she was squeezing his balls under the table at that very moment as she spoke. Nobody noticed, though – or, if they did, they didn't care. This was the seventies, when everyone was getting their rocks off. And some, like Margot, enjoyed bragging about it.

A few weeks later with a pack on his back, he took off for Greece. Margot didn't go. She wanted to stay in London. By the time he returned, she'd taken up with someone else. Some guitarist, if Gary remembered correctly.

'No hard feelings,' she'd said, her face flushed by the heat and smoky air of the little corner pub they frequented in Fulham.

'None at all,' came his reply.

'We can still be friends,' she'd added, 'and go and visit the Cochranes up in Cambridge together some times.'

'Sure thing,' he remembered saying.

And they had indeed stayed friendly.

The phone once more rang out, interrupting his thoughts.

It was Ron.

'Your timing's bloody good, mate,' said Gary. 'I just got off the phone from Claudia.' And then without hesitation added, 'Margot died.'

'It's probably a godsend, if the truth be told. How's Claudia bearing up?'

Gary told him she seemed pretty good. Considering.

After an exchange of pleasantries, Ron explained that he'd call to say he and Mira were inviting some people over for a little house-warming party on Saturday afternoon at the place they'd just bought in Stanmore. It was to be their pied-à-terre when they came to Sydney and wasn't too far from Leichhardt. It would be in two weeks' time. Would he like to come along?

'I'd love to,' was Gary's response.

'Great,' said Ron, 'but Mira thought I'd best ask you first if you'd mind very much if we also invited Kate Ward…'

'Jesus, Ron, what am I supposed to say to that? It would be nice to see her again but then if she and I are the only two guests, it's going to look like a set-up, isn't it? And if that's the case, I know I'd feel a bit uncomfortable, not to mention how she might feel.'

'That's not the case. Not at all. It's not a set-up. I wouldn't do that to you, mate, but I have to say it's not going to be a huge gathering either. It's like I've told you before, the place is tiny. There'll be no more than twelve to fourteen people here. We wouldn't be able to fit any more in. So what do you say? Will you be joining us?'

'Of course,' said Gary, wondering how else he could respond. By the time he placed the receiver back in its cradle, he was feeling rather overwhelmed by the morning's events. It had been quite an emotional start to his day.

*

He stripped off and took a long, cool shower. It didn't make him feel any better, so he dressed in shorts and an old T-shirt and took himself to the river. He needed to relax. He needed to think. He ducked into the tin shed down by the old jetty and grabbed his battered straw hat and one of the ragged rattan chairs that he kept there. They both looked like he felt. He stepped up onto the pier and plonked the chair down, sat on it and gazed out across the water. Morning light was still dancing on top of it.

He'd always liked this time of day, especially down here on Salt Pan Creek. As a kid, he'd spent many weekend hours either observing the construction of the elevated sewer pipeline that ran across the river or just mucking about, looking for treasure along the creek's bank with the neighbourhood kids like Roy Sadler, the Leggott boys and of course his best mate Ron and his older brother Paul. Theirs had been a Huck Finn kind of childhood. He and Ron had even made a canoe once. Took them days. And when the job was done, they carried her down to the shore and launched their handiwork. She floated serenely at first, and he'd yelled at Ron to hop in, which he did, but their proud little vessel immediately capsized. They gave up boatbuilding after that. Little wonder he later took up welding and Ron chose to specialise in bridge design and construction.

Over the years of their friendship, they'd often talked about bridges together. He'd never forget the first time. That was in Cambridge. He'd gone to visit Ron and Denise there. Just for four or five days. As a registered nurse, it had been easy for Denise to find work at the newly moved premises of Addenbrooke's Hospital on the southern edge of the city. Ron was a research scholar in civil engineering at Kings' College. His special interest was in the safety of bridges, so within an hour of Gary arriving and with Denise on day shift, Ron suggested a walking tour of Cambridge that, naturally enough, focused on its bridges – the Bridge of Sighs, the Mathematical Bridge and, of course, Clare Bridge, which on first sight became Gary's personal favourite. Gary learnt a great deal that day, particularly about the kind of man Ron had become, which was all tied up with his passion for bridges.

'I love the very idea of them,' Ron had said, as they made their way from the old Mathematical Bridge to the Eagle pub. 'They're solid. They've got heft. They can withstand massive amounts of weight. But more than all that, there's something wise and truly noble about them too: they span chasms, traverse obstacles and can reach across an abyss. They unite, they don't divide. They connect one side of a waterway with another. A bridge knows and understands both sides, both shorelines, but has no allegiance to either one.'

This memory made Gary smile. Ron had hardly taken a breath. But by the end of the day, he and Ron were as drunk as fish in a freshwater stream. And it had been that night, when the two of them had tumbled and stumbled through their Cambridge front door, that Gary had seen a side of Denise that he'd wished he'd never seen. He and Ron could barely stand and, looking back now, Gary conceded that, though unintentional, they were probably making quite a racket in the hallway, where she suddenly appeared before them as if from nowhere. She was wearing a long white cheesecloth caftan that was made transparent by the light from the kitchen behind her. Her arms were firmly folded beneath her breasts, accentuating their magnificence. Her expression, though, was withering, and her stare deadly. There was no doubting the state of her emotions, which were as cold as an ice maiden's kiss.

'If you dare come anywhere near me tonight, Ron Cochrane, I'll cut your fucking dick off!' And with that she was gone.

Now, for the life of him, Gary had no other recollection of that night. It was as if almost everything that had taken place on that visit, after Denise had spoken, had been wiped clean from his memory bank. Certainly, he and Ron had never talked about the incident, and Gary wondered if that was because Denise had humiliated him in front of his best friend. He knew for sure that he'd stayed four more nights with the two of them in Cambridge, yet all that remained in his mind was an abiding, but hazy, impression that the rest of his stay had been pleasant.

And despite him now holding Denise in contempt for the

despicable way she'd treated Ron, to say nothing of their daughters, he did in some way have her to thank for Claudia. If it hadn't been for Denise introducing him to Margot in the first place, he might never have known the joys of fatherhood. As for his friendship with Ron, it had weathered the heartlessness of time. And that's what counted after all. Yes, he had much to be thankful for.

He stretched out his legs. He was feeling more relaxed, as he always did when he was down by the river. Except of course for that one time when he and Kate had broken up. It was a life time ago really. And besides, they were only kids. A lot of water had flown down this river since then. Surely, he could face her now. He hadn't worried about meeting up with her again when he'd agreed to go to the school reunion with Ron. In fact, he hadn't even given the possibility of seeing her there much thought. It had only been after Ron had given him the rundown about the afternoon – how he'd seen her; how great she looked; how, in essence, she hadn't changed; how it had just been like old times – that Gary had realised he'd enjoyed hearing about her. But since then, he'd forgotten all about her again. He had enough on his plate to think about, what with Claudia's departure for the UK. His only waking thoughts ever since she'd left were for her and, by extension, Margot.

And now this. The prospect of meeting Kate at Ron and Mira's little get-together made him feel uneasy. Sure, it might not be a blind date, but perhaps he'd feel a whole lot better if fifty or more people were invited. He could avoid any embarrassment by getting lost in the general throng of partygoers, rather than be vulnerable in the cosy comfort of a dozen guests. And what would she think of him after all these years? He was grey-haired and not as fit and agile as he once was. She'd been a teacher, and he was a tradie. They'd have nothing in common. He wouldn't even know how to start a conversation with her. And really and truly, did he even want to?

A woman's laughter and the sudden sound of an outboard motor made him look to the south. These people were having fun. He needed to cheer up. After all, what on earth could Kate Ward judge him about? He'd found happiness in his life. This property, for starters, had contributed to that. He'd been smart to buy out Lorraine's share in the place after Les and Hazel died. She hadn't wanted it. She and her husband were all for selling it, so he'd made them an extremely generous offer. He didn't want any recriminations later, especially now since he'd finished the renovations on the house.

His sister and brother-in-law wouldn't recognise the place now. Though the jetty would be a dead giveaway. He hadn't touched it yet. Probably wouldn't either. It was an antique really, a little bit of his old life, a piece of his childhood. This jetty was a bridge to his past, the part he was happy to remember.

The river had never bored him. Its waters were constantly on the move, mostly steady, sometimes sluggish, occasionally rapid, but ever changing. And there was always something to look at – a glimpse of a galah, a floating limb of a tree. As far as he was concerned, it was the centre of all the beauty and wonder of nature. And just being near it made him feel rested, at peace with himself and the world.

Warming the House

Camilla has the job of welcoming people at the front door of the small, semi-detached, inner-city cottage that the Cochranes have just bought. And although this is the first time Kate has met Ron's youngest daughter, Kate is certain she would've recognised Camilla anywhere, because she looks so much like Denise. She's about to say something to that effect, when the younger woman, having shut the door behind them, turns back round to Kate and hands her a business card.

'This is for you,' she whispers. 'It's from Mum. I told her you were coming here tonight. But please don't say anything to Dad or Mira about this, will you?' She looks down the corridor, half expecting to see one of them suddenly appear.

'Of course not. It'll be our little secret.' Kate smiles at her and pops the card into her shoulder bag.

'Don't get me wrong. It's just that I don't want to hurt my father, that's all.'

Kate takes Camilla's hand and gives it a gentle squeeze. 'It's OK. I won't breathe a word.'

'Follow me, then. Mira's dying to meet you.'

The whispering disappears and suddenly, as they reach the end of the slender hallway, there is Mira, more exquisite than Kate had ever imagined. She's wearing an embroidered mauve silk *salwar kameez*, and her long panther-black hair is plaited in one thick, loose braid that falls over her left shoulder.

'I'm so very pleased to meet you,' she says, then thanks Kate for the flowers she'd had delivered earlier that day. 'They're simply beautiful, as you will see.' Taking Kate's hands in her own, she adds, 'Hopefully,

we'll get a chance to talk later, but let me introduce you around first.'
Then as an afterthought, 'Almost everyone's here now.'

And, indeed, they are. The Cochranes are consummate hosts. Ron
dispenses champagne and bonhomie in equal measure, while Mira
glides around the softly lit living room, shaping the mood of this
special gathering of friends.

Having been introduced to all the guests inside, Kate looks about her.
It's not a huge space, but the cedar bifold doors are open, which let in the
courtyard with its intense musky fragrance of night-scented jasmine and
the sultry voice of Chet Baker. Laughter also drifts in from the nest of
people standing beneath a string of Chinese red paper lanterns.

'It's a glorious evening,' says Ron.

Then someone suggests they all join the others outside. There's
agreement and movement and more introductions.

Murray Delmar-Jones, poet, novelist and academic, is holding
court to what appears to Kate to be a rapt audience. 'No one reads
literary fiction these days,' she hears him say. 'Partly because no one's
writing it any more, and publishers are only interested in making a
buck, so it's all low-brow, cheap-thrills crap and a million bloody
memoirs by nobodies besides.' He pauses for effect. 'There's absolutely
no Beauty. No Art for Art's sake. No love of the word, the bon mot. It's
all about me, me, me…how I overcame adversity – be it from
misfortune, a grand perversion, a regrettable affliction or some form of
nasty abuse. It's all market-driven. And the market we're living in just
so happens to love the victim.' He sips thoughtfully from his glass as
his eyes circle his audience. 'I'm afraid to say it, but in this kind of
world, it's the self-promoter who rules.'

Kate thinks Delmar-Jones quite magnificent in a sententious sort
of way. She begins to listen to the conversation between one of Mira's
colleagues, Nysha Singh, and the Cochranes' next-door neighbour and
café proprietor Carol Benson. Kate hears the words reconciliation,
indigenous and healing and so moves in closer.

'We can harbour all the illusions we like,' says Nysha, 'but the fact remains that in the name of Empire, the British robbed this land from its people.'

And we're all still clinging to the wreckage of those brutal beginnings today,' says her husband Surinder, 'spinning stories that we find more palatable.'

Kate is about to speak but Carol beats her to it. 'What I can't stand is the way people seem to think that Aboriginal people need to stop their whinging and negative mindset and just build a bridge and get over it!'

And Kate finds herself wondering if Gary is coming to the party at all, then suddenly remembers Denise and of course the business card that seems to be burning a hole in her shoulder bag. She's eager to see it, so she can begin to imagine their next meeting, to prepare and rehearse for it.

She decides to go in search of the bathroom and, excusing herself from the group with a wordless bow of her head, she moves back towards the interior of the house.

And then she sees him.

A sharp flash of heat surges through Kate's body. She wants to fan her face, but knows she has no fan. She must keep calm. Composed. As he walks towards her, smiling, she tells herself she's being ridiculous. He stops and stands there. Closer than he should, she thinks.

'Well, look at you,' he says.

She wishes she'd prepared herself for this moment – seeing him again. Why had she thought this wouldn't affect her? She hopes she looks unruffled and self-possessed. They measure the years on each other's face. Her smile is setting – rigid, unnatural.

'It's good to see you again,' she says. And it is. It truly is. But she sounds insincere. The ice is not yet broken. She doesn't know how to do it. 'How long has it been? Forty years?'

He ignores her questions. He doesn't care how long it's been. It's just great to see her again, to be with her. 'Ron's been telling me you visited the old neighbourhood recently.'

She can't help wondering what precisely Ron may have told him about her, but she tells him she's been doing a bit of family history, resurrecting her ancestors from anonymity – all those migrants to Australia. She maintains a temporal distance and doesn't mention her childhood or Salt Pan Creek, but she does talk about Adam and his recent return from the States. The ice between them begins to crack.

Gary tells her about the renovations to his property and talks proudly of Claudia. Then he asks Kate if she remembers Margot Henshaw and tells her she was a nursing mate of Denise's. That's how he'd met her. Denise had introduced them. In Cambridge. He says he and Margot had a bit of a fling in London, but when they broke up, they remained friends.

'That's nice,' says Kate, and wonders if he's rebuking her about how she'd cut all ties to him when they'd split up and how they'd managed not to speak to one another for almost four decades. But he continues talking about Margot and proceeds to tell Kate that some years later, Margot asked him to be her sperm donor, and he'd agreed.

'Absolutely no regrets either,' he says.

Kate's a little astonished at his directness, but then reminds herself that he'd always been like that. But back then, she'd called it being blunt.

'Ah!' says someone. 'Something smells like Spain.'

Everyone turns to admire two immense paella pans piled high with steaming mussels and giant prawns that are being carried by Camilla and Ron to the rectangular table.

'Dinner is served!' says Mira, brandishing a plate of lemon cheeks.

'How wonderful!'

'I love seafood.'

'Me too.'

Everyone seems to be talking at once.

'It's Camilla you should thank,' says Ron. 'She's responsible for this feast.'

There's applause and a tinkling of plates and glasses as food is distributed and water poured.

'I've got some rosé here, if anyone would like some…'

Bottles are opened, and joy surrounds the table as Costa Poulos, another of Ron and Mira's new neighbours, entertains the party with the story of the night he went fishing for squid.

Kate's not sure how it's happened, but she's sitting between Ivan, one of Ron's engineering colleagues from Newcastle University, and Doug Benson, Carol's husband. No partners are sitting next to one another. So it's by design, thinks Kate.

The conversation turns to King Street, Newtown, where the Bensons have their café. How the area has changed, someone says. Jocelyn Finch, a commercial artist, lets it be known that this street alone provides her with the bulk of her business, that she'd be penniless without it. Ivan says he loves the razzle and the dazzle of Newtown – the ethnic mix of it, the cultural grunge, the arty and student splendour of its streetscape. But Delmar-Jones begs to disagree, preferring the way it once was – rough around the edges and everywhere else as well. The table is laughing.

Directly opposite Kate is Gary. Now and again she observes him, discreetly. He's unshaven and looks fit. He's still a handsome man. She wonders what he thinks of her; if he's noticed she's put on a little too much weight; if he finds her attractive. And she's unnerved by this train of thought and so begins to pile more rice onto her plate. She continues to eat, unaware that several large flat bowls filled with warm water and slices of lemon appear on the table.

'They're communal,' Mira announces, while passing around more paper serviettes.

Kate looks up. Her eyes meet Gary's. His are shining in the candlelight. He's placed his hands in the water bowl in front of them. She does the same. His fingers brush against hers. She avoids his gaze and removes her hands. She knows she might seem prissy, but she can't help it. Laura, the pharmacist married to Ivan Matiss, asks her to pass the serviettes.

And it seems it's time for dessert. The table falls silent as all the guests begin to spoon their servings of a luscious chocolate mousse cake into their mouths. Gary stands and raises an almost empty glass for a toast. 'Here's to our fine hosts – Mira and Ron.'

'And let's not forget Camilla,' says Surinder Singh.

Everyone's glass is held high and a chorus of voices call out the names of Ron and Mira and, lastly, Camilla.

But Gary's not finished. 'May this house always be filled with the warmth of friendship and love as it has been tonight.'

'Hear, hear,' says Doug.

'Amen,' says Costa.

'I'll drink to that,' says Murray Denmar-Jones. And he empties his glass down his throat.

There's more laughter, but the party is coming to an end. There's general movement. People are starting to go. There's a sprinkling of goodbyes, lots of thanks, and everyone agrees it's been a wonderful party. Kate gathers up her bag and stands up. Before she says a word, Gary is whispering in her ear that he'd kiss her if there weren't still people present. She feels embarrassed and knows she's blushing like an empty-headed schoolgirl.

And then he says, 'Mine's the white ute parked two doors down on this side of the street. I'll wait for you there.' He's moved away without waiting for her reply.

Kate presumes the cocky bastard is now somewhere inside the house. She's wrestling with her thoughts. What should she do? What should she say? It's completely absurd – well, he is, for sure – wanting to kiss her. After all this time? And now – just like that…he must think he's irresistible…that she'll fall into his arms. God, he must've seen her get all hot and bothered when he arrived tonight. The last thing she wants at her age is a sexual relationship! Sure, it's been quite a while since she last went to bed with a man. But she's grown quite accustomed to celibacy. In actual fact, she finds it quite liberating. She doesn't miss sex at all. Not one bit. But then…

Perhaps he just wants to be friends. Like he was with poor Margot Henshaw. Perhaps that's the point of the story he told her earlier.

Kate decides she'll just go home and get a good night sleep. Alone. But once out on the footpath, she sees a pair of headlights flashing on and off two doors down the street, and so strides towards them.

*

The interior light goes on when she opens the passenger door.

'So what's all this about?' she asks.

'Can you please get in the car,' says Gary.

'What for? Why should I?' Kate knows she sounds shrill and unreasonable. She tries to breathe more slowly. She's desperate to appear serene.

Gary looks glum. 'Come on, Kate. I didn't mean to offend you. I just want to talk to you. Privately. Without the likelihood of interruptions.' He waits a moment. 'Please get in the car. We'll just talk – five minutes, max.'

His pleading works. She gets in and closes the door. 'OK. You've got five minutes then.'

'I'm not sorry I wanted to kiss you, but I am sorry I told you I did.'

Kate bites her lower lip, trying not to laugh.

'It was great talking to you tonight. It was natural. It felt right. And I was wondering if I could see you again.'

'Oh, I'm not so sure that'd be such a good idea.' She looks straight at him then.

His eyes are closed. His head leans back onto the seat's headrest.

She decides to press on. 'It's just that I'm not sure what you have in mind. I'd be happy to see you, to be friends. But I can't promise anything more than that.'

Gary's eyes spring open. 'That's great. Perfect.' He's grinning.

'You are aware that I live in the Blue Mountains? In Wentworth Falls, to be precise.'

'Yeah, Ron did tell me. Why? Is that a problem?'

'Not that I can think of. It's just that it makes spontaneity a little difficult.'

167

'I'm sure we can work around that.' He whips out his phone from his shirt pocket. 'What's your number?'

'Could I please ask for an extension of time?' She is smiling.

'How long do you need?'

'As long as it takes you to tell me why Denise and Ron broke up.'

'That shouldn't take too long,' says Gary, moving slightly in his seat to face her. 'You know they came back to Australia together?'

Kate nods.

'At first, everything was fine. They were living in Melbourne. They'd married by this time and had two girls – Alice and Camilla. Alice, the older one, has two kids of her own now – Max and Cleo.'

'Yes, yes.' She knows all this. 'And…then what?'

'Well, Denise didn't work when the girls were little. Ron was on a pretty good salary by then. Anyway, around the time Camilla turned three, Denise got an invitation to meet up with some old schoolfriends in Sydney for a weekend.'

'I wonder who they were…'

'Yeah, well, hold your horses. All will be revealed.' He breathes in. Kate could see he was revelling in the role of raconteur. 'Anyway, that's how it started. Every month or so, she'd fly up to Sydney or over to Adelaide for the weekend to meet up with one or all of these school friends. When she went to Sydney, she'd take the girls with her and leave them with her mother, but when she was off somewhere else, Ron would look after them. She even flew to Hobart one time, but Ronnie, the poor bastard, never suspected, never saw it coming and then one day, he comes home from work and discovers she's cleared out. But she'd left him a lovely little note, telling him where she and the girls were now living and that she was sorry, but it was over between them; that she'd never really loved him and if she had, she certainly didn't any more.'

'Oh God, so there was someone else?'

'You and I might have thought so, but Ron truly believed there was no one else. He'd asked her straight out, and she was adamant – even flew off the handle at him for thinking that of her. Some of their friends asked her too, and her family and it was always the same response: there was no one else and, moreover, why did everyone assume there was? Naturally, Ron was devastated. He couldn't understand it. He was a mess. He was missing the girls badly too. Whenever he saw them, they'd be clinging to him, bawling their eyes out and saying how they wanted to live with him, not their mother. Anyway, from what I was told, he started to hit the booze, and then, in the nick of time, the chickens came home to roost.

'Out of the blue, his in-laws, Denise's folks, ring him one night, pleading with him to go around to Denise's flat and check if she and the girls are all right. What had happened was the Reids had just rung Denise, who was hysterical, saying she'd been an idiot, that she'd lost everything, that she didn't want to live any more, et cetera, et cetera. So around Ronnie goes, and there she is, lying on the floor, and she starts begging him to take her back, that it wasn't supposed to end like this, that she hadn't planned it that way, and then out it all comes. She finally comes clean…'

'Oh no!' Kate has her head in her hands. She can't look at Gary. She's hoping that what she's thinking is wrong. 'Surely not, surely not. She couldn't be that stupid.'

'And you won't guess who she was meeting all those weekends either?'

Silence.

'Graham Ingram. You'd remember him, wouldn't you? Lived with his family down by the river at the end of Clarendon Road. A pack of hillbillies, they were. Wasn't his sister involved somehow with that bloke who murdered Mr Attard?'

Kate nods a yes but says nothing. In her mind's eye, she can see him – the Rat with his sleazy grin. Amazed, she shakes her head. How could Denise have fallen for all his low-life bullshit a second time? What was wrong with the woman?

'According to Denise, Ingram was the love of her life, but he was married too and had a couple of kids himself. He and Denise had agreed to tell each of their spouses around the same time. The plan was that he'd leave Sydney, and they'd live together happily ever after in the Melbourne flat that Denise would set up for them. But, as far as she was concerned, it was all taking a bit too long to eventuate, so she decides to speed things along a bit. She figures the sooner she ends it with Ron, the sooner she'd be living with Ingram. So she does just that, but old lover boy is still dragging his feet, and when she finally confronts him, he fesses up, tells her he can't split from his wife right at that moment, because she's three months pregnant, and he just can't leave her like that – what with the other two kids and now this one on the way. Can you believe it? What an arsehole!'

'I'd laugh if it wasn't so bloody tragic,' she says.

'It's more like a pathetic soap opera,' he says in a conclusive tone. Then adds, 'But if you ask me, Ron's much better off without her.'

'So he didn't take her back, then?'

'Are you kidding! How could anyone ever trust her again? After all that? Nah,' he says emphatically, 'she deserves everything she gets!'

Kate is glad she hasn't mentioned the business card. 'Thanks for telling me, Gary. I have wondered…'

'You want to give me your number now?'

And she does.

*

Later, back at Salt Pan Creek, Gary feels sad and tired and ridiculous. He leans on the railing of his deck and replays the evening in his mind. For a moment he considers swimming out into the river's depths and dumping all his stupid, petty vanities, letting them sink into oblivion. He'd love to start the night over again, but then he recognises this thought for what it is, a daydream without a shred of possibility. No, he must start with what's possible, going with the clock, not rewinding it. Meeting Kate again hadn't gone as well as he'd hoped, but at least she'd given him her number. The evening hadn't been a total write-off. Something had definitely passed between them – an understanding of mutual feeling, perhaps?

He hopes he's not clutching at straws. Seeing her again tonight made him realise that she is what he's always wanted and always would. There was no getting away from that. And as for the past, their shared past, he'd forgiven her long ago and he wants to tell her that it doesn't matter to him any more and that it never should have mattered to him. He'd been a first-class idiot, too proud and stubborn for his own good. But things are different now. He's older and much, much wiser. As he should be.

So why the hell did he go and act like a complete sleazebag at Ron and Mira's? God almighty, she must think he's such a stupid old fart!

But she did give him her number. He must remember that. She's also a decent person, is now and was back then. And he's always played a straight bat with decent people. Well, has done until tonight.

If he could be given another chance, he'd dam up the river of time and try to convince her he'd never confine or constrain her, that they could each flow free and find a new way to navigate the rest of the time they have.

Together.

Lunch by the River

Within seconds of Kate knocking on the front door, Gary is standing before her, his arms wide open in greeting.

'Welcome, welcome!' he says, sweeping her into an embrace. Then, 'Where did you park your car?'

'I didn't. It's at home. I came by train and grabbed a cab from the station.'

He looks taken aback but makes no comment. She pulls a bottle of wine from her bag and hands it to him.

'Totally unnecessary,' he says, 'but thank you. Fancy a glass of champagne? I've got some on ice.'

'That would be lovely.' She feels awkward. She knows she needs to relax.

'Why don't you wander on out to the deck, then,' he suggests, 'while I get the bubbly and some glasses. It's such a beautiful day, I thought we'd have lunch out there. If that's OK by you.' He disappears before she can respond.

Kate thinks he's probably feeling awkward too. She looks around her. The interior is not how she'd remembered it. It's completely changed. Back in the sixties, the house had been like most of the other houses in the area – a cube-like building with matchbox-sized rooms either side of a central hallway that ran into a dining room with an adjoining kitchen and a small covered veranda beyond that. Nothing of that remains. Now there seems to be no interior walls at all. The entire house has been extended both in its width and its length. There's a discernibly European feel to the place with its liquorice-coloured timber floor and whitewashed walls. It appears to be a single open-plan space that spreads out onto an exterior deck that in turn gives complete access to the backyard and beyond to a distant view of a decrepit jetty jutting out into Salt Pan Creek. The effect is rather magnificent.

She surveys the cavernous room as she makes her way to the deck. It's clutter-free except for one enormous abstract painting – all blues and greens and reds – that adorns the south-facing wall. The furniture is sleek, stylish and functional. Kate likes it. She likes it a lot.

Gary reappears from behind what is a clever use of partitioning that hadn't been obvious before. He's carrying an ice bucket and smiling as he walks towards her. 'So, Katie, what do you think of the place so far?'

He's called her Katie. She hasn't been called that for a long, long time. 'It's stunning.'

'I'm glad you like it. I really am,' and bends to place the ice bucket on a coffee table, then moves closer towards her. 'But before I pour the bubbly, there's something I want to say.' He pauses, only half an arm's length away from her now. 'I want to tell you how sorry I am for all the lousy things I said and for the way I behaved towards you back in 1969. I was way out of line and…'

'And nothing. There's no need.' Her eyes search his. 'I said a lot of horrible things too, you know. We were a pair of kids, Gary, and…'

'Well, I'm so glad you're here now…that we can be friends and…'

She takes a step back, away from him. She's sure he's about to kiss her. Which is not what she wants. Not now, at any rate. It's too soon. They don't even know one another. Not as adults, that is. Yes, he's attractive, but she's not sure she even wants a sexual relationship with anyone, let alone one with her childhood sweetheart. That would be too corny for words.

She sees he's about to say something more so she raises her index finger to her lips. 'Shoosh,' she whispers, and he seems to know what she means.

He gives his head a little shake and passes a hand through his hair. He looks like a little boy, who's just woken up from an afternoon nap.

'What say we have a drink?' He doesn't wait for an answer. After he's filled two glass flutes, he gives her a tour of the house, then refills their glasses and takes her back out onto the deck.

They stand side by side at the railing, a discretely slender stretch of steel, and look down the length of the yard. There is little of immediate interest: no garden to speak of except for an angry strip of greying kikuyu, and a pile of rubble beneath a scrawny silver gum on the north side of the property. Closer to the water's edge sits a stand of bamboo that someone years before had wisely constrained within a raised and fenced bed. Even by Sydney standards, it's a big backyard but it needs a lot of work.

'So, what do you reckon? All gardening ideas will be gratefully received,' Gary says.

'Like they say,' she answers, 'it's got loads of potential. Apart from the bamboo, it's pretty much a blank canvas.'

'Would you like to walk down to the river?'

'I'd love to.'

They leave their glasses behind and Kate tells him about her Wentworth Falls garden, how Richard had designed and carried out most of the work himself. She also tells Gary about the recent restoration of it and how it now requires very little maintenance, which suits her perfectly.

'That's what I'd like for this place,' he says.

They are standing on the jetty, and as they talk, he turns away from the river to face the house. Kate follows suit.

'If you want my opinion, you've got to keep this jetty.'

'And not restore it?'

'It might need some structural repair so it doesn't collapse completely but, if I were you, I'd retain its character, its old-world feel. It's a beautiful object, a relic of the past, and it really ought to be the focal point of your whole garden. And I don't just mean the jetty here. I'm including the river too, of course. It's one of the best water features I've ever seen.'

Gary laughs at this. 'OK,' he says, 'and what about trees and plants? Anything you'd recommend?'

'Lots of them.'

As they make their way back to the house, she mentions some natives and recommends lilly-pillies for fast-growing mass plantings that are great for lining boundaries. Gary takes it all in, and Kate suggests he checks out his local garden nursery.

'They'd know what plants suited the soil and weather conditions of this area. And you mustn't forget to tell them your property backs onto the river though.'

'You sound like you could be on one of those TV gardening programs.'

'Don't be fooled. I know very little compared to avid gardeners and, while I love being in gardens, I'm not all that crazy about working in them.'

'Now you're sounding like me,' he says laughing. 'Hope you've worked up an appetite.'

*

Over a lunch of barbecued king prawns and salad, Gary tells her about the old cardboard shoebox filled with postcards and photos and an audio cassette that Les, the man he called Dad, had left him and that he'd only recently gone through it all and how, when he'd listened to the tape, it had reduced him to a blubbering mess.

'Why? What did he say? What was on it?' asks Kate.

'I'll let you listen to it some time,' he answers. 'If you'd like to, that is.'

'Oh, that'd be wonderful,' she says. 'I'd like that very much.' Then she tells him about her own recent discovery; that she has First Fleet ancestry, via the convict Edward Goodin; and that when he married Ann Thomas, another convict, who'd arrived with the Second Fleet on the *Lady Juliana*, they'd both signed the marriage register with the mark X. 'And because what interests me most of all is the inner lives of people, I couldn't help but notice how Ann's sign looked extremely shaky, which made me think she was either really nervous or just plain terrified.'

'What about Edward's X? What's it like?'

'It's thick and masculine and it's been written over several times, which I guess shows a certain level of determination on his part.'

Gary snorts. 'Or his enthusiasm for the present moment.'

Kate raises her eyebrows in amusement. 'Whatever's the case, both signs are open to interpretation. And that's what I find so frustrating about family history. If your ancestor didn't write letters, or kept a diary and stuff like that, you haven't got much to go on and you have absolutely no idea about the personalities of individual people.'

'Unless your culture has an oral tradition…'

'Of course. But even that would have its own inherent problems, I imagine.'

'So what kind of inner lives do you imagine your Ann and Edward had?'

'Well, I can't help speculating about their first meeting. I mean, was Ann given to Edward as some kind of servant-prostitute, which was a fairly common practice at the time? Or had he selected her from what was left of the women convicts who'd already been used and discarded by the British military?'

'You don't suppose they might have been in love with one another, do you?'

'I'd love that to have been the case,' Kate replies. 'That would be a magical stroke of luck, don't you think? It'd mean that my Edward was a good-hearted man and that he didn't use Ann as some kind of sexual commodity – some kind of breeding machine.'

'Have you found out anything else about them then?'

'Well, Edward was granted sixty acres of land at Kissing Point, half of which they cultivated. They also bred livestock. But everything belonged to Edward. Ann didn't appear to own a thing. The way of the world back then, I know. At any rate, together they managed to have at least thirteen children. And she died in 1830. Nine years later, Edward was buried with her in St Anne's Cemetery in Ryde.'

'If they were buried together, surely that tells you their relationship couldn't have been all bad.' He sips at his wine.

'Yes, but what I find interesting is that by the time their daughter Margaret dies in 1865, Ann has been written out of history altogether. On Margaret's death certificate, her father's name is given as Edward Goodin, but in the space provided for her mother's maiden name there appears the word *Unknown*.'

'That's a bit sad, I know, but then maybe the person who made the official notification of her death simply didn't know.'

'But surely it would've been a family member or, at the very least, someone close to Margaret, who notified. This person knew the name of her father.' She looks at him, seeking his approval. 'My hunch is that the quavering X that Ann signed on her wedding day is a symbol of her oppression. She knew she was being tyrannised and exploited, and then to be omitted from her daughter's death certificate is just more evidence of the kind of patriarchal, misogynist society that existed back then.'

'Not to mention the many injustices done to the First Peoples…'

'But of course – that's a given. I'm sorry, …' She feels flustered and stupid.

'No need. It's OK.' His voice is calm, reassuring. He smiles as he stands up and, reaching across the table to pick up Kate's plate and cutlery, says, 'But I tell you something. You and Claudia will get on like a house on fire. She's quite the feminist, you know.'

Still sitting, Kate clears her throat and asks, 'Can I help you with the washing-up?'

'I'd be delighted.'

*

The dishes have been done. He washed. She wiped. While Gary puts the last of the plates away, she finishes telling him about her marriage break-up, about Richard's death and their son's response to it. She chooses to omit how several months after her husband's death, she'd come home late one night, after a parent– teacher evening at school, to find Adam drunk from vodka and crazy with grief. She doesn't mention how he'd verbally attacked her; how he'd blamed her for his father's death, claiming Richard had died from a broken heart, that his father had told him that he'd only ever loved one woman and that had been her but that she'd loved someone else. Like some mad Hamlet, her son called her a slut and a whore, and she'd wept and wept for hours at the vile injustice of it all. But when he woke the next day, he claimed he couldn't remember a thing. Kate decided to believe him and then she helped nurse her son through his first hangover.

What she does tell Gary is that Adam will soon be coming to pick her up.

'That's great,' he says. 'I'd like to meet him.'

She looks at him, nods a yes and feels her face redden under his gaze.

He suggests they go outside.

As they walk out onto the deck, Kate says, 'This is my favourite part of the day.'

The afternoon sun has lost much of its power now, and the sky has turned a streaky violet blue.

'It's the day on the point of change, about to tip over into something other, something more moody and mysterious. Do you like it?'

'Yes, I do,' he says.

They stand side by side at the railing as they'd done earlier that day. And again, they look down to the river. There is a long stretch of silence.

'You know, ever since you told me about Denise and Ron, I haven't stopped thinking about them,' says Kate. 'I mean, I wouldn't give two hoots if Denise had an affair or even stopped loving Ron. What I actually think is morally bankrupt about this tawdry story is all the lies and deceit, that caused so much misery and suffering – and for what?' She was thinking of Ingram here, how at the very start he would've spun Denise a fine yarn about the loveless state of his sexless marriage. He'd have convinced Denise that she was the one, the only. So it would've been a double blow for her to learn his wife was pregnant. The selfish cruelty of the man was staggering.

'It's what we human beings do so well, and that's our tragedy.' He hopes he's not sounding too pompous. 'We keep doing dreadful things to one another.'

Kate is silent. Then suddenly she bursts out, 'Oh Gary, you've got to believe me, I'm sorry about the way we ended. I really am. I'm sorry that I hurt you.'

'Now, come on. Like you said earlier, we both were to blame. We both hurt one another, but all that's behind us.'

'I never had the abortion.' These words seemed to hover in the air then echo across the river.

'What? You mean…you had the baby?'

'No, no. I didn't have a baby. But I'd told my mother I was pregnant and she was planning everything. But then the next morning I started to menstruate.'

'Why didn't you tell me?'

'I was angry with you. And I knew it was over between us. You can't patch up things like that.' She turns to look at him, then adds, 'Besides, we were babies ourselves.'

Neither one of them moves. Gary is still facing the river, but Kate is wondering if she should seize this silent moment to tell him how much she'd like him to hold her in his arms. That she would never leave him again.

As if on cue, he turns towards her, but she's now beset by fears. Is he sizing her up, aware that her body is ageing and is no longer firm and supple? Does he realise her breasts are large and pendulous and that her youth's been crushed and her beauty's fast fading? Could he be that superficial?

But he lets in the light and says, 'You know you're still a stunner, don't you?' His arms are round her waist, and his eyes talk to hers.

Gently, he pulls her towards him. Their lips meet. His kiss is tender but tentative. She closes her eyes. Yes, yes, she wants this and she feels his lips lingering. They begin to part, and the moist tip of his tongue is there, there, yes, yes, entering her mouth. And then he moves his head back from hers.

'I can't tell you how good it is to be with you,' he says. The warmth of his breath is close to her cheek. 'Would you care to dance?'

'Oh yes. Very much.' She's smiling.

And it's then that she hears the distant drone of didgeridoo and sees the setting sun, golden in his eyes.

*

On the drive back home, Adam asks her more about Gary. He tells his mother he likes him but asks why she didn't tell him that he's Aboriginal.

'I didn't think it was relevant,' says Kate.

'But you told me he'd been your first boyfriend and lots of other stuff besides. I'd have thought you'd have told me about his Aboriginality… I mean, I think that's pretty significant, don't you?'

'Well, of course it is.' She looks at him, his eyes straight ahead as he drives into the night. 'And I would've told you but it didn't occur to me to mention it at the time. Sorry.' Then, watching him more closely, she adds, 'I'm glad you like him, though.' She sees he's smiling, so says, 'You and Claudia seemed to hit it off.'

He quickly glances at his mother. 'You never miss a trick, do you?' And there is no animosity in his words. 'So what do you reckon? Do you think if I asked her out, she'd say yes?'

'She'd be an idiot if she didn't.'

The Audio Cassette

As you well know, I'm not what you'd call an educated man. Never pretended to be neither, but I've been thinking about making this tape for quite a while now. Hazel always said I could talk under water with a mouth full of marbles. So here goes.

I've lived a long life, and it's been a good and happy one. Mainly. I've seen a lot of changes in my time. Some good. Some not so good. And I also have a lot to be thankful for. I met Hazel, didn't I? And we had our beautiful daughter Lorraine too, but then we lost two baby boys and what with Hazel being told she couldn't have any more kids, she was pretty sad. So when you came along, it was like a miracle. You were a terrific kid. Have been all your life, always making us feel real proud of you. That's why I'm doing this now, before it's too late. I want to tell you everything I know and everything I remember about our family, our people. Then, when your time comes, you can pass it on to Claudia and her kids. When she has them, that is. And then they can pass it on to theirs and so it'll keep going on and on, always remembering, never forgetting our story – what's gone before, what's taken us and all the others to this place here, now and in the future.

First of all, I'm going to talk about you, Gary. And explain, man to man like, how you got to have Hazel and me for your parents. And I won't be telling you no lies either. I'll be straight up, the whole truth and nothing but. So help me.

Now, my father's name was Gareth Jones Saunders. He's your grandfather and he was born in Wales in the early 1890s. I remember him telling me that his mother was a Jones, and his father was a Saunders, and that's how he got such a highfalutin name. He came out here to Australia not long after the First World War. He'd fought on the Somme, poor bastard, and he told me he'd decided to come here because, he said, he was so sick and tired of all the cold and rain and mud of that stupid war and, because every Aussie he'd ever met was happy-go-lucky and always wore a smile, he thought he was sure to have a better life in this country, where he'd heard the sun shone bright.

Anyway, he was a good worker, my dad, and he got himself a job as a linesman with the PMG, the government organisation that was responsible for all the postal and telegraphic services in this country. At first, he lived in a boarding house with a lot of other single working men round Surry Hills, and then one Sunday afternoon he went for a bit of a tram ride with a few of his mates to see the snake handler Mr Cann, who put on shows for all-comers down at the Snake Pit at La Perouse.

And that's where he met my mother, Dulcie Roberts. She lived out there on the La Perouse reserve. She and her sister and brothers used to collect shells for their mother, who made souvenirs for all the tourists and visitors flocking there on the weekends to buy them. By all accounts, my mum was a beautiful-looking woman, cause Dad always said that no one in their right mind could ever blame him for falling in love with her. That's how lovely she was. Anyhow, they got married. That was in 1920. A year later, they had me. I'm not sure where they lived, but when my brother Fred was born, I was two, and we were living in Leeton, as Dad had accepted a promotion down there with the PMG. I only have happy memories of being there. I still remember the citrus scent of the orchards and going swimming in the Murrumbidgee.

But it wasn't until the early thirties, during the Depression, that we returned to Sydney. There was six of us kids by then – me and Fred, then came Billy, Doris, Jack and little Ivy, your mum. And although we didn't realise it at the time, we were dead lucky, cause Dad was one of the few men who kept his job back then, so we weren't too badly off compared to lots of other people, especially our black fella rellies.

What's more, it was around this time that an uncle of my father's fell off his perch back in England and left him a little bit of money, which allowed Dad to buy outright a large block of land that backed onto Salt Pan Creek from some Chinese market gardener or other. At any rate, Mum and Dad were well acquainted with the area around Peakhurst and Herne Bay, as they'd often visited friends of Mum's family, who were part of an Aboriginal community living down by the river there in Peakhurst. So, on weekends, Dad and some mates built a dunny down the back of his land and then they put up a huge single-room house. Like a giant shoebox, it was. Of course, much later, once a proper house was built, they partitioned off the shoebox that we'd all lived in for a couple of years, and made it into a garage, a laundry and a tool shed.

But I'm getting a bit ahead of meself.

For a short time after leaving Leeton, we had to live somewhere, so we'd set up camp at Frog Hollow near to the reserve at La Perouse. And you know, all the kids living around there played together without a care in the world. It didn't matter if we were black, white or in between. It was like we were colour blind. We couldn't see any difference between Aboriginal and non-Aboriginal children. As far as us kids were concerned, we were all the same. And of course, we were right. We were the same. We are the bloody same. But try telling that to some people.

Nevertheless, I was twelve years old and I had enough brains and a pair of eyes to start to understand that the so-called Aboriginal Protection Board wasn't really serving the best interests of Aboriginal people. And I remember there being an awful lot of talk about a black fella called Joe Anderson, who was the son of Ellen and Hugh Anderson, and I'll tell you a bit about them a little later. But as for Joe, he was now the leader of this Aboriginal camp at Salt Pan Creek I was talking about and he was making quite a name for himself defending the rights of his community to remain on the public land where his family had long lived. He was sometimes in the newspaper and magazines and suchlike. He even made a big speech demanding equal rights in a newsreel that screened in all the picture theatres across the country.

Until the day he died, Joe kept protesting against the idea that him and his people might be relocated from their little corner of Salt Pan Creek. But eventually everyone living there was moved on to the La Perouse reserve. Against their will, of course. But we're a tough and adaptable mob. Plenty of Aboriginal people have grown up close to Salt Pan Creek and the Georges River. And we'll continue to do so. Don't you worry about that!

But I almost forgot to mention 1938. That was a real big year for all our mob. The twenty-sixth of January was the 150th anniversary of the First Fleet's arrival and, rather than celebrate it, most of us wanted to mourn it. Many of the people who organised the Day of Mourning used the day to call for Aboriginal rights. And a lot of them activists had visited the Andersons' Salt Pan Creek community many a time. It was where they learnt all about protest.

Anyway, I might've only been sixteen but I'll never forget that day. We'd spent it with family and friends at La Perouse, and late that afternoon I got to see Pearl Gibbs set several floral wreaths into the sea as an act of mourning for all the things our people had lost since 1788. And I can still see myself standing there watching those flowers float far away and wondering what it must've been like to see those sailing ships floating right into the bay with all their finery and flags and fearsome weapons.

There's a slight pause in the tape.

The following year, of course, war was declared, and I was no different to most young blokes back then. Dad had raised me and my brothers to believe we were the equal of all men. Consequently I was damn eager to serve my country. And so I enlisted as soon as I could, which wasn't until after I'd turned nineteen, which was then the minimum age of entry. As a gunner in the 2/12th Field Regiment, I saw action against the Japanese in the Huon Peninsula campaign and then later in Borneo. Enough said.

But it was because of my experience driving trucks and jeeps during the war that, once I'd been discharged from the army, I managed to get a job driving government buses, but not before I'd reunited with Hazel. She was a local girl I'd known before I'd joined up. We'd gone out together a couple of times. Nothing very much – just to the pictures and the like. But she wrote to me right through the war. Never stopped writing, she did. And I can't tell you how good that made me feel. Some of the fellas never got a postcard, let alone a letter or a parcel. A couple of my mates got one of those Dear John letters, which most of us reckoned was more painful than a bullet in the guts.

Anyhow, Hazel kept writing to me, even though I wasn't the greatest letter writer in the world. And when I got home, I couldn't wait to see her. I'd forgotten how beautiful she was, and so when we met up again, well, you can imagine. One thing led to another. You know the rest.

Looking back, things were fairly tough after the war, not that I noticed much. I had a job, a wife and a baby on the way. We were living in the garage that Dad and I had converted into a single-roomed flat. So part of what we all called the Shoebox was back being a smaller Shoebox, but it was big enough for Hazel and me and baby Lorraine. We had a bit of privacy and all the love and support we needed. Two of my brothers, Fred and Billy, had gone jackarooing. Doris was training as a nurse, and my youngest brother Jack had an apprenticeship as a glazier. We were all off our parents' hands, all of us making an honest living for ourselves.

Except for Ivy. Let's just say she got herself into a bit of trouble. Mum of course blamed herself. Reckoned she'd turned her back for five minutes and when she'd turned back round, Ivy had taken up with some young country lad she'd met. He'd come to the big smoke to look for work but ended up in the Settlement at Herne Bay on account of the housing shortage in Sydney after the war. That's about all we ever knew about him really. And that was only after Dad found her, thanks to a couple of friends of his in the local constabulary. I'll never forget the day he brought her back home, kickin' and screamin' the place down she was.

Naturally, we all felt sorry for her. I mean, she was only a kid of sixteen, and when she learnt that lover boy had been moved on, she cried her little heart out for weeks and weeks and weeks. But she was safe and well, and that's all we cared about. Plus she wasn't pregnant, which, as far as Mum was concerned, was very good news. Everything was hunky-dory really, even though Ivy firmly believed that Mum and Dad had ruined her life. Well, that was what she kept telling Hazel. They'd become very close, Hazel and Ivy. I suppose Ivy didn't have much choice, seeing as she was banned from stepping outside the front gate. 'Until you've showed your mother and me that you've got some bloody sense,' said Dad.

And to Ivy's credit, she did as she was told. Hazel was advising her, though. She taught her to have some patience, to not start wishing her life away, that there'd be plenty of time once she'd come of age to do as she pleased – that kind of stuff.

At any rate, what with Lorraine and all, she was over our place all the time, practically living with us. Only went back to the Big House, as we called it then, to sleep. You just couldn't keep Ivy away from that baby and, understandably, Hazel appreciated the extra pair of hands, as well as her company.

Anyway, after a while, Ivy got herself a little job working for Tom Virgona, the man who owned the Melody Picture Theatre in Herne Bay. She used to man the box office selling movie tickets, or else she helped clean up the cinema after the shows, particularly after the Saturday matinees. That was when all the local kids went to the pictures, mainly to pelt one another with Jaffas. Well, that's according to Ivy. And she loved working there. She'd always been a bit movie crazy, but especially then, seeing as she got to see all the latest films and cartoons from Hollywood for free.

But during those years, Hazel and I lost two babies. The first one was stillborn and that was bad enough. Hazel grieved and grieved for that boy. Then, when the next one came along, he was such a tiny little thing. Premature he was, but he never left the hospital. As for Hazel – well, she was in a bad way. There'd been a few problems during the birth, and it was touch and go there for a while. The doctors said she shouldn't have another baby because it would be the death of her. Hazel was devastated. And it took her a long time to recover, but my little sister Ivy was magnificent. She upped and quit her job and started looking after young Lorraine full-time, while Hazel got herself better. She had a good heart, my sister, your mother. No one can ever tell me different.

And what happened to her was just a bloody shame really. But once Hazel was back on her feet, I don't reckon Ivy felt as needed as before. At any rate, she wasn't at our place so much. But we weren't suspicious or anything. Neither were Mum and Dad. Ivy's country boy was a thing of the past. And what with Hazel and me wanting a real place of our own, we were saving like crazy so we could make a down payment on a block of land. We weren't thinking about Ivy, and what she was or wasn't doing. She was working again back at the picture theatre, but only on weekends this time round, and she seemed happy enough. She said it suited her and she started hanging around Hazel and Lorraine again. And Hazel certainly wasn't about to complain. So it suited everybody. Until, that is, we all start noticing that Ivy's putting on a whole lot of weight and finally, she confides in Hazel, tells her she's pregnant, and of course that's when all hell breaks loose.

I'd never seen Dad so worked up. He was toxic, demanding Ivy tell him who the lad was who'd done this to her – as if she'd had no part in it. Mum was howling and crying, and there was Ivy, just sitting there in the corner, her face like stone, not saying a bloody word, refusing to give us a name. Dad said some terrible things that night, things he soon regretted, like he was ashamed of her and she wasn't to darken his doorstep again and not to expect any help from him and Mum, cause they were done with her. Forever. And then all his words just hung there, floating in the air, so that we could hear them, again and again. And there was no taking them back, even when Dad wanted to. Those words turned Ivy granite-hard, even more determined not to speak the fella's name.

And Hazel and me were no help to Mum and Dad. We had no idea who it might have been. We knew it couldn't have been the lad from the bush, but that was all we did know. And close as your mother was to Hazel, she wouldn't tell her either. But there was no way we were going to kick her out onto the street, so she lived with us. It was a bit cramped, I can tell you, but Lorraine, who was then about four, just loved having her Auntie Ivy staying with us.

And soon enough, you were born and you were the cutest little fella. Right from the start, we all loved you. Dad thought Ivy had forgiven him when she called you Gary, a version of his Welsh name, Gareth. He begged her then to come back and live with him and Mum in the Big House, but Ivy went all stony-faced on him again and told him she and you weren't budging.

'Let him think what he likes,' she said to Hazel and me. 'But I named my baby after Gary Cooper. *Not* after him.' And boy, did she emphasise that 'not'.

Anyway, to cut a long story short, you were seven months old when she cleared out. You were still sound asleep in your cot that morning when I discovered she'd fled. She'd left a note, telling us she'd be back, that she'd let us know when and that we were not to worry. She also asked us if we'd look after you in the meantime. Of course, she knew what our answer to that question would be, and we were certain she'd return, sooner than later.

We knew she'd headed south along the coast. She'd sent us post-cards, one each week: Thirroul, Kiama, Nowra, Huskisson, Ulladulla, Bateman's Bay, Moruya, Tuross Head, Narooma, Bermagui, Bega, Merimbula, Eden. They're all still here – the postcards, along with her letters. I'll put them with this tape so you can see for yourself. We always intended to show them to you, but it never seemed to be the right moment to drag them out and then, what with one thing and another, we just forgot about them. I found them, though, after Hazel passed on, and I guess that's why I decided to make this tape, to explain properly to you. And so you could take it in. A bit at a time – at your own pace, like.

Anyhow, where was I?

Ah, yes. The postcards. Well, after Eden, they kind of dried up. We didn't hear from Ivy for some time. We were never worried, though. We knew she'd turn up some day. And she did.

You'd started walking and you were talking – saying words. You were a bright spark, right from the word go, and there we all were, the four of us, one afternoon, hanging out the washing on the line, you playing hide and seek between the sheets that were flapping in the breeze. And she suddenly appeared, as large as life. She called to Lorraine, who just stared at her, not sure who she was, I suppose. But Hazel had thrown her arms around Ivy, and I followed suit. We were so happy to see her, though we must've looked pretty silly – the three of us hugging and kissing and jabbering away. And suddenly, you came running through the sheet tunnel, calling out, 'Mumma, Mumma.' As soon as Ivy heard your little boy voice, she broke away from us and extended her arms out to embrace you, but you went running right past her and wrapped yourself around Hazel's legs. Hazel picked you up and carried you over to Ivy but, like most kids that age, you were shy with people unfamiliar to you and you clung to Hazel like the cuddly koala you were, refusing to budge. My sister and I exchanged glances. I knew she knew I'd seen a flash of sadness cross her face. And what was left was just this face of stone like some kind of statue staring out at me.

Anyway, she stayed a few days and made a kind of peace with Mum and Dad, and in that time, you too warmed to your mother and you even sat on her knee once, and she'd cuddled you. And when Ivy saw I'd noticed, she put you down and told you to run along and play. Old stony face was back! That was how it was to be, you see. Off she'd go for months at a time and then come back home for a couple of days and off she'd go again.

Once, when pressed, she told Hazel that your father had come from around Salt Pan Creek. Another time she said he was married with kids, and he couldn't leave his missus. And then she said she'd loved him once, but not any more, that she had someone else now and she loved him instead and that next time she'd bring him to meet us. She also told us, we could keep you for good, that she'd sign adoption papers, whatever it took to make it legal.

That was the last time we saw her. Several months later, she was dead. The car she'd been travelling in had hit a tree. She was killed instantly. The man who was driving lingered a bit longer, then died of his injuries. He'd been drinking, and she was five months pregnant.

All very, very sad, I can tell you.

As for getting legal custody of you, it wasn't too difficult. We discovered Ivy hadn't even registered your birth. As far as the authorities were concerned, you didn't exist. Now, this was the early fifties I'm talking about. It was a period when the government encouraged all us half-castes and quarter-castes, as they liked to call us back then, to assimilate into the white community. And they must've thought I was some kind of perfect example, being married to such a lovely white woman like Hazel. Why, I'd bought land with my own hard-earned cash near my white father's place. I was holding down a good job and building my own house. By their standards, I had turned my back on my Aboriginality and adopted their way of life. And in some respects, I suppose they were dead right, because Hazel and me would've agreed to anything to keep you. We were a family of four and we were determined to stay that way by hook or by crook. We told the authorities everything they wanted to hear. We looked pretty assimilated to them. And that's how we got to keep you. And in our hearts, we never once stopped thanking Ivy. She gave us such a precious gift. And I know she'd have been as proud of you as Hazel and me have been.

Now, I'm a bit tired, doing all this talkin' and I think I'll take a break and come back tomorrow and finish it off. OK? Good. Until tomorrow then.

A crackling noise can be heard.

Hello again. I'm back now.

Before I finish what I want to say, I need to get something straight with you, Gary, and that is, I hope you realise how very proud I am to have Aboriginal blood running in my veins. I probably played it down when you were growin' up. But I had my reasons. I wanted you to make something of yourself and I didn't want you ever feeling you were second-rate because your skin was browner than most of the people living round here. I thought if I harped on about all the injustices done to our people, you might start feelin' sorry for yourself. I was afraid you'd start thinkin' you were worthless or somethin'. But I should've realised that would never have happened, that you had the fighter's spirit in you, that you came from a long line of warriors and rebels and people who stood up for what they believed in and what they knew to be right. And none of them took too kindly to being told by white fellas what they could and couldn't do.

I have to hand it to my father, though. He was a good, decent man, who taught me to stand tall and be proud of who I was and to never judge a man by the colour of his skin. He reckoned externals didn't matter, that it was what was inside a bloke, what was in his heart and how he treated others. For him, that was what really mattered. I had to learn that. But with you, all that was pure instinct. Like from the time you were a little nipper, you never seemed to doubt yourself. You always looked past the colour of someone's skin. It was like you knew straight off that the people who tried to offend you were just plain trouble and probably not all that bright. You understood they weren't thinking people and that no good would come from stooping to their level.

And in some ways, that's why I'm doing this tape, to tell you what I should've told you long ago, the stories of your bloodline – the stories

I can remember, that is. And what I tell you now will probably also explain why you've always had such a strong connection to this place here at Salt Pan Creek. You see, from my mother's side and probably from your father's side as well, this is your country. We're river and coastal people. That's why you've always found a kind of freedom here. It's in your blood, see, or what they now call your DNA.

It was your people, our people, who managed this land and its rivers. They knew everything about it – its flora, its fauna, its secrets, its songs. Our mob were hunters and gatherers, and we've always been drawn to rivers. It's not hard to see why either. They provided us with food, and their banks gave us shelter. Rivers and waterways have been our roads, our highways and byways. They allowed us to move around, to be free to hunt and fish, feast and socialise, trade and celebrate and to live in peace in any little inlet our hearts had a hankering for. And we've been doing that here for over 65,000 years. And no one can ever dispute that. No matter what lies they tell you, we have all the evidence we need now, thanks to scientists. And of course, when it comes to around here, there's plenty of rock art and middens galore if you know where to look.

You see, ever since the white man first came to this country, Salt Pan Creek has been a great little hidey-hole for many, including the likes of Pemulwuy, no less. It's also been a place of protest for a long, long time. It didn't just start with Joe Anderson when he made his stand against the guzzling greed of the white fella. No fear.

I'll try to explain with a little history lesson of my own.

Now, the area of land that stretches from Botany Bay south of the Cooks River, and then west along the Georges River and up Salt Pan Creek to just south of Bankstown, is part of your mob's territory. It's the land of the Bidjigal people and so, like I've said, it's the homeland of the warrior Pemulwuy.

Now, my mother's people, that's your grandmother's mob, they are Gweagal, a clan of the Dharawal tribe and they lived mainly on the southern shores of the Georges River. The Bidjigal and Gweagal often intermarried. They understood one another. Among other Aboriginal languages, we could all speak Dharawal. All of us knew the George's River very well because we were canoe cultures and we were there when the British came in their ships and, let me tell you, none of us liked it.

When Cook and his men rowed up to the shore at Kurnell, what we called Kundul, two brave Gweagal warriors shouted at them to go away, '*Warra warra wai.*' And they kept yelling at them, and when one of them threw his spear, some of Cook's men wounded our fellas with their gunfire. After eight days and with about four dozen of our spears and lots of other stuff too, they finally took the hint and buggered off.

But as everyone knows, eighteen years later in 1788, they came back – this time with eleven sailing ships filled with convicts, soldiers and marines, and again we brandished our spears and yelled at them to piss off, but Captain Arthur Phillip had no intentions of leaving, cause he was on a mission.

But we were, and still are, an inquisitive mob. These British people were like Martians to us. Firstly, they spoke differently, yet we picked up their language quicker than they ever learnt any of ours. Secondly, they looked peculiar. They were beardless and wore silly hats and red coats. They also had very powerful weapons and more than anything else, they had extremely odd ways of going about things. Like when they'd set up camp at Sydney Cove, our mob just shook their heads in disbelief when they saw this British mob stringing their own people up on trees and whipping them senseless until their backs were matted with blood, shredded skin and gore. And I tell you we were horrified to see them cutting down trees willy-nilly and then the way they put their men in chains and made 'em carry rocks from one place to another. We couldn't believe it. And boy, oh boy, did they hate sharing. I mean, they stole our spears and took far too many fish for themselves, yet when we took corn they'd grown or one of their iron shovels, they'd get pretty damn hot under the collar, I'll give you the drum.

And then came the smallpox that they'd brought with them. It decimated our people, and soon the colony began to expand and wherever colonists appeared, we'd always be obliged to stay away…

As you know, our country that we lived on for thousands of years was slowly taken away from us. It's also a historical fact that massacres took place. There's no denying it. Even in my lifetime, there's been two prime ministers who in important speeches mentioned the murders and injustices done to our people. And there are even books about the atrocities that caused so much pain and suffering then and continued to do so, on and on down through the generations to today.

Things have really got to change, Gary. Fair dinkum, they do.

Now one of the stories I remember my mother telling me was about a woman called Biddy. She was Botany Bay Dharawal of the Gweagal clan and was born around 1820 near Kurnell and often used to speak about her uncle who saw Cook's landing. Unfortunately, in her teens, she was unhappily married off to a much older well-known fella from the Georges River named Cooman or King Kooma. Word was, he didn't treat her too well, so she soon ditched him and married Paddy Burragalang and moved to the Five Islands near Wollongong in the southern part of Dharawal country, where she lived for twenty years. They had two daughters, Rosie and Ellen.

When Paddy died, sometime in the early 1860s, Biddy went back to the Georges River and hooked up with a Pommie bloke by the name of Billy Giles and she was known as Biddy Giles from then on, until she died. Together, they lived on the western side of Mill Creek, another tributary of the Georges River but upstream from Salt Pan Creek, where they had a bit of a farm and orchard. But they made a decent living from being hosts and guides for many European travellers, who wanted to go hunting and fishing or who just hankered for a bit of adventure in what seemed to them uncharted and undeveloped territory.

So Billy and Biddy became well known for their warm hospitality, with Biddy preparing meals for their guests in the traditional way, like goanna wrapped in clay and roasted in the campfire. She'd also serve local oysters and fish she'd caught herself, as well as wild honey. And then she'd tell them stories about the bush and the animals. She'd tell them about her country, her river, her people.

I reckon she would've been a shrewd old bird, that Biddy. She cottoned on pretty quickly how to make a buck by satisfying these white folks' need to experience the real thing. You've got to hand it to her. She had dignity and was well respected by everyone who met her. She was also one of the survivors, who lived and worked as she pleased up and down her beloved Georges River that was part of her country.

Her daughter Ellen was a survivor too. She was also a bit of a traveller. From her childhood at the Five Islands, she first moved to the northern end of Botany Bay, then went by train to Maloga on the Murray River, where she met and married the Goulburn River man Hugh Anderson. This was all in the time of the Protection Board, when it amalgamated the Maloga mission with the Cumeragunja reserve adjoining it.

Now, this Hughie Anderson was a special fella. He was a practising Christian, but not one of those let's-not-rock-the-boat types. He was a fine speaker and a man who believed in his right to protest against injustice. Because of the many problems in Cumeragunja, Hughie and Ellen moved around a bit, often staying with relatives in the Shoalhaven and around Kangaroo Valley – but they were always close to a river.

When they moved up to Sydney in the early 1900s, they bought a block of land on the eastern side of Salt Pan Creek, where there was a huge midden close by. Their friends the Rowleys from Weeney Bay bought the block next door, which was at the end of Ogilvy Street in Peakhurst on the bend that's now known as Charm Place. At the time, it still had a great deal of bushland surrounding it, not too many mangroves like there are now, and as for the river itself, well, its waters were pure and clean and provided William Rowley and Hugh with a decent living from its fish and prawns and oysters. There were also swamp wallabies and plenty of rabbits close by, and in springtime the bush came to life like the Garden of Eden with wildflowers every-where.

Ellen was as smart as her mother Biddy. She knew a thing or two, let me tell you. You see, a lot had happened since Federation. There was a lot of nationalist feeling in the air. Thanks to the likes of Henry Lawson and Banjo Paterson, people were finally seeing the beauty of the Australian bush. Native plants had become real popular, and Ellen cashed in and made a tidy little profit for her family by selling the best of the native blooms and gum leaf tips to local and city markets. Life was good. Just how it should be.

Because Hughie and Ellen's camp at Salt Pan Creek was a bit of a distance away from so-called respectable society, it became the perfect place to get together to discuss our problems and plan how we could solve them. It was where our mob could go and hear Hughie Anderson rail against the Aboriginal Protection Board and the terrible way it intruded into our lives.

But things started to change after Hughie and Ellen passed on. But I know you know all about that; about how Joe, their eldest son, kept up the fight. Right up until his death, he never gave up.

And nor should any of us.

I know that some folk could say I've never done very much in my life for black fellas. I guess I was too busy living. And I've always been a bit of a late-starter. But to speak the truth, it just wasn't in my nature to stir the pot. Plus, I've never been much of a talker. Though I reckon you're probably thinking I'm a bloody liar, after listening to me yabbering on here.

But in my defence, I learnt a thing or two about keeping your trap shut when I was discharged from the army at the end of the war. I was like most veterans then. When the guns fell silent, so did we. Few of us saw the point in speaking about the unspeakable. We wanted to bloody well forget the war and the senseless waste of it. What we all wanted and dreamt about in the jungle was the future. Why in the world would you want to dredge up all that blood and horror when you were back home, safe and sound? Some of us, I know, managed better than others to live our futures. I kept almost all of my pre-war memories at bay, so I could live my future. I'm sure you'll understand what I'm trying to say here, Gary, and why I've chosen to tell you now about the most important parts of my past and yours. It's the story of our family, our bloodlines. It's the story of our river.

From the beginning of time, Aboriginal people have migrated up and down it. They've lived on it and adapted to the changing flow as well as the erosion and destruction of it. They've been dreaming, singing and dancing near it long before the mighty Pemulwuy rowed along it.

Now I hope you understand why I've made this tape, Gary. And I do hope you'll remember all I've said here.

The noise of the recording button being released can be heard.

Meeting at the Hilton

Kate looked out the window as the express train raced through Sydney's suburban sprawl, flashing by factories, shunting yards, apartment blocks and graffiti, graffiti, graffiti, all of which hug the Blue Mountains railway line until the watery splendour of the Nepean River is reached, marking the western edge of Sydney. It could not have been a more perfect blue-skied day. But Kate had seen little of it.

*

For this particular reunion, earlier that day, she'd wanted to be the first one there, so she'd arrived at the Hilton fifteen minutes before the scheduled time. But there was Denise, already waiting for her. She was sitting at the bar facing the entrance. As Kate approached her, she sensed that her old friend was observing her carefully, evaluating what time had wrought on her face, her figure.

Denise waved a greeting as Kate drew closer. 'I couldn't wait any bloody longer,' she said, 'so I ordered a bottle of bubbles to get things underway. Hope you don't mind.' She laughed and turned to the bartender. 'Be a darling and fill my friend's glass, please.'

Inwardly, Kate cringed. The boisterous, look-at-me voice made her feel estranged from her old school friend. Had she always been like this? Was her memory so faulty? One thing was certain, she would have recognised Denise anywhere, despite the Botox and her colossal mane of silver hair. By anyone's standards, she was still an attractive woman – one who was obsessed by appearances and dressed with an eye on high-end designer labels.

The two women embraced and once they were both seated on their stools, Denise declared how wonderful it was for them to be together after all these years.

'I used to avoid coming to Sydney, but now with Mum living in Boronia Vale aged care facility, I fly down from Byron fairly regularly. Not that she'd know I ever visited her. She's well away with the pixies, I'm afraid. I used to fly down and back on the same day, but I've rather taken to doing a bit of shopping round town, so more often than not, I stay a day or two in the Hilton. They look after me here, don't you, darling?' And right on cue, the young barman smiled and nodded, then refilled the women's glasses.

'Would you like another bottle, Mrs Reid?'

Denise, glancing at Kate, who'd barely uttered a word since she'd arrived, reminded the fellow that they had a reservation for lunch in the brasserie, so no, they'd wait till then. 'And,' she said, turning back to Kate, 'it's my treat. I'm picking up the bill.'

'But...'

'No, no, Kate. I absolutely insist.'

*

Later, once they'd ordered their meals, Denise asked Kate what she'd been doing since they'd last seen one another. She listened attentively as Kate pulled back the years, summarising the main events of her life: university, overseas trips, teaching, marriage, Adam's birth, her divorce, retirement, and reconnecting with Gary.

'It's a wonderful stroke of luck really – getting back together, that is. I mean, it's one thing to meet up again after all these years, but for both of us to be simultaneously unattached and at a time in our lives when neither of us has that overwhelming desire to possess the other...'

Denise looked incredulous. 'Are you saying you don't fuck any more?'

'No, I'm not at all saying that. What I am saying is,' and Kate took a deep breath here, 'that sex is not the be-all and end-all as it was when we were younger. We just enjoy one another's company. We like being together, but neither of us feels the need to live together day-in, day-out. We're a couple, but not in any traditional sense. We trust and respect one another, but each of us is free to do as we please.'

'Sounds like you've had to make that little speech quite a few times before, but it all still seems a bit weird to me.'

Kate nodded, almost dumbly. She felt sick. 'Maybe you're right. But it's working for me and Gary.'

'Good for you,' said Denise.

The dismissive, patronising tone of her old friend's words aimed to wound and Kate knew it. But if Denise was looking for an argument, she wasn't going to get one from Kate. Not then at that moment and not there in public. She decided to defuse the situation by changing the subject. She spoke of Claudia and Adam, how the two of them had been virtually inseparable since meeting over a month ago. 'But I can't help wondering if he isn't being too precipitous, too unthinking. I mean it could all very well end in tears.'

'Oh Jesus, can you hear yourself? Have you forgotten what it's like to be blind with desire, Kate? To be so in love you think you'll never get enough of this person, so you fuck all day and all night and wake after an hour's sleep and want to do it all over again and again? Or am I the only woman in the world who's ever experienced such shameless wantonness?'

If only she knew, thought Kate, though she was not about to enlighten her. 'Of course I haven't forgotten,' she said automatically, now more than a little irritated by Denise's overt rebuke and criticism. What the hell was wrong with her?

'So tell me, where's Margot Henshaw living these days?'

Kate told Denise what she knew of Margot's death.

'You know,' said Denise, 'I could never figure out what Gary saw in her. I know I introduced them, but by God, she was a mouse of a woman. Couldn't get a word out of her – as boring as bat shit, she was. All I can say is, she must've been damn good in bed.' She laughed, then stared at Kate, waiting for a response.

But there was now no doubt in Kate's mind that Denise was baiting her. For what reason, she didn't know, but there was no way Kate was going to satisfy her old friend by giving her the argument she wanted. Right at that moment, all she wanted was to get through this lunch without losing her temper. And the only way to do that was to change the subject. Yet again. 'What went wrong between you and Ron? When did you split up?'

'Let's order some coffees, and I'll tell you *everything*.' And when she stressed the word 'everything', her tone was blatantly salacious. She signalled for the waiter, who scurried away after they'd given him their orders.

'Gary must've told you that he was our best man when Ron and I got married in Cambridge.' Kate nodded and Denise continued. 'Everything was fine between us while I was nursing and he was finishing off his PhD, but when I fell pregnant with Alice, we decided to come on home. Ron had been offered a great position at Monash University, so we moved to Melbourne. And I suppose that's when things started to go downhill for us.'

'How? What do you mean?'

'Ron changed once we got back to Oz. He became a complete tightwad. Maybe he'd always been like that, and I'd just never noticed before. But I sure as hell noticed once we'd established ourselves in Malvern. I wasn't working as such and twelve months after Alice was born, I found myself pregnant again with Camilla.' She rolled her eyes theatrically. 'I'm sure you can imagine what it was like for me. There I was with a newborn baby and a toddler, stuck in this imposing bloody mansion we'd bought, slowly climbing walls. I had no friends or family for support and that's when good old Ron started coming home every night full of complaints about my cooking and housekeeping, and, what's more, demanding I account for every dollar I spent at the supermarket. I tell you Kate, our marriage wasn't what you'd call living in a love nest.'

She paused when the waiter brought the coffees and placed them on their table along with a little plate of petits fours. Denise popped a tiny ball of dark chocolate into her mouth and said, 'I could eat a dozen of these in one sitting.' As she ate, she continued her story.

'Anyway, one day my mother phoned me, and I started to cry and I couldn't stop. Mum was convinced that I was suffering from a bad case of postnatal depression and next thing I know she's somehow persuaded Ron to buy me a plane ticket to Sydney so I could have a little rest. So up I fly with the two kids, and it was an absolutely wonderful break for me. But not in the way my parents or Ron or even I had imagined. You see, I met someone…'

Kate hoped her face did not betray her. She wanted to hear Denise's side of things, but she definitely wasn't prepared to reveal she had any knowledge of what had happened. So instead, she said, 'Come on, out with it.'

'Well, one afternoon when the kids were having a nap, I went for a walk. Down to the river, to be exact, and I was on this little track, when I got a spooky feeling that someone was following me. I swung around and guess who it was?'

Kate tried to look thoughtful then said: 'Graham Ingram?'

'What made you pick him?'

'You…Salt Pan Creek…who else would I think of?'

'Well, you're right.' Triumphant and aglow with the memory, words rushed from her. 'He said he'd thought it was me and to make sure he'd followed me, that I looked terrific and that he'd never stopped thinking of me.' She shook her head slightly. Her voice was unmoored now. 'And Kate, you mustn't judge me when I tell you I was so starved of compliments, so hungry for affection that I couldn't help it…we started fucking. And it was so good…out in the open, up against a tree – the most natural thing in the world – and the weight I'd been carrying around just lifted. And when I went back to my daughters I was happy, happier than I'd been for years.

'Of course, he was married and had kids too. We met one more time before I had to go back to Melbourne to my sexless marriage. But we made plans to stay in touch and we did. I don't remember exactly how we managed it, but we spent some secret, wonderful weekends together and started planning our future, but it all went horribly wrong – a case of bad timing really.

'Anyway, I didn't see Graham for years. But Ron and I split up. I moved out with the girls and once they started school, I went back to nursing. I scored a fantastic job at the Royal Adelaide Hospital, which meant I had to move interstate. At that point, the kids went to live full time with Ron. He'd remarried by then, and I loved Adelaide. That's where I met my second husband, Steve. He was a patient of mine. He was in real estate. He bought old houses and did them up, then he'd sell them off for a huge profit. He was a smart man, a good man, really. Quite a bit older than me, but we were happy enough. I had an open chequebook, so who was I to complain? We lived in Sydney for a while there too.'

'When did you move to Byron Bay?'

'Around the time of the Sydney Olympics. Steve was semi-retired by then, so we decided to spend the colder half of the year up north and the rest of the time in our Rose Bay apartment. It was great for a while, until Steve dropped dead on the golf course. Left me very well off, mind you, but didn't stop me thinking my life was pretty well stuffed.' She paused to down her, by now, cold coffee. 'And then one day, I was feeling pretty miserable and I'd probably had one too many drinks, but I plucked up the courage and I rang Graham and, like they say, the rest is history. We've got this perfect, little arrangement. I come down to see Mum once or twice a month, and he comes and spends a couple of nights here at the Hilton with me, and I go back to Byron with a smile on my face.'

'You wouldn't consider living closer?' asked Kate.

'No way! I'd be a bloody idiot. I mean, Graham's still married to the same bimbo he's always been married to. Except now she's got MS, and things aren't too good because, even though he'd like to, he can't leave her, not now when she's like she is. And of course, I'm letting him think he can move in with me whenever he's able to. But the tables have turned, Katie. I'm not the idiot he's always assumed I was. He would dearly love to live with me. I know, because he likes my lifestyle. He also loves my money, and I can't wait for the day when his wife finally carks it, and he's standing on my doorstep with all his suitcases, and I tell him point-blank to piss off, because all this time I've just been using him, and I'll tell him he's not even a good fuck any more, and that I never want to see his sorry arse again.' She paused a moment. 'I can't wait to see the expression on his face. What sweet revenge that's going to be.' Her mouth curved into a smile. 'Does that shock you, Kate?'

'No, not really.' But she was lying.

*

By the time Kate got back home, she was exhausted. It had been one hell of a day. She'd spent the entire trip from Central Station to Wentworth Falls trying to make some sense of her reunion with Denise. It had been Denise who'd reached out to Kate and initiated the meeting. So why the aggression?

Sipping at her milky tea and staring at her reflection on the black screen of her television, Kate knew she'd lost a friend, one she'd considered to be her very best friend. However, it hadn't happened today, but decades ago. In 1970. And nothing could change that fact. It was only now that Kate realised she shouldn't have trusted her memories of Denise.

She thought she might have even made her up. Because the person she met today was not the kind of person she'd imagined her to be. Maybe she'd conflated Denise with their carefree youth, all the laughter and joy of it and added a good dose of nostalgia to the mix. It was nothing more than a fantasy. Except for their shared schoolgirl past, she and Denise had little in common. Kate felt disillusioned and bereft.

Denise's life had become all about the accretion of wealth. She'd even found it hard to believe that Kate didn't have a property portfolio. To her, accumulating houses was a speculative sport. It fortified and energised her. But the worst thing about it, as far as Kate was concerned, was that her childhood friend was not a very nice person. She took no responsibility for anything. She saw herself as an innocent victim who never questioned any of her own decisions, because in her view she was blameless. It was always someone else's fault. Her life was one big lie.

Kate looked at her watch. Her brother Mark would probably be having dinner about now. She'd phone him in the morning. He'd have something to say about all this. And she would like his opinion. But she knew she never wanted anything to do with Denise Reid again. Life was simply too short. They were two very different people, who didn't share the same values any more.

Of course, she wondered how it happened. Was it simply a matter of circumstances, of life experiences that create the people we are? Does personality influence the choices we make? And just how much do the patterns of behaviour we develop during our childhoods determine the adults we become?

She gulped down the last of the tea from her mug. Why hadn't Ron and Gary drifted apart? And how had she and Gary managed to reconnect in such a profound way after so long?

Too many questions to answer at once. She wasn't the slightest bit hungry, but her brain was tired. She'd have an early night. But first she'd spend some quality time in front of the telly. Then to bed.

Coupling

Their mouths meet and melt together in a long, gentle kiss. And then he tells her that he loves her and that he'll never stop loving her.

She feels her back against the wall and she clasps him to her. His breath is hot on her neck. He's pressing into her.

'Do you love me?' he whispers. 'Do you love me?'

And suddenly, her knickers are gone. She feels his hands. They're clutching her buttocks. He lifts her up and there he is, inside her, inside her, pushing, pushing. There's a violent shudder and then a stillness. Adam doesn't move. They're still pressed together, but his head has slumped onto her shoulder. She can hear his heart beating in his chest.

Somehow, she tells him she needs to sit down. He helps her slide down the wall. They both then sit on the floor side by side.

'You haven't answered my question.' His voice is thick, his words muffled.

After a time, she says, 'You know I do. I wouldn't be here beside you with my naked bum on the floor, if I didn't.' She kisses him on the lips, on the tip of his nose.

'Go on then. Say the words.'

She takes his hand and raises it to her lips. 'I love you, Adam Nelson. Now do you believe me?'

'Of course, I do. It's just sometimes, I have these moments when I can't believe how lucky I am to have met you.'

*

Later, in her darkened room, they lie naked on her bed. Claudia will remind him that her father and his mother are in the room across the hall. She will place her hand around his penis and stroke it slowly – up and down, her movements slow and dream-like. And when she feels his fingers inside her, she will gasp. He'll ask her if he's hurting her, and she will laugh and say no, no. Not at all.

His mouth will find hers. They will kiss – their tongues playful, delicious. Then he will move, taking her with him. They will roll together until he's lying on his back, she on top of him. She will kiss his eyes, his forehead, his cheeks and feel again his heart beating in his chest. Then without thought, she will ease herself onto him.

And when he's moving inside her, he will make her laugh when he says, 'Let's try not to wake our parents.'

It's then when she'll move on him faster. And faster.

*

Much later that night, Gary is lying on his back in bed, waiting for Kate to return. What is keeping her? He stares at the slender strip of moonlight that crosses the floor. He must remember to talk to her about the white-bellied sea eagles they all saw this afternoon.

The house is still. Then a sudden creak of the bedroom door and a patter of bare feet – at last!

He rolls onto his side as she gets into bed and whispers, 'What on earth have you been doing?'

She snuggles up close to him and tells him she'd gone to get a glass of water and couldn't help but hear Claudia and Adam.

'Doing what?'

'Well, they weren't playing tiddlywinks, that's for sure.'

'How do you know?'

'I listened at the door, and it sounded pretty damn heated to me.'

'Oh Katie, what if one of them came out and saw you there – spying on them, as if they're kids? Then what would you've done?'

'I don't know. But they didn't, so it's OK.'

'Of course it's OK. They're both consenting adults.'

'I know that. It's just that… I don't know. It sounded like they were fucking their brains out.'

He inches closer to her, and she feels his erection butting against her. She resists the urge to take hold of it and feel its stiffness. But his hand is already inside her nightie between her legs. He leaves it there, his fingers playing idly with her pubic hair.

'And what's wrong with that? Here's hoping they're enjoying themselves and, who knows, something wonderful might come of it all.'

'And what if it doesn't? What if it all goes terribly wrong?'

'You've got to stop being so anxious about things, Katie. You've got to relax. What will be will be…' His voice trails away as he kisses her very lightly on her lips, on her cheek, on her earlobe.

She looks at him then, and this time when their eyes meet, an agreement passes between them that is beyond words, beyond the mundane and the surface of things. They both know that it can't be given expression. But nevertheless, it's timeless and heartfelt and true.

*

Gary wakes up covered in slats of fractured light. He'd forgotten to close the shutters the night before. But who could blame him? He had had more important things to do.

He rolls onto his side and props himself up on his elbow so he can observe Kate, who is still sleeping. Her naked body is tangled in the whiteness of the sheets. Her hair is splayed out across the pillow. She looks to him like some Grecian beauty captured for all time in stone.

They'd managed to slow down time last night. He wants to believe that something momentous, something wonderful, happened between them and that it wasn't some kind of crazy dance to beat off death. He lets his head fall back on his pillow.

Staring up at the ceiling, he feels her stir beside him. He turns back onto his side to face her. She's only centimetres away from him. He inhales deeply and smells all the salty, sweet loveliness of her. Her eyes open. She smiles at him. And then he hears her speak.

'Good morning.' Just two words of greeting – but it's the tenderness in her voice. Her head moves closer to his, and their lips meet. She kisses him lightly once, twice.

And of course, that's it. He's filled with a sudden surge of feeling – of being alive. Right here – this minute. There's never been any other woman who could do that. It's wonderful and terrible, and he knows he must resist being haunted by thoughts of the lost possibilities of all those years gone by when they hadn't been together. For that kind of thinking is life-negating. And this, after all, is their second chance.

A shriek of cockatoos outside fills the room with their delinquent morning chorus. He smiles and says he'd arranged it all for her. Then he tells her to stay where she is; that he'll get them both some coffee.

She moves to the middle of the bed and makes herself more comfortable. She knows she's happier than she's been in a long time. She and Gary understand one another in an essential, fundamental kind of way. They share the same sense of humour, the same way of looking at the world as they did all those years ago. He's still a really nice bloke. When she'd told him yesterday evening about her disastrous meeting with Denise, Kate's words hovered in the air, then floated off the deck and out above the garden, to sail the darkness of the river.

'That's really sad,' he'd said. 'She must be a very unhappy soul. I feel sorry for her.'

You have to love a man who responds like that, thinks Kate.

A distant smell of freshly brewed coffee invades the room. She sits up straight with the pillows at her back and pulls up the top sheet to cover her breasts.

He's coming back to her.

And later in the morning, she will speak of her fear that she may one day discover that her First Fleet ancestors or others after them may have harmed an Indigenous person and how the thought of that makes her feel sick with guilt. And he will face her directly and say that even if they did, no one can change what happened. There's no turning back the clock to stop the British from invading. No amount of white guilt can do that. But a treaty would be nice.

Then she will say that all the denial, the lies, the cover-ups must stop. And he'll remind her that she won't get an argument from him about that.

The day will glide by with talk of the past. She will ask him if he'd be surprised to learn that her father in his later years, when his world was shrinking along with his memory, had been terrified of being exposed for having concealed a midden on the family block of land at Salt Pan Creek – this from a man who'd spent his working life in pursuit of the truth.

*

It was late in the afternoon when they heard it. A voice on the jetty, 'I LOVE YOU. I LOVE YOU.' And then. 'CLAUDIA, CLAUDIA, MARRY ME, CLAUDIA' – carried by the wind, in the air. Everyone breathing and feeling the lunatic joy and wonder of it.

One Last Thing

My work is almost done here. It is to other rivers I soon must go, for I belong everywhere and nowhere, and my ancestral roots are timeless, boundless and everlasting.

Some folk claim I'm a high discloser but, unlike mere compulsive tittle-tats, I speak truth for truth's sake. It is preordained within the name you know me by – Alethea. Google me, if you must. For there, you'll glean all that I represent - everything that Lethe, that timeworn river of amnesia, is not. Its waters murmur irresistible invitations to sleep, while its banks deliver drowsy dreams of poppy magic.

Dismiss the past, Lethe whispers. Forget, forget. But I cannot.

I am history's handmaiden, the keeper of stories and, like some colossal iCloud library, I am the museum of memory. I archive what I know is truth. So please forgive my fondness for fact over fiction. A preference some have failed to share when they've written history in the ink of fluid prejudice.

But let me tell you, I do not wish to teach or preach. I want only to shed light.

History is always complicated and fake history is sheer delusion.

Sometimes we must look at the past from another angle, from another's perspective. Sometimes we must rethink what we've learnt.

There is no us. There is no them. Only human beings with stories and silences. So pay heed.

Be not like the Ancients, who drank from the waters of the River Lethe and thus had their memories wiped clean to sleep in perfect oblivion.

For eternity.

Wedding Day

Kate came in from the garden. She'd done enough weeding for one day. Besides, it looked and smelt like rain was very close by. The entire sky to the south was a single roiling mass of black cumulonimbus cloud. There'd be no need to turn on the sprinklers for the lawn this afternoon. Before closing the doors of the outer deck, she lingered awhile, surveying her handiwork.

And there it was, spread before her in an atmosphere of fading light – the happy union of native and exotic flowering shrubs and the promise of statuesque trees pleased her enormously. She let her eyes stroll along the curved gravel path, one side of which was the border for a carpet of deep green grass. It looked so soft and inviting that Kate had a sudden urge to roll naked over it, which she suppressed by focusing her attention on the tumbledown jetty at the end of the property. She was glad Gary had made it more structurally sturdy and given it a new coat of paint, for it really had become the stand-out feature of the garden. She was sure that at the wedding reception on Saturday it would beckon guests to go down to the river. Of course, that's as long as the rain that was beginning to pepper the deck cleared off within the next thirty-six hours.

Since she'd been spending so much more of her time at Elwin Street, she'd grown to love gardening. She'd stopped regarding it as a chore and began to see it as a rewarding, creative exercise. And the design of this garden had been easy. She and Gary were in agreement. They'd follow the natural contours of the block, construct a pathway to the river and, except for the creation of an expanse of lawn, the rest of the yard would be covered by a layered profusion of flowering gums and low-growing plants with drifts of seasonal blossoms and bulbs. While colour was important to both of them, what was absolutely obligatory was the production of an air of wildness, and so they'd planted several varieties of boronia and bottlebrush, a wattle tree, some Christmas bush and, of course, waratahs. This garden was not only to be a sanctuary for them, it was also meant to be an ecological gift to the river, a tribute to the fertile natural beauty of the bush that had once, not so long ago, bordered Salt Pan Creek.

For 2018 was not shaping up to be such a good year. The planet was in crisis. Kate was sure of it. Random terrorist attacks and mass shootings plagued the world still, while numberless refugees continued to flee wars, hunger and persecution. More than that, here it was – almost September, and already severe droughts and heatwaves had been sweeping the northern and southern hemispheres. The world, no matter the season, was ablaze with wildfires – Greece, Portugal, Spain, the US, Russia, the UK, Australia, even inside the Arctic Circle. The future looked bleak.

But at heart, Kate was an optimist. As long as there remained a clutch of small mercies, like the beauty and delight to be found in the natural world or in a work of art, there was good cause to be hopeful.

Besides, she said to herself, I am here – the prodigal daughter returned to where I belong, where I best fit. She thought then about how she wakes beside Gary. Sometimes she's lying on her back, his head on her breasts. Other times, it is he who is lying with her head resting on his shoulder. And there are also times when, half dreaming, half awake, he holds her to him and they cradle together with such love and tenderness that they wake smiling into the morning light.

*

'The garden looks lovely,' someone said. The statement hung in mid-air.

Staring across the backyard, people raised their glasses and, as suddenly as the conversation had ended, it erupted once more, then fanned out and splintered. Everyone, it seemed, had a memory of a particular garden he or she wished to share. Kate surveyed the scene.

People appeared to be mingling well. The sky was unending blue. The caterers were busy in the kitchen. For a moment, a silver tray of loaded champagne flutes was suspended above the heads of guests and then whisked away empty. The sound of chatter and laughter muted the music that was playing in the background. And then a boisterous exchange of hugs and greetings came from inside the house.

'Kate, look who's here!' It was Gary.

She swung round, and there they were – her brother Mark and his partner Tom – two men suddenly boys again, walking towards her, smiling in the sunlight of the day. Mark embraced her with such obvious affection, she felt her spirits soar. Oh, this was truly a very special day.

Platters of sushi drifted about the deck, and more drinks were proffered and taken. The doorbell rang again, and Gary hurried away and returned seconds later, ushering in Mira and Ron Cochrane. More introductions followed, and they were all soon talking together, at ease in one another's company, which made Kate wonder if the younger generation felt as relaxed and as comfortable when meeting new people. Glancing about her, it was apparent that the living areas of the house were now full of geniality and people of all ages. Kate decided to grab herself a glass of champagne and stop worrying about everyone getting on with one another.

*

The bride and groom had wanted the ceremony itself to take place in the garden beside the sunny profusion of the weeping wattle, and despite some initial fears about the wisdom of having a tinkling of bells to announce the commencement of the wedding service, everything went to plan.

When Claudia appeared at the top of the lawn, there was a communal intake of breath. At that precise moment, she became the embodiment of everyone's notion of the romantic bride – elegance in ivory lace and tulle. The ceremony was simple and heartfelt, with only one false note as far as Kate was concerned, and that was when the celebrant, a little too pompous for his own good, read in overblown style a passage of his own choice from Victor Hugo's *Les Misérables*: 'When two mouths, sanctified by love, come together to create, that ineffable kiss is simply bound to set the mysterious stars shuddering throughout immensity. This is the real bliss. There is no joy beyond these joys. Love is the sole ecstasy here. Everything else weeps. To love or to have loved is enough. Don't ask for anything more. There is no other pearl to be found in the shadowy folds of life. To love is an achievement.'

Kate was surprised that several people applauded him. Gary gave her a wink, which forced her to suppress her laughter. She knew he understood that she always found cheap sentiment amusing. But it was all quickly over and, when Adam and Claudia kissed, a collective cheer from the guests erupted spontaneously and music swirled above the garden. Soon, people were on their feet, and after photos were taken and champagne and laughter spilled here and there, the guests were directed to various tables and lunch was served.

Once Kate and Gary were able to relinquish their roles as hosts going from table to table, they took up seats next to Mark and Tom that Ron and Mira had saved for them at the long banquet table close to the deck. And so the formalities became less formal as they stretched into the afternoon with dancing on the deck until someone called out, 'Look at that!'

All eyes moved in unison and turned westward and up into the sky to see two giant pairs of wings soaring high above the river.

'Now that's got to be a good omen,' someone else said to general laughter.

Kate felt a tap on her shoulder. It was Adam. She stood up, and his arm went round her.

'I've never seen you look so happy as I have today,' he said.

'I could say the same to you,' and she smiled as she stood on tiptoe to kiss her son. She knew he and Claudia were ready to leave.

There remained a few couples on the deck swirling about in time with the rhythm of the music. It had all been a great success. But the party was almost over.

In Flight

Mark had no idea why Tom, a nervous flier, had insisted upon taking the window seat. Ever since they'd boarded the plane, he'd been as silent as air and incredibly still. And as the aircraft began to reverse away from the dock, Tom had hunched his shoulders and pressed his forehead against the windowpane so he could stare out as if he'd had a lifelong fascination with tarmac.

When the chief steward's well-oiled words of welcome began to fill the cabin, Mark reached across the armrest and took his partner's hand.

Tom straightened up and leaned back in his seat. 'Wait for it,' he said, turning his head towards Mark and smiling. 'Next thing will be the crew's turn to perform their predictable, little pantomime.' And of course, he was right. But Tom took no pleasure in his accurate prediction, because the plane started to lurch and creak as it made its way towards the runway. Tom grew pale.

'It's OK…it's OK,' Mark said, hoping he sounded reassuring, despite knowing from past experience that no amount of soothing words would dispel Tom's perception that he was in dire risk of obliteration.

When the plane lifted off the ground, Mark noticed he'd shut his eyes to the world around him, including the clear, translucent blue that now filled the oval frame of their cabin window. He knew Tom would now remain quiet and wouldn't begin to relax until the crew started moving about the cabin, dispensing drinks and courtesy. But that was fine with Mark. After the weekend they'd had, he'd tolerate any whim or foolishness on Tom's part.

Last night, when they'd finally got to bed, Mark had thanked him for accompanying him to the wedding. 'I know you never wanted to come back to Sydney again, so I can't begin to tell you how much you being here with me these last two days has meant to me.'

Tom was dismissive. 'Don't be silly. It's been great fun. It was a fantastic wedding!' He paused, then added, 'Anyway, I bet you agree that it was about time I stopped blaming this city and its entire population for one homophobic moron beating me senseless.'

And Mark recognised the kernel of truth in what Tom said, for the attack had occurred way back in 1980. Tom's mum Pam had been teaching with Kate at the time. The school year was almost over. Tom had just finished his HSC exams and he and a friend had taken themselves off to Oxford Street in search of a good time. But they got more than they bargained for when they were set upon by a pair of thugs in some back lane. Tom's mate managed to run off, and one of their assailants gave chase, which left the other one to thrash and kick his victim as he pleased, until Tom was a bleeding mess lying in the filth of the gutter.

But that was only when the first thug returned to the scene. He surveyed his partner's handiwork and said, 'Jesus, mate. Now look what you've done. You've gone and fucking killed the poofter.' That's when the pair bolted.

A lengthy period of hospitalisation helped put Tom back together again. Like many other gay-hate crimes in Sydney at that time, no arrests were ever made, which was all too much for Pam, who promptly packed up and moved with her traumatised son to Melbourne, where she'd been raised and where she believed Tom would be safe from the excesses of the harbour city.

It had been Kate who'd first told Mark about the incident. And then reminded him of it five years later when she'd given him Pam's number. 'I told her how you'd accepted an offer to write for the *Age*,' Kate said, 'that it was part of some kind of exchange program for young up-and-comers like you to expand their professional experience.'

Mark had cringed when she'd told him that.

'Anyway,' she continued, 'give her a call. She's a really good friend of mine, and I know she'd love to hear from you. She's a brilliant cook, so who knows? She might ask you round for dinner.'

The so-called exchange was supposed to be for a period of six months, after which Mark would return to the *Sydney Morning Herald*. But in his case, he'd rung Pam in the first few days he was there, and before the week was over he was sitting at Pam's table, eating her food and getting to know her son. The rest, as they say, was history. Melbourne became his home. And he still had no regrets. Which is what he should've said to Tom last night, when he'd mentioned the assault again.

'You know,' he said, 'I often look back at that time in my life and think to myself that, if all that had never happened, if I hadn't been beaten to a pulp and you hadn't contacted my mother, I might never have met you.'

That was the perfect opportunity for Mark to propose. But he'd said nothing. He'd just stared up at the ceiling while Tom continued to speak about the wedding and Kate – how well she looked, how laid-back and contented she seemed. Then he spoke of Gary. 'Such a nice guy,' he said. 'Makes me so angry about the Uluru Statement. How can any Australian not be moved by it? And to be rejected by the federal government…it's terrible…bloody terrible.'

Yes, it's a national disgrace, thought Mark. Yet another opportunity missed. The march of folly never seemed to stop.

Suddenly there were refreshments on offer, and Tom's eyes were open and ready for action. 'And I have to say that was a great take-off,' he said, turning his head to face Mark. 'Very smooth. But even so, when we come back to Sydney again, let's drive up…take our time… I mean, stay a few weeks. I've always loved your sister, but now that I've met Gary and Adam and Claudia, well…they're really terrific people, good people, and I'd like to get to know them all better. What do you say?'

Mark laughed and nodded in agreement, but he still hadn't proposed. So what was stopping him? What was he frightened of? He knew that a proposal wouldn't come as a surprise to Tom. They'd discussed the possibility of getting married during that anxiety-ridden period of the national same-sex marriage postal survey. But once the positive result was announced and parliament had ratified it, the sheer joy of finally having the choice to marry or not, made them both realise they had no real need of a certificate to prove their love and commitment to each other. They'd been together now since 1985 and despite the usual petty irritations all couples experience, they had stayed together. Because they'd wanted to.

But now Mark wondered whether they might not like a ceremony to acknowledge and solemnise that fact. A celebration would uplift everyone's spirits. He remembered how delighted his parents were when Kate got married. Or did it only appear that way? Perhaps pleasure had little to do with it. Perhaps they merely felt a sense of relief. Certainly, Betty had been worried about her daughter for quite a while. Mark had noticed subtle changes in his mother from around the time Kate had left home to go to university in Canberra. At first, he thought she was simply missing her daughter, until he asked her if that were the case, and he'd never forgotten how she'd answered without a hint of emotion.

'No, son. I do not miss your sister and I definitely don't miss her defiance. You'll understand when you're a parent one day. But I do get a little anxious about her sometimes, down there all by herself, not knowing a soul.'

And basically, Betty had continued to be a little anxious until the day Kate introduced Richard to her and Milton.

'What on earth are you thinking about? You look like you're in pain.' The voice was Tom's.

Mark turned to him, as if seeing him for the first time. And he was suddenly filled with a kind of euphoria, a sense that he was one of the lucky ones. Married or not – it didn't matter. What did, was this smiling man beside him, his best friend, his life's partner. And that here they were, strapped into this plane, speeding into their futures and out there beyond the window, all he could see was the brilliant bit of blue sky behind the head of the man he would always love.

Out of Mind

Kate is looking out the window, trying to remember how she came to be here: it had been her turn to cook the Sunday roast, Adam and Claudia were coming for lunch and as always they would join her and Gary in the kitchen, something all four loved doing, because these Sundays were always the most relaxed of days, for they were able to ignore time, each one of them helping out in a leisurely, almost dreamlike way; some Sundays, they'd talk a lot and sometimes they spoke to one another without words, and at those times, no one ever seemed curious about what the other three might or might not be thinking, which was just as well, but this last Sunday was different, it had been unseasonably cold, a very grey morning, perfect for a roast, and Gary suggested they rug themselves up and go down to the river so they could 'survey our empire' before the kids arrived, and so the two of them, carrying mugs of morning coffee, had walked through the stillness of the garden and no sooner had they stepped up onto the jetty than they'd spied them – a pair of white-bellied sea eagles, their long, black talons clinging onto two bare branches at the top of a lifeless gum that was sticking out above the mangroves on the other side of the creek – and quietly she and Gary observed their pride and watched as their beady, little eyes scrutinised their territory, and then there was a sudden shimmer of light on the surface of the water, which flickered and wavered, and for one moment Kate had a strong sensation that something extraordinary was about to happen, and then she heard it – someone was chopping down a tree on the riverbank, not far from them, and she saw it was her father, and he began to drag the casuarina behind him, and she was running beside him, trying to keep up with his strides, for they were taking it home to her mother and brother to decorate, and Kate was saying: it's perfect, Daddy, it's perfect, and she is happy, crazily Christmas happy, and her eyes blur with tears, then it was gone, and she looked at Gary and saw he'd seen something too; they were both without words and his arms went round her shoulders and he shivered and said it was time to go back inside because it was a bit too cold for his liking but before turning to make their way back to the house, her eyes scanned the other side of the river again, and she saw that their friends had disappeared but then she woke up – here, in this horrible box of a room, and now here comes a young woman in a blue uniform, all smiles and good cheer, who says she's delighted to see Kate awake at last and asks how she's feeling and when Kate tries to respond, she can hear only silence; exasperated, she moves her head this way and that, then the smiling blue uniform tells her not to worry, that she's in good hands, that she'd been in a coma and all the scans have shown she'd had a brain haemorrhage, and she'll soon be moved to the neurosurgical wing, and that's when Kate wants to ask what the likelihood of recovery is, but still she can't get the words out and she wants to cry and howl and rage, rage against the dying of the light but the nurse tells her that her family will be visiting soon and she'll help her to sit up a little and so she gently places several pillows behind her back, then starts combing her hair, to make you more presentable, she says, and Kate submits, wondering what the nurse means, for she feels sleepy but will not close her eyes in case everyone thinks she's slipped back into a coma, that wouldn't do; 'Sleep no more! Macbeth doth murder sleep' and this way she takes heart, for it comes to her that she still has her memory, she's remembered lines from Dylan Thomas, as well as Shakespeare, which must surely be a positive sign, for without memory there's no language, no words, no way back and that would be a terrible thing, for she wasn't yet ready for that great enigma, death, to take her and she wonders then if the dead remember, or is it all everlasting darkness and solitude or maybe, if what physicists keep telling everyone is true, that time is an illusion, then we're reincarnated over and over again, or perhaps we get to live all our lives at once; now wouldn't that be interesting, thinks Kate, but she can't complain because the narrative of her life, this life she's been leading, has been quite wonderful really; sure, the ending she's now experiencing is none too pleasant, but perhaps that's the price she must pay and when the final moment arrives, she wonders if her entire life will flash before her eyes, like some giant YouTube clip, made from all her memories, one dissolving into another, then another, in no particular order, beginning with the faces of her many, many students, the ones she recalls, that is, and they dissolve to the faces of the children still in refugee camps across the globe, one after the other, and even now, she laughs and shakes her head to think she even feels the need to make some political point at the end of her life, for whom and for what purpose, she'd like to know; but surely there'd also be a shot of her mother, Betty, probably blowing endless smoke rings in the air and of her father, swinging a sledgehammer into a mound of oyster shells and other debris, and she decides then and there that if she were to choose what she would or would not see before she shuffles off this mortal coil, she'd definitely want some archival footage of all the wonderful and terrible events that occurred in her lifetime like Neil Armstrong walking on the moon and a replay of Martin Luther King delivering his 'I Have a Dream' speech back in 1963, which would fade to the cinema images of a pink-suited Jackie Kennedy crawling from the back of the moving limousine moments after her president husband was assassinated, and of course that would cut to the two hijacked American planes crashing into the Twin Towers of the World Trade Centre, but that's such an awful, awful memory, there must be something more uplifting, more Australian than all of that, and then Kate sees Kevin Rudd making the National Apology to the Stolen Generations, which fades to Julia Gillard delivering her misogyny speech, and she hears a man's voice say, what's so funny, and it's Gary smiling, and there beside him are Adam and Claudia, all here to see her, and she tries to tell them about the silly things she's been thinking, but there's still no sound, and Gary leans closer to kiss her, and she hopes her breath smells not too rank, for it's been some time since she last cleaned her teeth and she hears him whisper I love you and she looks him in the eye and trusts he understands that she loves him too, but death, that great spoiler, has dropped by to remind them both not to be so damn complacent, that no one lasts forever and she can tell that her son thinks she's about to die, for he looks quite pale as he and Claudia move from where Gary's standing to take up positions on the other side of the bed, and she feels Adam's hand take hers and she squeezes it, and his eyes light up and then out it all tumbles: how Claudia is pregnant and how happy they both are, and of course their happiness is glaringly obvious, Adam is now grinning like a loon, and Kate wants to say she's delighted, but there's only silence from her, and Gary tells her she must get better, she's got a lot to live for, but all Kate wants to do is sleep, perchance to dream and she hears the old nursery rhyme singing itself in her mind – row, row, row your boat gently down the stream, merrily, merrily, merrily, merrily, life is but a dream – and her eyes well with tears and tiredness so they leave her alone with the ferocity of her recollections as well as her thoughts for company, and she sees the river moving, forever flowing through time, and she's sitting with Gary on the back deck in the fading light of the dying day and they're watching Adam and Claudia down by Salt Pan Creek and as they step up onto the jetty, they trigger the sensor switch that Gary had only recently installed for the wedding and the couple is suddenly enveloped in a mantle of soft yellow light, where they remain motionless within the centre of the glow, for Adam has wrapped Claudia in his arms, and Gary grabs at Kate's hand, and they look at one another and smile, then return their gaze to their children clinging together beneath the shimmering light, and perhaps that's what death is, thinks Kate, when all the words have been said, and all the small illuminated moments in one's life coalesce, there's nothing left but to end it there, to call it a day. Full stop.

Acknowledgements

Many people have encouraged and supported me in various ways throughout the writing of this book. But there are some who deserve special mention.

I am most grateful to Emeritus Professor John Carter, School of Engineering, University of Newcastle, who gave so generously of his time, knowledge and childhood memories.

Words are inadequate to express my gratitude to Nicolle Lowe, who, some years ago, shared her family's history with me and in so doing helped me to see how integral Aboriginal history is to Australian history. As Bruce Elder remarked, '…the sense of despair and hopelessness which informs so much modern-day Aboriginal society, is a moral responsibility all white Australians share. Our wealth and lifestyle is a direct consequence of Aboriginal dispossession.'

I am also indebted to my dear sister, Jan Grinham, as well as Donna O'Grady and her brother, the late Kevin Vogel, and to sisters, Diana Russell and Ann Woodward, all of whom kindly shared their reminiscences of growing up close to Salt Pan Creek.

Warm thanks must also go to Robert Adamson, Wayne Asboth, John Baltaks, Dr Rhonda Barringham, Philippe Desveaux, Jo Gardiner, Terri Katsikaros, Jenny Marchionni, David May, Anne Nicholson and Nella Perovich.

And lastly to my first readers, Wendy De Paoli and Kerry Herger – thank you both for your meticulous editing skills, your insightful observations and your astute suggestions.

And of course, as always, my heartfelt thanks go to Peter – for everything.

The following publications have been particularly useful to me in the writing of these stories:

Blood on the Wattle: Massacres & Maltreatments of Aboriginal Australians since 1788, Bruce Elder, New Holland Publishers (Australia), third edition, 2016

Damned Whores & God's Police: The Colonization of Women in Australia, Anne Summers, Penguin Books, Australia, 1976

Dancing with Strangers: The True History of the Meeting of the British First Fleet and the Aboriginal Australians, 1788, Inga Clendinnen, Text Publishing Company, Melbourne, 2003

Deep Time Dreaming: Uncovering Ancient Australia, Billy Griffiths. Black Inc., Australia, 2018

Don't Shoot, It's Only Me: Bob Hope's Comedy History of the United States, Bob Hope with Melville Shavelson. G.P. Putnam's Sons, New York, 1990

EORA: Mapping Aboriginal Sydney 1770–1850, State Library of New South Wales, June 2006 <www.atmitchell.com>

Hidden in Plain View: The Aboriginal People of Coastal Sydney, Paul Irish, NewSouth, Australia, 2017

Portraits from Memory and Other Essays, Bertrand Russell, Simon & Schuster, New York, 1956

Rivers and Resilience: Aboriginal People on Sydney's Georges River, Heather Goodall & Allison Cadzow, UNSW Press, Sydne,y 2009

The Australian Dream: Blood, History and Becoming, Stan Grant. Quarterly Essay, Issue 64, 2016

The Fatal Shore, Robert Hughes, Pan Books, Australia, 1987

The History Question: Who Owns the Past?, Inga Clendinnen,. Quarterly Essay, Issue 23, 2006

The Journal of Philip Gidley King, a digital text sponsored by University of Sydney Library, Sydney 2003

'"The Several 'Discoveries" of Sydney's Georges River: Precursors to the "Tom Thumb" Expedition', Robert Haworth, in *Journal of Australian Colonial History School of Classics, History & Religion*, University of New England, Volume 14 (2012)

Websites

Barani – Sydney's Aboriginal History

Dharug And Dharawal Dalang – language is culture

The Dictionary of Sydney

The Koori History

https://aso.gov.au/titles/documentaries/lousy-little-sixpence/clip3/